Mattie's

UNSPOKEN VOW

Ruth~

I hope you enjoy
this final book in the series!
Share His Word!

Margo :)

MARGO HANSEN

Mattie's

UNSPOKEN VOW

· A NEWLY WEDS SERIES ·

TATE PUBLISHING
AND ENTERPRISES, LLC

Mattie's Unspoken Vow
Copyright © 2013 by Margo Hansen. All rights reserved.

No part of this publication may be reproduced, stored in a retrieval system or transmitted in any way by any means, electronic, mechanical, photocopy, recording or otherwise without the prior permission of the author except as provided by USA copyright law.

This novel is a work of fiction. Names, descriptions, entities, and incidents included in the story are products of the author's imagination. Any resemblance to actual persons, events, and entities is entirely coincidental.

All Scripture quotations in this book are taken from the King James Version of the Bible.

The opinions expressed by the author are not necessarily those of Tate Publishing, LLC.

Published by Tate Publishing & Enterprises, LLC
127 E. Trade Center Terrace | Mustang, Oklahoma 73064 USA
1.888.361.9473 | www.tatepublishing.com

Tate Publishing is committed to excellence in the publishing industry. The company reflects the philosophy established by the founders, based on Psalm 68:11,
"The Lord gave the word and great was the company of those who published it."

Book design copyright © 2013 by Tate Publishing, LLC. All rights reserved.
Cover design by Jan Sunday Quilaquil
Interior design by Caypeeline Casas

Published in the United States of America

ISBN: 978-1-62510-907-1
1. Fiction / Christian / Romance
2. Fiction / Christian / Historical
13.02.05

Dedication

To the pastors
who have faithfully taught me
God's Word through the years.

And to Bruce,
who has truly shown me
God's love through the years.

Acknowledgments

It is hard to say good-bye to my Newly family in this final book of the series. They have been in my life for a long time now, and I know there are many more stories I could tell about them, but I'll let your imaginations take them where you wish them to go from here on out. It has been a privilege to share my stories with you. None of these books would have been possible without the encouragement of others, so I would like to acknowledge the following:

Again, my praise goes to God the Father of our Lord Jesus Christ for blessing me each day with all spiritual blessings in heavenly places in Christ as Ephesians 1:3 tells me. What a privilege to know and serve him!

Bruce, you are the best support of all. You are always willing to listen to my ideas and offer suggestions and give encouragement. What a privilege to be your wife!

My children, you are my biggest fans and my best salesmen. You are the reason I began to write and the reason I enjoy it so much. I hope you pass these on to your children and their children. What a privilege to be your mom!

My friends, I would try to name all of you who have encouraged me, but I am afraid I would miss someone. I can't tell you how much I appreciate all that you do through your prayers and your support. Thank you for always asking when the next book will be out. What a privilege to be called your friend!

My readers, I call you my friends as well. Each of you has been a blessing to me with your comments, your reviews, and your recommendations. Thank you to those who have written to me. I pray these stories have touched your hearts and either caused you to want to know my Savior or, if you already do, to want to serve him with the life he's given you. What a privilege to write for you!

And once again, my friends at Tate Publishing, thank you for seeing me through the series and giving me the means to share my Newly family with others.

Sand Creek

Russ and Sky Newly
TYLER (M. JADYNE CRANDALL)
LUCY (M. BUCK RILEY)
DORCAS (M. CAVAN NOLAN)
EMMA (M. SIMON CHAPPELL)
REX (M. IRENA JENSON)
ABEL

Hank and Randi Riley
BUCK (M. LUCY NEWLY)
DUGAN (M. MELODY WELLS)
MALLORY (M. MICHAEL TRENT)
JETHRO
PARKER
RODNEY
ROSS

Jonas and Bridget Nolan
ROONEY
BERNADETTE (M. STEVEN ROWAN)

Jasper and Martha Riggs
PERCY SCOTT (M. REBECCA TUNELLE)
PETER SCOTT (M. ROBIN TUNELLE)
DEXTER (M. ESTHER TRENT)
BERNARD (M. PEARL MADDOX)
CLAYTON
RHODA
PENNY

Evan and Ella Trent
MICHAEL (M. MALLORY RILEY)
GABRIEL (M. LEIGH SHELDON)
ESTHER (M. DEXTER RIGGS)
MARTHA (M. ROB TUNELLE)
JOHN

Duke and Angelina Tunelle
REBECCA (M. PERCY SCOTT)
ROBIN (M. PETER SCOTT)
RALPH (M. PHILIPPA GRAY)
RAY (M. CORA MACARDLE)
ROBERT (M. MARTHA TRENT)

Harry and Gretchen Nolan
ANNIE (M. MONTY DAVIES)
CAVAN (M. DORCAS NEWLY)

Taylor and Violet Gray
PHILIPPA (M. RALPH TUNELLE)

Bert and Gertie Davies
MONTY (M. ANNIE NOLAN)

George and Janet Spencer
MALACHI

Gerald and Bertha Nessel

Rex and Irena Newly
ANIKA
NIELS

Rob and Martha Tunelle

Clyde and Belle Moore

Cavan and Dorcas Nolan
LEON
FIONA

Dexter and Esther Riggs

Grandville

Tyler and Jadyne Newly
EDMUND
PAMELA
BOONE

Buck and Lucy Riley
MOLLY
FINN

Ralph and Philippa Tunelle
JOSEPH

Malcolm and Hermine Tucker
PAUL
MARK
JESSE

Simon and Emma Chappell
TROY
TRUDY

Michael and Mallory Trent
MARCY
MARTIN
MILLARD

Bernard and Pearl Riggs
THOMAS

Ray and Cora Tunelle
MINERVA
REUBEN

Palmer and Hazel Granville
SIDNEY CRANDALL

Way Station

Gabriel and Leigh Trent	Dugan and Melody Riley
ADELE	JASON
ARLENE	JANELLE

Chapter 1

Grandville

The old farmer warned him not to set out for home today, but how was he to know the temperature would drop so suddenly and that the wind would whip into a frenzy, turning the mild rain into freezing pellets of ice that hit his face like slivers of glass? The road, once softened and rutted by the warm spring thaw, was now frozen solid again, and the puddles formed by the rain were now frozen into treacherous patches of ice on which he slipped repeatedly. Abel Newly struggled to keep his balance and still lead his wearied horse along, their heads bent against the onslaught of the biting wind.

During the worst of the storm, when the rain had changed to sleet, making it impossible to see or travel, he had taken his horse to shelter under the branches of some towering white pines. But Abel knew that with his clothing soaked by the rain and now freezing against his skin, he had to find better shelter and quickly. When several branches began to crack from the weight of the ice on them, Abel urged the reluctant horse out into the wind again with the mission to get to safety and a fire as soon as possible.

There are other farms along this road somewhere. Abel had made note of them when he hurried to answer the urgent call for a doctor. He paused to rub at the horse's nose and gently break loose the ice that was forming there. "Don't worry, fella, we'll find you a warm place yet." He spoke into the horse's ear, but his words were snatched into the wind. The sleet now changed to fat snowflakes that swirled all around them and rapidly turned the ground white, making each step he took a risk for a fall and an injury to himself or the animal. Suddenly a flash of light made him look up, causing a gust of cold air to sweep down his neck and back. He huddled back down into his collar and clutched it close with his free hand. *Lightning? In a snowstorm?* A rumble of thunder boomed overhead, and Abel knew his situation had just gotten worse.

It was only a few days earlier when Abel arrived in Grandville by stagecoach, his black doctor bag proudly held in his hand. He was done with medical school in Boston and ready to join Sand Creek's aging doctor in caring for the people in the area, but first, he wanted a little time for a vacation. And spending time with some of his relatives in Grandville was what he needed to unwind.

Abel rubbed his hand down the side of his pant leg. It felt so good to be out of his city suit and back into the comfort of his old clothes. He took just a few moments to look around the small town, relishing its simplicity. In Boston there was already talk of horseless carriages, and he had even seen a couple of the steamer cars pass by on the streets. Their noise and hot, sputtering coals had cleared a path ahead of them as horses and people scattered in alarm. No, he was more than happy to be out of the city. He jumped down from the high seat on top of the coach and turned to thank his cousin Gabe, who was the driver.

"Tell Leigh and Melody thanks again for all the great cooking they did for me," he told Gabe. "Your way station sure makes the trip a lot more pleasant than it would be otherwise."

Gabe laughed as he handed down the other customers' bags. "Did being a city boy make you soft, Abel? You're back in the Minnesota woods now. You better toughen up."

"Did I hear you accuse my little brother of being soft?"

"Tyler!" Abel bear-hugged his older brother and then stood back to take a look at him. "You better watch that *little*-brother talk, old man. I seem to be half a head taller than you."

Tyler grinned and stepped aside to let Abel greet Jade and their children.

"You look so much older, Abel, and so handsome!" Jade hugged her brother-in-law with one arm while she held her newest baby with the other. "Meet your nephew Boone." She unwrapped the baby for Abel's view and then turned to her children. "Eddie. Pamela. Say hello to your uncle Abel."

The children held back a bit, but Abel knelt to their level. "Jason wants me to tell you that he is practicing jumping his horse over a log now, Eddie. And, Pamela, the girls want to know when you will be coming to play with them."

"You were at the way station?" Eddie's eyes lit up.

"Yep, and they want all of you to come stay with them for a visit."

Eddie tugged at his mother's skirt. "Can we, Ma? Can we?" Pamela smiled shyly at Abel.

"Thanks, Abel." Tyler's tone was dry. "Do you have any idea what it will be like at our house now until we actually take the kids for a visit?"

"Yep." Abel smiled in return and then tapped Pamela on her nose. He rose to his full height.

Gabe jumped down from the coach and joined them. "That's right, kids. Adele and Arlene, Jason and Janelle told me to invite all of you for a visit." He turned to Tyler and Jade. "It's been too long since you've been there," he reminded them. "And it won't be long before Dugan and Melody's new baby arrives."

Jade looked to Tyler. "We really need to plan a trip, Ty. I haven't seen Melody and Leigh in so long."

"Well, first, let's visit with our wayward brother. Then we'll talk about a trip," he advised. "Come on, Abel. Let's get you settled." He flung an arm around his brother. "So you're a real doc now, huh?"

They went straight to Buck and Lucy's home connected to Grandville's only hotel. Lucy greeted her brothers with delight.

"Abel! I haven't seen you in so long! When was your last visit home? Rex and Irena's wedding, wasn't it?" she jabbered on while directing her company to sit in the parlor. Buck came from another room, carrying Molly, their little girl, in one arm and his new son in the other.

"Abel, great to see you again." He handed his daughter over to him and then shook his hand. Abel jostled and bounced her until he was rewarded with smiles and giggles.

"All these new babies!" Abel gently rubbed his thumb along the newborn's cheek. "Hey there, Finn," he said softly to Lucy and Buck's son. "And the other children have changed so much in looks," he commented to his siblings. "The rest of you just look older," he teased.

"I see you haven't changed much." Lucy laughed. She stood back to get a better look at her younger brother. "Well, maybe you've changed in looks somewhat, maybe a little more mature, but you're still full of jokes just like when we were kids."

"Who's joking?"

They all laughed.

Supper was a time for catching up on news and family events. They all ate at the hotel dining room so Abel could visit with other members of the Grandville community before heading out to Tyler and Jade's for the night. The next day, he made the rounds to see the lumber mill and visit with more of his friends and meet the newest members of their families. Grandville's population was growing steadily every year with new babies being the prime reason. The young couples who started the town seemed determined to help its expansion.

The next couple of days, Abel spent with his other sister Emma and her husband Simon Chappell on their dairy farm just outside of town. It was Simon's family who housed Abel during his time at medical school in Boston, and Abel had gifts and messages from Simon's parents to deliver to their son's family. The twins Trudy and Troy were delighted with their uncle's visit and promptly informed him that they were going to get a new brother or sister.

"That's great, Emma. Congratulations!" Abel held a twin on each knee as he watched his sister prepare the evening meal. It was good to catch up with his family, but he felt he was missing out as he saw all the happy couples around him. Emma caught the wistful look on his face.

"Something bothering you, Abel?" she asked as she carried the dishes to the table.

Abel set the children down and began helping Emma with preparing the table for the meal. "Why do you ask?" He was aware of her studying him. Of all his brothers and sisters, Emma was the one who knew him best. Maybe it was because she was the youngest of the girls and he the youngest of the boys in the family, so they often had paired up when they were younger, but more likely, it was because for a time, Emma had been the schoolteacher in Sand Creek, and she and Abel had formed a special bond during that time when he was not only her little brother but also her student. He waited for the question he knew was coming.

"I was watching you with the children, and I…well, you're finished with school now and can settle down so…I guess I'm just wondering if you…you know…if you're sweet on someone?"

Abel chuckled. "I was wondering when one of you was going to ask me that."

"What do you mean? Did someone else ask you?"

"No, everyone has been politely avoiding asking me anything too personal. How out of character for my sisters!" He chuckled again.

Emma slapped at her brother's arm. "You rascal! You know we've all been dying to ask if you found a girl in Boston, but we decided that we would not pry." She gave him a sheepish grin. "Honestly? None of them questioned you? Not even Lucy or Jade?"

He laughed again. "Oh, I could tell they wanted to ask, but they obviously have more self-control than you do, sis. Ouch!" he yelped as Emma smacked his arm harder this time.

"So now that I asked, what's the answer?"

Abel grinned again but remained silent while he watched Emma study his face.

"There *is* someone! I knew it!" She pulled him down to a chair and sat down next to him, leaning forward eagerly. "Tell me!" she demanded in her best no-nonsense teacher tone.

"I never meant to keep it quiet," Abel began. "I was waiting for someone to ask, and somehow I knew it would be you."

Emma smiled.

"Her name is Delphinia Digby. She lives with her family in Boston, and her father is also a doctor and is a member of a distinguished practice in the city. I worked a term at the hospital with him, and that's how I met his daughter."

His eyes gleamed as he began to tell Emma what he had been anxious to share ever since he arrived. "I've asked her to marry me, and she said yes, Emma! I can hardly wait for you to meet her. She's so beautiful, and even though she is a city girl, she's willing to move out here to live in Sand Creek. I'm going to get established with Doc Casper first, and then I'll invite the family for a visit, you know, to meet Mom and Dad and see the town and all. Then I'll go back to Boston with them to be married. Delphinia's really wonderful! I hope to have them come here before the summer is out. I don't really want their first impression to be of a Minnesota winter. That is something she'll discover soon enough. But I know she'll be happy here. She told me she'd be willing to go wherever I set up practice."

Emma jumped up to give Abel a hug. "I'm so happy for you! I knew that you had met someone. Something was in your expression that told me you had a secret to share! She sounds very sweet. What does she look like? Does she have brothers and sisters? Is she short, tall, big, or small? Come on, Abel, tell me more!"

Abel was relieved at his sister's enthusiastic response. Somehow her approval mattered the most to him.

Simon entered the farmhouse kitchen and heard Emma's last few questions.

"Ah, so your guess was correct, my dear wife! Abel, Emma has been speculating on your romantic involvements ever since you left for the big city. I think she even made a list of eligible young ladies between Grandville and Sand Creek in case you came back empty-handed."

Emma smacked her husband's arm. "Hush, Simon! Abel will think I'm a busybody if you keep telling fibs like that."

Simon sneaked a wink at Abel.

"Congratulations are in order then?" Simon asked.

"Thanks, Simon. Yes, I'm hoping Delphinia and I can get married by the end of the summer. I can answer all your questions about her, but I know you haven't asked the most important one yet." He paused and could tell by their expressions that they knew what he was talking about. "She is a believer. She and her parents invited me to attend their church with them, a rather large and prestigious church. Delphinia was saved as a young girl. She's a little bashful about sharing her faith, but she helps out at the orphanage and even comes in to the hospital to lend a hand by reading to patients and visiting them."

"That's wonderful news. She sounds like a treasure! Have you told Mom and Dad? I know you haven't been to Sand Creek yet, but have you written to them? Do they know anything?"

"Not yet. I've been waiting to tell them in person. It's going to be a busy summer getting ready for my bride and starting my work as a doctor. I imagine we'll start out with a small house in town first like Doc Casper to be more readily available to patients, but I hope to live on some of my own land eventually and just keep my practice in an office in town. We'll see how the Lord directs our lives. I know how plans can change."

Emma resumed her supper preparations as Simon helped the twins get washed before their meal. She peppered Abel with more questions and learned quite a lot about her future sister-in-law.

"So she's taller than me? That's no surprise. Most people are, except maybe for Irena. Speaking of Irena, you remember that this used to be her home when she was married to Nels Jenson? We just love living here. It is ideal for Troy and Trudy and this little guy." She patted her abdomen. "And I have to say that even though Irena went through a terrible time after Nels's death, she and Rex are doing very well and are so happy together. Rex loves Anika as if she were his own little girl, and their new son, Niels, they named after Nels. I suppose you are getting impatient to get home and see them and Dorcas and Cavan and their family too. How much longer can you stay with us?"

"I really should leave in the morning. Buck lent me a horse so I'll be able to travel faster than by coach even though I may decide to stay over at the way station again. I'm not as used to long trips on horseback as I was when I lived here," he admitted ruefully.

"Just watch the weather," Simon warned. He helped his son and daughter take their places at the table. "This warm spring has been a bit of a surprise, but the old-timers are warning of some cold coming, maybe even some snow."

Abel grimaced. "Snow? I really have gotten soft!"

It was early the next morning when a rider came and pounded on the farmhouse door. Simon and Abel, who were in the barn taking care of chores, came running when they heard it. Emma stopped breakfast preparations to see who it was. She opened the door to find a young boy about fifteen years old, panting heavily as he tried to get his message out.

"I was tol' to come here to git the doc. There's no doc in town right now. There's bin an accident at the Halbergs," the boy announced. "We live on the farm next to theirs, and Mr. Halberg's wife rode over to ask us to go for help. Old Mr. Halberg dropped a tree on hisself and broke his leg or somethin', I guess. It's bin bleedin' too, she said." He stopped for air, and Emma hastened to get him a glass of water, which he drank gratefully.

Abel was already headed into the house for his things. "I'll be right with you," he called as he raced past the boy.

"I'll get you a fresh horse, son. Why don't you sit down and eat something while I saddle him and one for the doctor?" Simon suggested.

"But...how will I git my horse back?" Clearly the youth didn't want to risk losing his horse.

Emma took the boy by the arm and led him into the kitchen and to the table. "We'll return him in a few days when we go to see how the Halbergs are doing," she told him. "We know where they live, and we'll want to check to see if they need help. You just take good care of our horse in the meantime, okay?"

"Yes, ma'am."

Emma quickly dished up some eggs, ham, and potatoes for the boy and another serving for Abel. It was about an hour's ride to the Halbergs, and they would need the sustenance. Abel joined the boy at the table and wolfed down the food while he asked more questions about his patient. They were ready by the time Simon had their horses saddled for them.

"Sorry to cut our visit short, Emma," he said as he hugged her good-bye. "I'll go on to Sand Creek when I'm done at the Halbergs. Thanks for everything and hug the twins for me."

"We'll be praying for you and for Mr. Halberg. I do hope it's nothing too serious." She laid her hand alongside his cheek. "It's so good to have you back home, Abel. I'm so proud of you."

They left with the boy leading the way and setting a reasonable pace for the horses. In no time, they arrived at the farm, and the boy took Abel's horse to the barn to care for it while Abel ran in to attend to the wounded man. He found him wrapped in blankets on the floor.

It was several hours later when Abel sat down to a hot cup of coffee that he learned more of his patient's situation from Mrs. Halberg. Abel had found the gash in the man's leg cleaned and bandaged, but the break in the bone needed to be set, and after several painful attempts and the help of the man's wife, Abel was finally successful in setting it to rights. The old farmer never uttered a sound during the process, but Abel was worn out from the exertion yet exhilarated at the same time. This was his first emergency on his own, and he had handled it well—although a lot of credit was due to the farmer's wife, he had to admit.

"You did an excellent job of cleaning out the wound, Mrs. Halberg." He thanked her as she refilled his cup. "I see no danger of infection if you can continue to keep it clean and dressed."

The woman nodded, and Abel could see weariness in her face. "You say that the tree he felled was some distance from here?"

She nodded again, and after some coaxing, Abel extracted more of the story from her.

"He didn't come in for lunch at the usual time, so I knew something wasn't right," she told him. "He had the horse and wagon, so I walked until I found them on the back eighty acres. I found my husband pinned under the tree, so I wrapped up the gash in his leg first thing and then chopped the tree into a piece small enough that I could push it off him. He never hollered even though I knew he was hurting, and he never passed out. Then I grabbed him under the arms and pulled him up onto the wagon bed and brought him home. I know I hurt him even more doing that, but I had to do it. I figured the best place for him was the floor until he got tended to by a doctor."

"And you say he ate his lunch?"

"He never misses his lunch," she replied.

Abel shook his head. "You are quite a woman, Mrs. Halberg." He was amazed at the endurance and strength the small woman possessed. Why, she was no bigger than Emma! He had helped the man to his bed after splinting his leg, and it was all he could do to handle the extra weight.

For just a moment, he pictured Delphinia in the small farmhouse and wondered how she would fare under these circumstances. He smiled to himself. He had no doubt his bride would pass through such trials with the grace and strength shown by the farmer's wife. He silently thanked the Lord for providing such a wonderful helpmate for him.

Abel spent the night with the older couple. The next day after he assured himself that the farmer's leg was going to heal correctly, he left them with instructions for his care and a promise that Dr. Arnett in Grandville would be by to check up on him. But the farmer then issued him a warning.

"There's a storm coming, Doc. Best you stay here until it runs its course."

Abel glanced out the window at the morning sky. It was a gray day with the promise of rain in the clouds, but he wasn't afraid of getting a little wet on his travels. "I'm sure I'll get to the way station before the storm comes," he assured the man.

But the farmer was insistent. "I can feel it in my bones, young man. A storm is brewing, a bad one."

Abel patted the man's shoulder. "I thank you for the warning and for the offer to stay, but I really want to get home. And I think that after an injury like yours, all your bones would be talking to you and telling you about the weather," he joked.

But the farmer didn't smile.

The farmer didn't smile, Abel reminded himself as he concentrated on putting one foot in front of the other. Each step was treacherous. The thick snow on top of the icy ground made it almost impossible to keep upright, and the wind was determined to knock him backward each time he stepped forward.

It was dark now. The only way he knew that he was still on a road was when the odd lightning would illuminate the way before him. The thunder continued, and the snow came down in surges. Abel didn't know what time it was, but it seemed to him that the light had left the day earlier than usual. His ice-crusted pant legs were like weights holding him down, and he was aware that his fingers and toes were dangerously numb.

Lord, I'm glad you know where I am because I sure don't. It never seemed strange to Abel to joke with God when he prayed. Even now when he was tired, lost, and, yes, he had to admit it, in danger of losing his life, he knew he had a relationship with his Savior that allowed him to speak freely what was on his mind. The way he figured it, God knew his thoughts anyway, so why try to put them into fancy words to pray to him?

I could sure use some help here. I'm ready to come home if you want me, Father, but I'm ready to fight on if you give me the strength. "*I can do all things through Christ which strengtheneth me.*" He quoted more verses and kept up his conversation with God as he trudged forward. He heard his horse whinny just as he bumped into something.

Abel forced his head up to see what he had hit. Another tree? He had run in to a few of them trying to stay on the road. He let go of the collar on his coat and gasped as the cold air hit his neck. He reached out to feel what was before him. Something rounded. This was bigger than a tree. Abel felt excitement as he let his hand guide him around the structure. Walking to the other side, he saw a glimmer of light in the swirling snow. He reached down and brushed the snow away from it.

A lantern. A lit lantern.

His numbed fingers tried to grasp the handle of the lantern to lift it out of the snow, but he found it stuck, frozen to the ground. He marveled that the flame still burned but realized that it was protected from the onslaught of the wind by the structure.

His heart was pounding. People and shelter had to be nearby, but where? Which direction? He couldn't see more than a few feet in the swirling snow, and if he just set out in any direction, he might miss the house or barn or town or whatever it was he had found.

Direct my paths, Lord, he prayed. *Please let me run into the side of a house.* He grasped his collar again and took one step, then two. He took another and tripped, falling to his knees. He had the horse's reins wrapped around his hand, so his fall pulled the horse's head down with him. The lantern, now cleared of some of the snow, lightened the area where he had fallen. He brushed more snow away from the mound on the ground that had tripped him. His horse snorted and pushed at the mound with his head. Abel peered closer to it and found he was staring into a woman's face.

Chapter 2

Near Grandville

Abel brushed the snow off the woman's face and tried to determine if she was still alive. He couldn't tell if she was breathing; the wind made that impossible to detect.

She lay so very still. With his numbed hands, he tried to pull her up but soon found that, like the lantern, she was frozen to the ground.

She must have come outside with the lantern to do something. Check the animals in the barn maybe? He peered once more through the swirling snow around him. Was that a building over there? He felt his horse tug at the reins and start to move in that direction. "Do you think you've found the barn then?" he yelled to his horse.

The horse whinnied and pulled again. *I don't dare leave her here, Lord,* he quickly prayed as the animal pulled him to his feet. *Help me find my way back to her.* If that truly were the barn they were headed for, he might be able to find something within to help the woman get loosed from her icy prison and then maybe get her back to the barn's shelter or, better yet, find the house.

He allowed the horse to lead him away from the lantern and the woman, and after much stumbling, he slammed into the side of the building. *Thanks, Lord. I guess sometimes you give me exactly what I pray for.* He ran his hand along the wall until he found the latch to the door and pried it open. It was a welcome relief to stumble inside and know that the shelter would save his life.

Okay, Abel, you're not done yet, he spoke to himself. *Most barns have a lantern near the door and a way to light it. Keep moving. Don't stop now.*

He let go of the horse's reins and allowed the animal to step away in the blackness. He knew the horse would be all right for now, and maybe after he took care of getting the woman to safety, he could come back and tend to him more. Right now she needed him worse.

He fumbled until he found the lantern, but it took several tries before he was able to get it lit. He was shaking now even though he was out of the wind. The barn offered a measure of warmth from whatever animals were in it besides horses. He could hear the whinnies and sense the movements of the creatures, but as soon as he had light, he ignored the animals and instead searched the area for something to help break loose the woman trapped outside.

Then he spotted the axe.

"That should do it." The words spoken out loud seemed strangely strong as if in competition with the howling wind beyond the walls. Abel rubbed his hands together to get more feeling back into them. His actions were clumsy at best.

The axe in one hand and the lantern in the other, he slipped out the door again, making sure it stayed shut behind him. No sense causing the animals any more discomfort than they already were feeling. The wind wasn't as strong now, and the snow seemed to be abating, or was it the knowledge that he was close to shelter that made it seem that the weather was under control? He could actually see the light from the other lantern, and he started for it.

As soon as he left the side of the building, he felt the wind's bite again. He had almost forgotten his own frozen state in his quest to rescue the woman, and he felt the sharp rub of his iced clothing against his skin when he moved. He wouldn't think about that now.

She was still there. Abel crouched down and again tried to pry her loose. With his lantern, he spied a bucket nearby her and realized that the rounded structure he had first encountered was a well. Had she come for water? Could it be that she had slipped and fallen to the ground and in the process doused herself with the bucket of water, and that's why she was frozen fast to the ground?

Her hair was loose and spread out all around her. Abel brushed at the snow on top of it and realized that the hair was encased in a clear layer of ice. He recalled the rain and sleet earlier in the day and wondered just how long she had been out here. She had on a coat, and there was a shawl frozen under her neck that she had apparently had wrapped around her head. The coat was stuck fast.

Abel sat back and debated how to free her. He had to hurry. They were both in need of warm, dry clothes and a fire. He looked up again and was able to see the faint outline of another building through the snow that continued to fall. *Must be the house.*

He could cut her out of the coat! He pried his way into his frozen pocket for the knife he always carried. *Good thing I'm not wearing a city suit today*, he thought. He never carried his knife in Boston. His hands were clumsy, and he feared hurting her somehow, but he had no choice. He fumbled with his uncooperative fingers as he undid the buttons on the coat and opened it as much as it would go. Then he reached into one sleeve with the knife blade upward and began sawing through the frozen wool. It was slow going, but he finally was able to get all the way down to her hand. He lifted her arm, and it was free. Quickly he moved to her other side and repeated the action.

Her heels were also embedded in the ice, so he took the axe and carefully chipped away at the frozen ground around her boots. He managed to loosen both of them, and her legs were free. Then he moved to her head.

He stared at the white face and then at the frozen hair under the pool of ice all around her head. *I don't even know if she's alive, Lord, but if she is and I chop off her hair, she'll probably kill me for doing it.* He hesitated only a moment longer, and then he began to carefully chop through the ice and through her hair until he had her freed.

He was able now to pull her head up, so he kept pulling until he had her body completely loose, and he started dragging her toward the building he hoped was the house. He looked back at the hair still trapped there and the coat and the shawl in the ice. *No one's going to believe this story, Lord. Thanks for helping me get her out of there. I pray she's still alive. If you don't mind, I think I'd like to run into another wall soon.*

Abel looked over his shoulder and found that they were at the door of the house. He let go of the woman with one hand and managed to swing the door open. Warmth greeted him from inside. Blessed warmth!

He dragged her through the door and swung it shut behind them. A faint glow of embers still burned in the fireplace, cheering him as nothing had since the storm began that morning. He set his burden down gently and hurried to toss wood on the embers and soon had a blazing fire going. He turned back to his patient and realized as he reached for her that his own hands were shaking and tingling as they began to warm again. He still couldn't feel his toes, but that pain would come later, he was sure.

The woman hadn't moved. He placed his ear against her chest and listened intently for a heartbeat. Yes, there it was! It was faint, but it was there. He looked more closely at her and realized that she was younger than he thought. *Maybe it's the haircut.* He smiled at his thoughts as he looked around the house. Warm clothes were the first priority. He stumbled to his feet and went through a doorway he thought might be a bedroom. It was. The clothes he found in it belonged to a man and a woman. He grabbed some garments he felt would work and hurried back to the room with the fireplace. Though he knew it wasn't a chivalrous thing to do, he had to take care of his own physical situation before he was in a position to help his patient. As quickly as his shaking fingers would allow, he removed his wet clothing and pulled on the man's shirt and a pair of pants. The warmth of the dry clothing against his skin was a feeling he knew he would never forget. A life-saving moment.

Next, he turned to the girl on the floor. Even though he was a trained doctor, he felt a bit uncomfortable as he pulled away her wet garments and replaced them with the nightshirt he found for her. It was much too big, but that just made it easier to get on her. He did a quick examination and found a lump on her forehead. *Yes, the bucket must have hit her.* He carefully checked each finger and toe for frostbite. Amazingly they didn't appear to have any of the telltale white spots. Her boots and wool mittens had offered the protection they needed. He was concerned about her ears. The scarf under her neck had kept them out of the ice, and they appeared fine, but he would check again. There was a small spot on her nose, not too deep, so after it healed, it should be okay as well.

Thank you, Lord! Maybe she hadn't been out there as long as he feared. She seemed to be young and healthy and fit. He found some bruising on her back and wondered if she had damaged anything when she fell, but no bones appeared to be broken. He couldn't leave her on the floor. He went back to the bedroom and dragged the bedding off the bed and brought it to the floor in front of the fire. Carefully he moved her onto it and wrapped her in the quilts.

He was still shivering. Seeing a stairway, he decided to explore. He found another bedroom and more quilts, so he took everything he could find back to the lower level. He wrapped more around the girl and wrapped the rest around himself. He checked her heartbeat again and saw that her breathing had gotten stronger, but he was concerned. He really needed to go out to the barn and get his medical bag. And the horse needed care too.

More searching revealed a worn coat that Abel shrugged into and a battered pair of boots that apparently were for barn use. He found scarves that he liberally wrapped around his head and neck and tucked into the top of the coat collar. He dreaded the chill air down his neck. Then he faced the doorway. It took a Herculean effort to go out that door into the cold again, but as he stepped outside, he found that the wind had drastically died down. Was the sudden spring snowstorm over? Now that he had time to think about it, he realized that the lightning and thunder had stopped about the time he found the woman. He made haste to the barn but stopped by the well to chip free the frozen lantern. Its light had now gone out, but the lantern he left there still burned. He took it with him to the barn and hastened to care for the horse that patiently waited. He quickly measured out feed and hay to the other two horses he found.

In the corner, he found some chickens huddled down together, and it occurred to him that the girl was going to need some nourishment when she woke up, not to mention that his own stomach was looking for food. Before he changed his mind by thinking about it too long, he grabbed a bird by the neck and hauled it to the door where he bent to pick up the axe again. Stepping outside, he walked to the nearest fence post and relieved the chicken of its head. He held it until it stopped flapping and then reached for his knife and swiftly cleaned it.

Haven't done that since before medical school.

There was no time for plucking feathers, so he pulled the skin right off, feathers and all.

On the way back to the house, he grabbed the bucket and hauled some water out of the well. The sky was lighter now, and he was puzzled. Was it only afternoon? The storm had darkened the sky so much, and he had battled in it so long that he thought evening had fallen.

He was weary as he opened the door again to the house. The girl still hadn't moved, so he took a moment to warm up by the fire and throw more wood on it. Then he started a fire in the cook stove and put water on to heat. He poured water into a large pot, scrubbed the rest of the bird, and dropped it in the water on the stove. Then he went for his medical bag.

Abel took out his stethoscope and laid it near the fire to warm up. He bent over the young woman again and began unwrapping some of the quilts around her. He then used the stethoscope to listen carefully to her breathing. He smiled. There were none of the rattles he feared he would hear. Maybe she'd recover from her ordeal without having bronchitis or pneumonia set in. Snow had covered her face, and no doubt she had breathed in droplets of the moisture. Infection could develop later.

For now he would just have to watch and see what happened. He turned to put the stethoscope away and heard her murmur. He looked back and saw that her eyes were still closed, but she was trying to move her lips.

She needs water.

He got up and went to the table to pour some water from what was left in the bucket into a glass. He could now feel the tingling in his toes as they regained life, and each step was painful, but it was a good pain. He sat down on the floor beside the girl and gently lifted her head so that he could send a few drops down her throat.

"That's enough for now," he said soothingly. "I'll brew you some tea, and soon there will be chicken broth. You just keep resting. You're safe."

He didn't know if she heard his words, but it made him feel better to say them. Some color was coming back into her face, and that was good too.

Abel spent the next hour cleaning up the water-soaked clothing on the floor. He hung the woman's garments over the kitchen chairs, and he took his own clothes and placed them as near to the fireplace as he dared. He found a broom and swept the puddle of water left by their clothes across the wood flooring so that it would dry more easily.

He made another trip to the barn and well. The snow-covered ice was still dangerous to walk on, but the weather had again changed and was now quiet and still. *I guess what the old-timers say is true: if you don't like the weather in Minnesota, just wait an hour and it will change.* Abel chuckled to himself, yet at the same time, he gave thanks to God for getting him safely through the sudden storm.

He was hungry. The chicken was cooked, so he spooned out some large chunks of the meat for himself and a small bowl of broth for his patient. He took their meals to the floor by the fireplace and sat down beside her makeshift bed. He cradled her head and spooned a few trickles of the warm broth down her throat. He was surprised and delighted when her eyes fluttered open, and she looked up into his face. Her lips moved again, and he realized she was trying to speak.

"Thank you."

The words were barely a whisper, and he had to bend closer to hear them. He felt her go limp again and saw that her eyes had closed. He laid her gently back and tucked the quilts around her.

"You're welcome," he said softly. "Don't worry. I'll take good care of you. I'm a doctor." He knew she didn't hear him, but he felt a measure of pride in telling her he was a doctor.

Then he leaned back against a chair with his legs sprawled out toward the fire and devoured his own meal, eating the chicken with his fingers. He thought of Delphinia and how she would enjoy hearing of his adventures. Finished, he pushed the plate aside and pulled a quilt around him. He would just lay back on the floor for a bit and rest before cleaning up. Just for a bit. In moments, he was asleep.

Chapter 3

Near Grandville Earlier That Day

Mattie Morrison continued with her chores, determined not to let the morning's incident disturb her any further. She shook her head and sighed. She needed to find a new job and soon; the Reverend and Mrs. Wynn had been quite impossible to work for. She bit her lower lip. It was probably wrong of her to think ill of a minister of God, but the more time she spent with the couple, the more of their true natures she had discovered. It wasn't that they did anything wrong, she reasoned. It was just *how* they did things and how they treated her that disturbed her.

She had hired on as a housekeeper for the minister and his wife after losing her job as schoolteacher in Norris. She still felt a twinge of anger at how *that* came about. The head of the school board had a nephew, recently out of school, who needed a job, and somehow Mattie had been replaced without so much as a say so on her part. Before that, she had worked at Buck and Lucy Riley's hotel in Grandville and loved her job there, but she left that position when the man she was sweet on married another woman, and she felt she couldn't bear to be in the same town as they were. Her sister Grace continued to work at the hotel, and Mattie knew she could go back as well, but Nels Jenson, whom she had once loved, was dead now, and she didn't want to go back.

Mattie sighed again. Life could sometimes be hard for a young woman. She was the oldest of seven children, and she needed to earn some money to help her family. The other children were old enough to help out with family chores now, so it was time for her to either get a job of her own or get married. She had no desire to do the latter.

Reverend and Mrs. Wynn were new to the area and had taken on the ministry of a small church south of Grandville. When word came that they required a housekeeper, many had expressed concern that maybe something was wrong with the new pastor's wife that she couldn't take care of a house on her own. Maybe she was ailing. The little congregation agreed to provide the extra money required to pay a housekeeper, and Mattie had jumped at the chance to get the job. She soon learned that there was nothing wrong with the pastor's wife. She was obviously devoted to her husband and his work and spent her time helping him and accompanying him on his calls, which won her the admiration of their little flock; this was true, but Mattie suspected that the real reason was that the woman was lazy. Her rounded figure was evidence of her lack of physical activity as well as her appetite for not only Mattie's cooking but also the baking and goodies provided by the women of the congregation.

This morning, Mattie had gotten up as usual to take care of the outside chores before beginning to prepare breakfast for the couple. She didn't understand how they timed it, but they exited their room at the exact moment that she had the meal ready, as was their practice. She decided that they must take care of their morning ablutions while she was in the barn. After a lengthy prayer, they ate in silence; then the reverend opened his Bible and read a chapter while Mattie and his wife listened. After that, they allowed her time to clean up the dishes; then she was expected to read her Bible for an hour before continuing with her other chores.

Mattie loved to read her Bible and had actually admired and respected the pastor at first for giving her this time to spend in God's Word. That was before she learned of the conditions. The couple was very strict that she must spend the entire hour reading and nothing else. No talking was allowed. As odd as it sounded, she complied, but the joy of searching the Word was taken away when she was reprimanded for flipping through the pages or for closing the book before the allotted time.

This morning's Bible time had been interrupted by a visitor to the house. Mattie heard the rider and waited for the knock on the door. She looked up at the reverend. He continued to read his Bible as if not hearing.

Mattie rose to answer the knock.

"Your time is not over, Mathilda," the reverend stated firmly, stopping her steps. Her lips tightened briefly at the use of her full name. She had requested time and again to be called Mattie, but the preacher wouldn't comply.

Mattie decided it was ridiculous to ignore the person at the door. Surely the minister understood that. "Yes?" She opened it. "Oh, good morning, Mr. Granger. How are you today?"

"Morning, Miss Morrison." The man took off his hat. He looked over at the pastor, who still hadn't moved.

"Morning, Reverend Wynn, Mrs. Wynn." He tipped his head in their direction. "Old Sam's on his deathbed, sir, and he's asking to see you. The doc says he won't last long now." He waited for a response and seemed puzzled when he didn't get one. He looked to Mattie for help.

"Would you like me to get the buggy ready for you, sir?" Mattie asked the pastor.

"No need for that. I brought my buggy so the preacher could come right away," Mr. Granger informed them.

Reverend Wynn closed his Bible and turned to look at the two by the door. It was obvious to both that he acquiesced out of duty, not desire. "We will kneel in prayer before our journey."

"Might be best if we prayed on the way, preacher. I don't know how much time Sam's got left in him."

The reverend scowled at the man. "God cannot be rushed," he admonished as he took the upper hand. He and his wife got to their knees and waited for the others to join them.

Mattie was frustrated with the indifferent reaction of the preacher and of his demanding tone. Just to hurry things along, she knelt beside Mr. Granger, for whom she truly felt sorry. The man was obviously in a hurry to fulfill a last request of a dying friend and knew as well as she did that God didn't require kneeling to be able to hear a prayer. There was a time for such things, but this wasn't it.

The preacher's prayer droned on, but Mattie ignored it and prayed for the dying man and for the correct way to handle her situation. *Give me patience and wisdom, Lord. I'm about ready to give this preacher a piece of my mind, so please help me control my tongue. I know I should be respectful of someone who claims to be preaching your Word, but I have my doubts.*

Mattie realized that the prayer had ended, and Mr. Granger was stiffly getting off his knees.

"I'll be waiting in the buggy then," the man said. He tipped his head to Mattie and gave her a look she couldn't interpret.

Mrs. Wynn went to the bedroom to gather what she and her husband would need for the journey, but the Reverend Wynn turned to Mattie.

"Mathilda, your services will no longer be required here after today. You have shown disrespect for my authority as God's minister and have disobeyed my commands. Be prepared to have Mr. Granger drive you to your home when we return. I will see to it that your parents are completely informed of your lack of respect."

Thank you, Lord! It took a valiant effort, but Mattie was able to keep the smile off her face as she demurely replied, "Yes, sir."

"I will expect you to finish your time in Bible reading and to complete your other duties, but I feel it is within my right to withhold your salary as a lesson to you. Perhaps it will cause you to be more respectful in the future."

It was all Mattie could do to hold her tongue, but she never dropped her eyes from his as he stared down at her.

"I see into your soul, Mathilda Morrison. God will indeed need to punish you to humble that rebellious heart you have."

Mrs. Wynn came into the room at that moment and announced that they were ready to leave. She seemed not to notice or care that there was tension between Mattie and her husband.

"Be prepared to leave by evening," the reverend reminded her before turning to exit the house.

The door shut behind them, and Mattie stomped her foot to expel some of the anger that had been building in her. He had no right to keep her pay from her! Then as she heard the buggy move out of the yard, she realized she was free from the oppressive atmosphere of the Wynns' presence, and she released a happy cry and twirled around in the kitchen. She paused a moment in thought. *God doesn't punish my sin. He took care of that on the cross when the Lord Jesus died for my sin. I do admit to being rebellious, Lord,* she prayed, *but you know my heart is not rebellious toward you or your Word. I do rebel, however, against anyone who uses your Word incorrectly.* She thought a moment about the self-important preacher; then she shrugged.

So she would have to seek another job, so she would have to listen to him rant on to her parents about her being disrespectful. She paused. *Ma and Pa will understand. I think they knew he was going to be trouble when they visited the church a few weeks back.* Mattie's folks attended a church in Norris, but they had traveled out to the country church for a chance to visit with their oldest daughter for the day. A comment her father made after the service came back to her: "The man seems to think that the people are here to serve him instead of him being sent to minister to the people."

At Mattie's puzzled expression, he had continued, "Maybe I'm speaking out of turn and just don't know the man well enough. Do a good job, Mattie. Let the Lord use you for his glory."

Mattie ran upstairs to her bedroom to pack her things. She wanted to be ready to leave and not have to spend another night with the Wynns. She hadn't realized how unhappy she really was in their home. She was almost through when she heard the rain and noticed that the day had started turning dark.

I better check on the animals before this gets any worse, she thought.

By the time she got downstairs and into her coat and boots, the sleet had started. She grabbed a shawl to throw over her head and hurried out to the barn. The ground was already starting to get icy, so she took her steps with care. A rider coming into the yard halted her progress, and as she looked up through the freezing rain, she saw Wally Beck stop his horse in front of her. Her heart sank.

"Howdy, Miss Mathilda," he shouted through the downpour. He grinned wickedly at her under the brim of his hat. "I see that your guardians are here." He indicated the two horses that were on their way into the barn for shelter, and she realized that he thought if the horses were there, the Wynns were also. She wasn't about to tell him otherwise.

"If only they were gone, I'd take shelter with you tonight instead of riding on home, but there's no way I'm going to get stuck in the same house with those two self-righteous biddies all night. Another time, my sweet. I'll be back," he called behind him as he rode off.

Mattie shuddered at her close escape. Had Wally known she was alone, she was sure he would have made himself at home. He had become a nuisance, making advances to her that she didn't welcome. Reverend Wynn had caught him talking to her in the yard on another occasion when Wally waylaid her and had actually accused her of having a tryst with the man. She had promptly denied it, but the pastor didn't believe her.

She moved on through the icy downpour to the barn.

"Hi, Misty." She patted the Appaloosa fondly then moved on to the palomino. "Hello there, Trouble." She went to the back door of the barn and closed it. The horses had come inside willingly out of the freezing rain. She noticed that the chickens had also made their way back inside their sheltered corner stall through the small doorway that led to the outside pen.

"Everyone's in?" she asked.

She took time to wipe down the horses and decided to feed them now in case the weather got worse and she couldn't get out later. "I wonder who will be tending to you when I'm gone," she talked to them while she worked. She knew that the people in the little church had provided the horses and chickens for their pastor and his wife. She wondered if the couple even knew how to care for the animals. Not once had she seen either of them even go into the barn. They had turned over all inside and outside chores to her.

"I guess they better hire someone else soon, or you guys will be on your own out here." She jumped as a boom of thunder rattled the barn, and she quickly moved to soothe the animals. She opened the barn door to see how bad the storm had gotten and was shocked to see the ground covered in snow and the snow swirling all about. The door was almost pulled out of her hands by the wind, and she pulled it shut with an effort.

"Oh no! Mr. Granger won't be able to return the Wynns home tonight, so that means I won't be leaving yet either, I'm guessing." She turned back to the animals one more time to check if everything was secure; then she took down one of the two lanterns that hung on nails near the door. "I think I better light this one and take it with me. I can't believe how dark it's gotten all of a sudden."

Mattie wrapped her shawl around her head and shoulders and pulled on the wool mittens that were in her coat pockets. "Well, here goes," she called to the horses. "I'll see you in the morning after all."

The wind nearly knocked her off her feet as she started for the house. Mattie had lived in the north all her life and knew the dangers of being out in a blinding snowstorm, even one that came suddenly in the spring like this one. She needed to get to the house and safety as quickly as she could and while she could still see where the house was. A gust took her scarf clear off her head, but she caught it before it could be taken away. She wrapped it around her neck with her free hand to secure it and felt the wind pull her hair loose from its pins and send it flying straight out behind her. It took her breath away.

She was near the well when she saw the bucket that hung there swinging back and forth wildly. *I better bring in water while I still have the chance. I don't want to have to come back out in this tonight.*

It was a struggle to stay upright and pull the filled bucket up from the depths of the well, but after setting down her lantern and using both hands, she managed to get the bucket up and free. She turned with the full bucket in one hand to reach for the lantern when her feet slipped on an icy patch and flew out from under her. She came down hard, flat on her back, and the bucket went sailing into the air. It came down hard too, right on her forehead, knocking her out. The water in the bucket drenched her and flowed to cover the ground around her. Her hair fanned out and was quickly trapped in the stream that seemed to harden to ice in moments.

But she was unaware of that. She was blessedly unaware of anything until sometime later for a few seconds when she felt someone hold her tenderly and offer her warmth.

Chapter 4

Near Grandville

Abel was dreaming. He knew he was dreaming because he was standing beside Delphinia, and she was wearing a wedding dress. She was so beautiful! He was listening to the preacher speak the wedding vows, but the man's voice was angry and condescending, not like the preachers he was used to. How odd! He needed to wake up, but his head felt so heavy. He tried, but he couldn't lift it.

The preacher was asking if he would take this woman to be his wife. Yes, of course. He loved his Delphinia! He was asked again. The voice was demanding an answer.

"Yes." Abel struggled to get the word out and was surprised to hear his own voice. How silly he felt to know he was talking in his sleep.

"I now pronounce you man and wife. What God hath joined together let no man put asunder."

What?

Abel willed himself awake. That voice wasn't part of any dream; that was a real person talking! He pried open his eyes and tried to figure out where he was and why there was a double-barrel shotgun pointed at his chest.

Shotgun?

Abel pushed himself up on an elbow and tried to make sense of his situation. Through blurred vision he saw a tall, thin man with a book in one hand and a shotgun in the other, towering over him. Beside him was a plump woman, her arms folded in front of her. She, like the man, was staring down at him with a menacing expression.

Abel took a moment to look around the room, but only a moment. That shotgun had his attention. He was on the floor—no, on a quilt or something. No, it seemed to be a bed of sorts on the floor, and he—

The girl! Suddenly Abel sat up and looked at the pile of bedding. The girl was still there, but she hadn't wakened yet. He turned back to the people standing over him and now noticed another man by the door. He was watching them all carefully.

"Is she—" Abel paused to clear his throat, but the words came out as a croak. "Is she okay? Don't worry. I'm a doctor, and I've been taking care of her."

"Yes, we can see that."

Abel was confused. He moved to stand up, but the man lifted the gun to follow his movements.

"Is there a problem?" Abel asked, motioning to the weapon.

"There won't be as long as you do as you're told," the man replied.

Abel stood. He studied the people in the room while he tried to make sense of their expressions. Suddenly he understood. "Oh! You think that I—that we—no, folks, nothing happened here with your daughter. I found her outside in the storm and got her back to the house before she froze to death. That's all."

The tall man looked Abel up and down. "Yes, we see where you attacked her by the well. By rights I should shoot you now and send your soul to hell where it belongs, but I've done the more righteous act and bound you to her in marriage. By God's law and the law of this land, you will take her now as your wife and do right by her."

Abel's jaw dropped. "Attacked her? Marriage?" He rubbed his face with his hands to try to clear his befuddled mind. *Is this a dream, Lord?*

"Let me explain to you what really happened here, mister. I was lost in the storm and stumbled upon your daughter by the well. She was frozen to the ground—"

"Don't attempt to lie to a minister of God!" The man's voice boomed out, and the girl on the floor gasped.

They all turned to her, and she stared at them with wide eyes. She pulled the quilts up to her neck and turned to look around her as if to determine where she was. Abel saw her groan with the movement of trying to sit up.

"Here, take it easy. You've had a nasty fall and will probably be very sore for a few days," he cautioned her.

"Who are you?" she asked in a whisper.

Before Abel could answer, the preacher spoke. "He's your husband, Mathilda. I now see that as soon as Mrs. Wynn and I left you alone, you carried on your love affairs behind our backs. First, it was that Beck fellow—that reprobate! And now we find you committing fornication right in our house. You thought we wouldn't return and that you would have time to cover your transgression, but your sin has found you out!" The preacher was ranting eloquently, and Abel could see he had fire and brimstone in mind for both of them.

"You have it wrong, sir." Abel's voice brooked no argument, and the steely stare he gave the minister didn't go unnoticed. Catching the man unguarded, Abel grabbed the shotgun from his grasp. When the reverend made a move toward him, Abel turned the butt end of the gun around and threatened to strike him with it. "I've had enough talk about lying and fornicating and sin! Nothing happened here! Now you're going to quit talking and listen to what I have to say."

Abel kept an eye on the man by the door, but the fellow hadn't moved and didn't appear to be a threat. The man and woman facing him, however, wore expressions that would have killed him dead if they could. *This guy's a minister, Lord?* He saw that the girl on the floor was watching him. "I was lost in the storm. I nearly tripped over your daughter when I found her frozen to the ground—"

"She's not our daughter. She's a lying, deceitful—"

"I don't care who she is or what you think of her!" Abel stopped the man. "She was frozen to the ground.

I think she slipped on the ice and doused herself with the bucket of water. I had to cut her loose."

Out of the corner of his eye, Abel saw the girl touch the lump on her forehead and then reach for her hair to feel the chopped ends. It was sticking out in every direction, having been wet when he laid her down. It was very short, and for that he was sorry, but he had to finish what he had to say before he could apologize to her.

"I brought her into the house and got her into dry clothes." Again, her movements caught his eye as she fingered the nightgown he had put on her as if seeing it for the first time. "She nearly froze to death. Do you understand that? I'm a doctor, and I saved her life. Nothing else happened here. In fact, this is the first time she's been awake since I've been here."

Abel motioned with the gun for the couple to step aside, and he gathered his belongings into his medical bag while he kept the gun ready if they should rush him. "I'm leaving now. I'm sorry for giving you a scare, but that's the gospel truth. Your daughter has nothing to be ashamed of, and neither do I. If anything, you should be thanking me for keeping her alive."

He motioned for the man by the door to move, and he opened it to let himself out. "You take care of her now," he told them. "She might still get pneumonia. Thanks for your hospitality." He looked at the girl named Mathilda. "Sorry about chopping off your hair, ma'am, but I had to do it to get you loose." And with that, he shut the door behind him and hurried to the barn.

Abel saddled his horse while he kept on eye on the house. He took a chance and changed back into his own clothes, leaving the ones that apparently belonged to the minister over one of the stalls. He left the shotgun too after he had unloaded it. He was just stepping into the stirrup when he heard a voice nearby.

"For what it's worth, I believe you, mister."

Abel spun around to see the man from the house standing near the door to the barn. "Don't try to stop me," he warned the man.

"Don't intend to. My name's Granger. I believe your story, and I'll see to it that Mathilda gets out of here today. I think I'll recommend we get a new preacher for our church too," he added.

"That guy's really a preacher?" Abel questioned him.

"Yep. He's Reverend Wynn. We had him checked out before we hired him. And"—he looked Abel in the eye—"he really did marry you two."

"Nonsense," Abel exclaimed. "Neither of us consented to a marriage."

"I don't know." The man scratched his head. "You did answer yes when he asked you, you know."

Abel's sense of humor returned. "That would never be a legal marriage, and you know it. Glad to hear she's not related to them anyway. You'll see to it she gets proper care?" he questioned the man.

Mr. Granger studied Abel a moment. "Seems like you kinda care what happens to her," he commented.

"I'm a doctor. I care about my patients," Abel informed him. "Well, I'm off. This has been an experience I won't soon forget." He asked Mr. Granger for a few directions, and then was on his way.

As stormy as the day before had been, today was warm and mild, and the snow and ice were rapidly dissipating. Abel had a lot to think about as he got on the right trail for Sand Creek and home. His first thoughts were that this would be a great story to tell; it was sure to get some laughs, but then he wondered if it were better not to say anything about it at all. After all, he wouldn't want word to get back to the girl named Mathilda. *Mathilda? What a name for a beautiful girl like that!*

Abel stopped his horse suddenly. *Beautiful?* That was a funny way to describe the girl with the chopped-off, deep-brown hair and huge, brown eyes and with a frostbit nose.

Chapter 5

Near Grandville

Mattie stared at the door after the man left. She was very confused. The last thing she remembered was pulling the bucket out of the well in the middle of a snowstorm with lightning and thunder all around her. Was it all a fantastic dream? Was she awake even now?

She closed her eyes and tried to recall anything of the night that would help her. For a second, she thought she remembered drinking something from a spoon. Yes, she had been held in the crook of a man's arm. The memory comforted her, and she smiled.

She opened her eyes in time to see Mr. Granger slip out the door. That left her alone with the Wynns, and she finally turned to face them, aware that they had been staring at her ever since the stranger left.

"How dare you lie there and pretend that nothing happened here last night!" Reverend Wynn's face was red with rage as he turned his fury on her. Having been outmaneuvered by the younger man, he now vented his frustration on Mattie. "You can't fool me, you Jezebel! The vows that were spoken here today are until death, and I will see to it with everything in my power that you abide by the vow you have made."

Mattie stared at the crazed man. "What are you talking about?" Her voice sounded raspy.

Triumphantly, the reverend explained, "Mrs. Wynn and Mr. Granger were witnesses to the wedding ceremony I performed to right the wrongs you and that debaucher committed. You are legally bound to him now and can no longer go on living in your sinful ways."

Mattie was astounded by his words. She hadn't heard anything of a wedding ceremony. "What do you mean about me making a vow? I haven't made any vow!"

"Mrs. Wynn spoke for you by proxy, and the man made his vow of his own free will. It was necessary that we take care of matters immediately due to the circumstances we found you in."

Mattie contemplated his words. Why would the man agree to marriage? She couldn't believe that, and she didn't believe for a minute that she was married to him. She stared at the couple as if they had gone mad. "Nothing happened here last night, and there was no marriage performed this morning."

"How do you know if you can't even remember?" Mrs. Wynn spoke for the first time.

Mattie turned to her. "I would know." With the quilts wrapped around her, she struggled to her feet. She swayed a moment while she got her balance. She felt weak, and her head throbbed, but she didn't want to stay any longer in the same room with the condemning couple. "I will get dressed and leave with Mr. Granger as soon as possible," she informed them. She hoped the farmer hadn't already left, but even so if he had, she would hitch the buggy and get out of here under her own power. She prayed she had the strength to do it.

They said nothing and did nothing to help her as she made her way to the stairs. She stopped when she saw her clothing on the backs of the chairs, and though her mind swirled with questions as to how they got there; nevertheless, she swept them into her arms as she passed by. The stairs exhausted her as did the struggle to get dressed. Her hands went to her head, and she felt the chopped ends of her hair. She took the small mirror in her room and held it up to view what was left of her locks.

I'm not going to cry now, she thought. *I've made it this far. I've only got a little ways left to go to be done and out of this house. I can't let a little thing like my hair being chopped off start me bawling now.* Mattie willed her self-control to stay strong. She had always considered her long, brown tresses to be her best asset. She reached into her bag for a scarf, made a triangle out of it, put it over what was left of her hair, and tied the ends under her chin.

Her bag was packed, and she slid it down the stairs beside her as she made her way to the lower level again. She reserved what strength she had left to be able to carry it out of the house.

Mr. Granger was outside by the buggy, so Mattie made no comment to the Wynns as she approached the door. But Reverend Wynn wanted his final say.

"I will see to it that you honor the wedding vows made today, Mathilda. If I find that you have not, I will make known your sin to others, and you will be an outcast in this community as will your family. It is my duty before God."

Mattie gasped. "You can't do that! You heard the man—nothing happened. He saved my life! We don't even know who he is!" She tightened her lips. "You leave my family out of this, or you'll regret it."

A slap to her face was the rapid response. She stared at the preacher in shock.

"Never threaten a man of God!" he hissed at her.

Mattie was stunned. Her hand went to her cheek. She wasn't frightened of the man, not with Mr. Granger nearby, but she was appalled at the wild look in the man's eyes. She turned away to get her coat but couldn't find it on the hook near the door. Not wanting to spend another moment in the house, she walked out the door without a backward glance.

Mr. Granger approached when he saw her coming and took the bag from her. He noted her lack of a coat without comment. Seeing her weakened condition, he held out his arm. It was then that he saw the red mark on her face from the slap.

"Who did that to you, Miss Morrison? Was it the preacher or the woman?" His features were set.

"It doesn't matter, Mr. Granger. I just want to go home, please."

"Yes, of course. Here, let me help you in the buggy." After he got her settled, he said, "I'll be right with you."

He was back in a few moments with two quilts, which he wrapped around her back and placed over her knees. Mattie noticed the red knuckles on the man's hand and guessed their cause. "Thank you, Mr. Granger."

"You're welcome, ma'am. He won't be striking any more women any time soon," was all he said.

He climbed in beside her, but before he signaled for the horse to move, he pointed to the ground by the well. She turned to see where he was pointing.

"Oh!"

The sun was already melting the snow and ice, but there was still plenty left to retain a hold on her coat. She saw that the sleeves were sliced open, and she could see the ends of the scarf now being lifted by the warm breeze. But it was the sight of her hair that startled her. There it lay under the ice. Her long, brown hair was fanned out with the chopped ends still framing the place where her head had been.

She didn't know what to say. The evidence was all there just as the stranger had said. How could the Wynns have not believed him? Mr. Granger slapped the reins, and the horse moved forward. Mattie found it hard to take her eyes off of what was left of her hair, but she finally turned away. Mr. Granger pointed to the fence post as they drove out of the yard.

"Looks like your stranger cooked up a chicken for you."

A mound of chicken feathers fluttered on the ground. Mattie stared at it, trying to recall anything of the night before. "I think I remember being fed some broth," she said.

Mr. Granger nodded.

Mattie had so many questions she wanted to ask the kind man, but embarrassment kept her silent for a time. Mr. Granger was on the church board and was well respected by the small group. What he must think of her! She cleared her throat.

"Mr. Granger, I just want you to know that I'm sorry about—"

"You have nothing to be sorry for," he assured her. "I talked with the doctor out at the barn, and I believe everything he told me about your night."

"Thank you. But what about Reverend Wynn marrying us? He claims that he will do everything in his power to make me abide by the marriage, but I wasn't even awake for it. Can he really do that?"

The older man rubbed his chin. "I don't know much about this sort of thing. Wynn is a real preacher with papers and all, and it looked to me like he performed a real marriage ceremony. I heard the young man answer yes to his question too, but maybe he wasn't awake yet like you. I didn't come into the house until the preacher was about done."

"But I don't want to be married! It can't be legal if I didn't answer."

"Mrs. Wynn spoke on your behalf," he explained. "No, I don't think it is legal, but that Wynn fellow may be out to cause you trouble. After I introduced his face to the floor, I told him that he was no longer a pastor at our church and that he and his wife had to move out of the house. We don't need his kind around here, preacher papers or not! I'll speak to the rest of the church board as soon as possible, but I'm sure they will agree with me."

Mattie was relieved to hear that and wanted to ask more, but her strength was gone, and she felt her head bob as she nodded off. The last thing she said before she fell asleep was, "I'm so sorry about your friend passing away."

"Thank you, Miss Morrison."

Mr. Granger kept the horse at a slow pace so as not jostle her, but he wanted to get her to her folks as soon as he could.

Chapter 6

Nolan Farm

Dorcas Nolan watched her husband walk to the barn after their lunch together. Something was bothering him, and she wished she knew what it was. He sloshed right through the puddles that remained after their recent spring snowstorm as if he didn't even see them.

She turned from the window and automatically began clearing away the dirty dishes. The children were getting their books out for reading time before their afternoon naps, and she was glad. She was afraid that there would be an argument about wanting to play in the puddles outside rather than settling down inside on this sunny day. She hurried to join them.

After tucking in Fiona, Dorcas stepped over to Leon's room. He was standing on his bed looking out the window, and she saw the longing on his face. He was such a good boy and always striving to please her and Cavan. She smiled at her four-year-old son when he spied her and plopped down quickly on the bed.

"You know what, Leon?" she asked him as she drew him close in an embrace. "I think you're old enough now that you don't need to take a nap anymore."

His eyes lit up. "Really, Ma? You mean I can go out and play?"

She laughed. "Yes, really, but be very quiet so you don't disturb your little sister. She still needs her rest because she's not as big as you are."

Leon squirmed out of her arms and bounced on the bed before jumping to the floor. He raced for the stairway but then tiptoed carefully down them after seeing his mother put a finger to her lips to silence him.

Dorcas laughed when she watched Leon rush outdoors and make his way straight for the biggest puddle in the yard. He would be wet and tired tonight, but he was having fun, and she loved to see him enjoying himself.

I wish I could see that joy in Cavan's face again, she thought. Her forehead puckered into a scowl as she tried to figure out just when Cavan had started to withdraw from her and the children. *No, not the children*, she realized. It was just her.

Maybe our visit to Mom and Dad's tomorrow will be just the thing to brighten his mood, she thought. *Seeing Abel again will certainly brighten mine.* She smiled at the thought of seeing her younger brother. It had been a long time since he had been home, just after Fiona had been born, she remembered. Abel, with his joking ways, had always been able to make her laugh. Now he was all grown up and a doctor. It was going to be wonderful having him home again.

Dorcas enjoyed her position as the third child in the Newly family. Being in the middle of the family meant that she was often the peacemaker between her brothers and sisters, but it also meant she needn't bear the responsibilities that the older siblings had, and she wasn't coddled as much as the younger ones. Russ and Sky Newly raised their six children on a ranch near Sand Creek, and now all the children except for Abel were married. Dorcas knew her folks were looking forward to having Abel home with them again, even though they knew it wouldn't be long and he would be on his own too.

Dorcas paused to remember. Tyler had been the first to marry after he and a group of young men from Sand Creek started the town of Grandville, which was a two-day ride from here. Tyler's wife, Jade, was from Chicago, and though Dorcas didn't get to see them often, she knew that they were happy and thriving with their family of three children.

Lucy was her older sister, and she too lived in Grandville with her husband Buck Riley. They owned Grandville's hotel and stables and had two children. And Emma was her younger sister. Emma and Simon Chappell lived near Grandville also and ran a dairy farm. Dorcas had only recently learned that Emma was expecting another baby to add to their family of twins, a girl and a boy.

Dorcas was between the sisters in age, and she missed them both desperately. Not having them near made visits even more precious. They had such a wonderful time growing up together, and now as adults, they seemed to have an even greater appreciation for each other. People often commented that the three Newly girls, with their blonde hair and blue eyes, could be triplets.

Rex was next in line, and he lived on land adjoining their parents' land. He was married to a lovely girl named Irena. Dorcas smiled to herself. Irena was so perfect for her brother. She was a woman who had gone through some hardships, being widowed with a baby girl when Rex married her. But Irena had a love for the Lord that Dorcas could only admire. She was an example to all of them of the importance of trusting Christ in every aspect of life.

Dorcas paused in her reminiscing. *That's what I need to do more of, Lord. I need to trust you to help Cavan with whatever burden he is carrying instead of me worrying about how to help him.*

And Abel was the youngest, Dorcas returned to her musings. Now the baby of the family was all grown up. *It's a good thing there are lots of grandchildren, or Mom would be awfully lonesome.*

The door slammed, and Leon stood inside with his hand on the handle, ready to go out again as soon as he delivered his message. "Pa says to tell you that he is riding into town for some supplies. Bye." And he darted out before he could be stopped.

Dorcas went to the window to watch Cavan mount the horse and ride off. He didn't even turn to wave, and her heart grew leaden as she realized that never before had he left her without a good-bye kiss. What had she done? Why was he acting so coldly to her?

Instead of allowing the worry to take over her thoughts again, she brought her concerns to the Lord. She decided that a special supper was in order for the evening, and she set about preparing one of Cavan's favorite dishes and desserts. With that under way, she called Leon in the house and gave him a bath after Fiona had hers. They would be clean and fresh and welcoming for their father as well as ready for church the next morning. She heard Cavan come home, and she rushed to change into a more attractive dress. Everything was ready. The children were waiting at the table, and she was standing nearby ready to dish up the food as Cavan entered the house.

Dorcas saw right away that Cavan noticed the extra efforts she made for the evening meal, yet he said nothing about them. The meal would have been a silent one if not for the children's chatter. Leon was visibly drooping by the time they were done, so Dorcas asked Cavan to get the children ready for bed while she cleaned up.

"Sure. Come on, kids." His tone was wearied, so she stopped him with a squeeze to his arm and a gentle smile. He nodded and walked past her.

Dorcas sighed. Whatever was on his mind was still bothering him, and she was going to get to the bottom of it. She couldn't stand any more of his silence and coldness. A sudden thought occurred to her. *It wouldn't be the money again, would it?*

Cavan was finishing tucking Leon in when she entered the bedroom. She bent and kissed her sleepy son's head. She whispered to Cavan, "His first full day without a nap." Already their son's eyes were closed, which caused the couple to smile at each other, and their eyes held for a moment. Cavan looked away first and got up and headed downstairs. Dorcas felt the sting of tears that she held back while she moved on to the next room to see to her daughter.

When she came downstairs, she looked for Cavan in his usual after-supper place, his chair. He would often read there, or they would sit together and visit about their day. He was nowhere to be seen. She checked their bedroom next, but he wasn't there either. She grabbed a shawl and stepped out onto the porch and nearly bumped into him. He was just standing there, looking out over their land.

"Tell me what's wrong, Cavan," she said without preamble.

He didn't turn to look at her, so she moved to his side and slipped her arm through his. "Please, Cavan, I don't understand your silence. Have I done something?"

"No."

"Then what's the matter?"

"Nothing."

"Cavan Nolan, you're acting like you did when your cousin Rooney sat beside me on the playground when we were kids!" She teased him with a scolding. "After that, you wouldn't speak to me for a week, and as I recall, it was a very miserable week for both of us." She looked up at him in the dimming light of the spring day. She saw a faint grin cross his face.

"And I made sure Rooney didn't get in between us again, didn't I!" he responded.

Relief washed over Dorcas that he was talking again. "I believe you gave him a black eye." She laughed softly. "You were my hero even then. What were we? Ten?"

"And I've loved you ever since," he whispered into her hair.

They shared a sweet kiss and then just held each other for a long moment.

"I need to check things in the barn, and then I'll be in," he said as he still held her. "Thanks, sweetheart, you always make me feel better."

Dorcas watched her husband walk down the path to the barn. She still didn't know what was wrong, but she knew everything was all right.

Chapter 7

Newly Ranch

Abel woke to the aromas of bacon, eggs, coffee, and his mother's cinnamon coffee cake, his favorite breakfast. It was good to be home.

His trip from Grandville after the storm had been uneventful. Because he got such an early start that morning, he decided to keep riding until he made it home, and he arrived worn out and hungry but happy to finally be there. He slept late the next morning, then he got reacquainted with running a horse ranch and spent most of the next day helping his father with the many jobs there were to keep everything in tip-top condition the way Russ Newly liked it. Of course, he and his dad visited all the time they were working, and he got caught up on more family news from his mother during meals.

He stretched before arising. His muscles were sore from the workout the day before. He really was as soft as his brother Tyler had accused. But there was nothing like good physical work to make a man feel useful. His doctoring practice would limit him on that. He needed to roll out of bed and get out to the barn before breakfast, but his thoughts held him back for a few more moments.

Should he tell his folks about the girl Mathilda and the strange minister's shotgun-wedding ceremony? He hadn't said anything yet, and they just assumed his delay in getting home was due to the farmer's leg injury he told them about. Was it wrong for him to leave out the happenings of a whole day? Without his confirming or denying it, they believed he sat out the storm at the Halberg's house.

Abel reached for his clothing as he pondered what to do. *Lord, I have no desire to be lying, and I have no desire to start gossip about a young lady whom I may never see again.* He determined to let the matter be.

But at breakfast later, he found that his parents were more discerning than he thought.

"Something's been on your mind, Abel. What is it?" Sky asked her son. She passed the serving platter to him and watched in delight as he heaped more food on his plate.

Abel filled his mouth to delay giving an answer. How she could always figure him out, he'd never know. He swallowed half a cup of coffee.

"What do you mean?"

"Come on, son," Russ joined in. "Your mother and I know you, and don't tell us that being away for a few years can change you this much. You're preoccupied.

Is it because of Delphinia? Are you unsure of marrying her?"

Abel nearly choked and had to cough before he could reply. "No! Everything with Delphinia and me is just fine. Of course I want to marry her! You'll see when you meet her in a few months. She's really special."

"Then what's been bothering you?" Sky demanded, but Russ held up his hand to stop her.

"If he doesn't want to talk about it, he doesn't have to. Sorry, son. We tend to forget that you're not a child anymore. Your mother and I are here if you need us. You know that." He pushed away from the table. "Well, I better get the buggy ready. It's almost time to leave for church."

"I'll do it for you." Abel quickly left the room.

Russ turned to Sky. "Is there anything you need help with? There will be quite a crew here after church with Rex's family and Dorcas's family coming."

But Sky wasn't listening. She was watching her youngest son walk to the barn. Russ slid his arms around her from behind.

"There's definitely something on his mind, but I don't think it's anything we need worry about," he told his wife. "He'll let us know if he needs us."

"It's not just that!" Sky blurted as she turned in Russ's arms to face him. "I've been hearing the ladies in town talking, and…I don't know how to say this, but… they are saying that they would be uncomfortable having Abel be their doctor."

"What?"

Sky shook her head. "I know, I can hardly believe it myself, but they are saying that no unmarried young man is going to deliver their babies or help them with their female problems. They say it will be all right to have him take care of broken arms and legs and such, but other than that, they want nothing to do with him."

Russ was perplexed. "What about all the babies Doc Casper has delivered over the years?"

"They say that not only is he married, but also he is an older man. Somehow they feel more comfortable with him. I know for a fact that most of them won't let Abel near their unmarried daughters." Sky looked so worried that Russ had to laugh.

"When did you hear all this?"

"When I was in town yesterday. I was so eager to tell everyone that Abel was home, but I kept getting strange looks from some of the ladies, so I asked Gretchen Nolan what was going on, and she's the one who told me—"

"Sounds like a bunch of gossip to me," Russ interrupted. "I wouldn't worry about it, dear. It's true that Abel is not married, but he is engaged and will be married soon. The women will get used to him before long."

But Sky wasn't convinced. "And just how are *you* going to feel about it when Irena or Dorcas has another baby? Will it bother you that Abel will be their doctor?" She was satisfied when she saw the startled look on her husband's face; then worry filled hers again.

Russ rubbed the back of his neck while he thought about what Sky said. "I think what we have to remember is that Abel is a trained doctor now. There was a time when Doc Casper was a young man too. Remember how you used to help him when you first came to Sand Creek? You told me that some of the women were uncomfortable with him too, but because you were there, they allowed him to care for them. Maybe Abel will need someone to help him too."

Sky nodded as she thought about that.

"Who's helping Doc these days?" he asked her.

"I know Rhoda Riggs, Martha and Jasper's daughter, was helping him a few months back, but Martha told me Rhoda was courting a man from Freesburg, so I don't know how long she'll be available."

Russ spied Abel through the window. "Look," he said quickly to Sky, "we can't change how people feel, and it could be that we're making more out of this than we should be. Abel may have to prove himself to the people of Sand Creek, but he doesn't have to prove himself to us. We're going to give him all the support he needs, starting with prayer."

Sky nodded and hugged Russ before Abel stepped into the house again.

"Everybody ready for church?" he called.

Sand Creek

Russ, Sky, and Abel rode into the churchyard a little early. Abel wanted an opportunity to greet the rest of his family and some of his friends before the service started.

"I think you'll really like Pastor Sweeney," Sky commented to Abel. "He's been here a couple of years now, and we are very blessed to have him, although we do still miss our first pastor and his family. They moved farther west to start a new church, but we still hear from them time to time." She scanned the faces of the people who were also arriving and was startled to see some of them avoid eye contact with the Newly family. She hoped Abel hadn't noticed.

But it was Sky herself who caught Abel's attention.

"You okay, Mom?" He turned to look at her carefully. The years hadn't changed Sky much. Her blonde hair, coiled in a bun at the back of her head, hid any gray hair that may have appeared, and the few lines that now deepened her frowns seemed to melt away when she smiled. Abel looked closely into the eyes that were the same hue of blue as his own. "You look a little tired. Perhaps you need a checkup. As soon as I get settled in with Doc at his office, you could be my first Sand Creek patient." He missed the startled glances his parents gave each other as he jumped down from the buggy and turned to help his mother.

"Hey there, Abel!"

Abel spun around to see his brother Rex helping his wife Irena out of their buggy. As soon as Sky was safely on her feet, Abel ran to meet them. Sky and Russ watched their sons slap each other on the back. Abel bent to give Irena a quick kiss on the cheek, and then he scooped up baby Niels to have a look. Anika clung to her daddy, a little unsure of the man who was holding her brother.

"This could get awkward," Russ admitted in Sky's ear.

"I never thought of him being *my* doctor," Sky whispered back.

They joined their children just as Dorcas and Cavan stopped their buggy nearby. Leon ran straight to his Papa Newly and was rewarded with a quick toss in the air. Then he threw his arms around Sky's legs, nearly knocking her over.

"Gramma! Ma says that Uncle Abel is home! Is he here?"

"Right behind you, Mr. Nolan. My, look at how grown up you are and how handsome you look in your Sunday clothes!" Abel handed Niels back to Irena and held out his arms to Leon, who ran into them without hesitation.

"Are you a real doctor now, Uncle Abel? Can you make sick birds get better? I got a bird that Ma is helping me make well. It flew into our window and hit the ground, and I rescued it and—"

"Whoa, son! Take a breath. Abel can't understand you when you talk so fast." Dorcas waited until Abel set Leon down, and then she gave him a welcoming hug. "So good to have you home, Abel!" Quietly she whispered, "Careful what you promise about the bird. Leon squeezed the stuffing out of it bringing it to me."

Abel squelched the laughter her words produced, but his eyes were filled with merriment. "I'll have to teach you how to care for a wounded bird. How would that be, buddy?"

"Time to go in, Leon." Cavan held out his hand to shake Abel's as he directed his family to the building. "Good to see you, Abel. We'll catch up over dinner."

Abel took a moment to say hello to Fiona and chuck her under the chin before following his family into the church. He paused often along the way to shake hands and return greetings of his friends and neighbors. Then he settled down on the pew beside his parents and took time to look around. Nothing had changed. Somehow that set his heart at peace, and he waited in prayerful silence for the service to begin.

He was happily surprised at the new preacher and his grasp of Scriptures. Abel was quick to admit to himself that during all his years of schooling, he hadn't devoted as much of his time to God's Word as he had his studies. He made sure he attended church every Sunday—at first, one that he had discovered on his own since the Chappell family attended one he didn't feel met his needs, but later, he joined Delphinia and her family at a larger, grander church. As he listened to the depth of Pastor Sweeney's teaching, he realized that he had just been floating along in his Christian walk. Suddenly he felt a renewed interest in getting back into the Word.

Doc Casper, Sand Creek's doctor since the town began, caught up with him after the service.

"Abel Newly, it's about time you got back home," he exclaimed. "Florrie's been looking forward to getting me to take her back east to see her sister, and now that you're here, that just might be possible." He looked Abel up and down while he shook his hand. "*Dr.* Newly." He smiled. "It's good to have you home, partner."

"Hello, Doc." Abel's eyes gleamed with excitement. "If you're ready for me, I'll come by tomorrow to get set up at the office. I can't tell you how much I've been looking forward to working with you."

"And I'm happy to have you. I'm slowing down, Abel, and I don't mind admitting to you that I could use a rest. Come by anytime you want, and we'll get to work."

Newly Ranch

Dinner was a happy, noisy time. Abel watched his mother serve the family, and he was interested to note that the tiredness he thought he saw in her earlier had disappeared. She was smiling and laughing and enjoying every moment. Maybe she just had something on her mind earlier; he had to be careful about his unsolicited doctoring, but it was a part of his life now. He looked around at his family, reveling in their closeness. He was particularly aware of Rex and Irena and Cavan and Dorcas. Soon he would have his wife at this table. With that in mind, he enjoyed answering all the questions put to him about his Delphinia.

"Abel, Dad says that you've already had a patient since you've been back." Dorcas spoke over her shoulder as she cut food into smaller pieces for her son.

Abel's fork stopped midway to his mouth. He darted a glance around the table, receiving questioning looks from the adults. "Oh, you mean Mr. Halberg. Yes, let me tell you about his wife." He regaled them with the details of how the farmer's wife had gotten her injured husband home and how the man wanted his lunch when he got there.

"They didn't mind you staying with them through the storm? I'm so relieved to know that you weren't out in it. Did you ever hear such thunder and see lightning during a snowstorm before, Dad?"

Russ answered his daughter's question, and the conversation continued, but Abel felt his father's glance return to him again and again.

Later the men took a walk outdoors while the women worked on cleaning up the kitchen. Russ stopped to lean on a fence post and turned to face the others.

"Something on your mind, Dad?" Rex questioned.

"Yes, there is. I didn't want the women to hear this, and I expect you boys to keep this in confidence." He waited for their attention.

"Word is out that there's a new gang in the area, and they're focusing on the banks. Now you know that it's no secret throughout the surrounding towns that the Newlys and Trents have inheritance money, so my old boss at the Pinkertons figures they'll try to hit Sand Creek or Grandville. We were fortunate not to have the Barnes gang try here, and ever since the James gang failed at Northfield, attempts have been fewer all over, so this new group of outlaws is probably feeling pretty cocky and sure of themselves that our guard will be down."

"What do you need us to do?" asked Rex.

"Nothing yet, but I wanted you to be aware and to help watch out for strangers in town. And that means to keep an eye on new women in town too. Remember Sophie Barnes posing as Sophia Barlow? She had a lot of people fooled."

Abel smiled.

"What's funny, Abel?" asked Russ.

"I was just thinking that I don't have much money left in this bank anyway after paying for my schooling, but I'm sorry, I know the rest of you do, and I'll be watchful."

"I'm sure you have plenty left," Cavan spoke for the first time, and his tone was dry and his face impassive.

The other three men looked curiously at Cavan, but he didn't elaborate on his statement.

Russ continued. "I especially want you to be aware, Abel, because if there is an attempt here, that means there could be bloodshed, and as a doctor..."

Abel nodded. "I truly hope it doesn't come to that, but rest assured, Dad, that I know how to care for bullet wounds too. It seems a shame to put it this way, but the Civil War taught the medical profession a lot about such things."

"Coffee's on, fellows!" Sky called from the house.

"You two go on ahead," Russ told his sons. "I'd like a word with Cavan. You mind?" he asked his son-in-law.

Cavan nodded, and the other two left.

"Let's walk, shall we?" Russ directed them down a trail. They walked a few moments in silence, giving Russ time to seek the Lord's guidance before he spoke.

But Cavan opened the conversation first.

"I'm sorry about that comment I made about Abel and the money," he said sheepishly. "I didn't mean anything by it."

Russ nodded. "But there is something about the money that's bothering you, isn't there, son?"

Cavan kicked a stone and sent it flying out in front of them. He shrugged as if he was struggling for the right words to say.

Russ stopped, causing Cavan to stop and look up at him. "Let me guess, and you can tell me if I'm wrong, okay?"

Cavan looked down at his feet.

"You and Dorcas got married pretty young, soon after you both finished school. You've worked hard to provide for her, and you're doing a pretty good job at it, and then one day, your in-laws show up at your door and tell you that they've put your wife's portion of an inheritance in your bank account for you to do with whatever you choose." Russ crossed his arms over his chest. "How did that make you feel, Cavan?"

Cavan turned his head away from his father-in-law to look out over a field. His jaw was set, and Russ could see he was embarrassed by the question.

"Let me tell you how I think it made you feel." Russ continued. "At first, you were pretty excited about it, but then as it sank in, you realized that your wife actually had more money than you did, probably more than you would ever make in your lifetime. You started to feel insignificant and wondered why she would even want to be tied down to you. You may have even thought about giving the money back or getting rid of it somehow. And you certainly didn't want to use any of it. After all, it is *her* money. Is that about it?"

Cavan squinted his eyes as he studied Russ. "Yeah. That's about how I feel. I almost wish those bank robbers would take the whole lot of it out of our bank." He spoke vehemently. "How'd you know?"

Russ chuckled. "Think about it, son. I was in the same position once that you're in right now. And so, might I add, was Evan Trent. That money came from Sky's inheritance from her step-uncle in England. She gave half to her brother Evan right away, and that left half for us. Quite an amount too."

Russ shook his head. "I didn't know what to do. There I was in love with Sky and wanting to marry her, but I was sure that people would think I only wanted her for her money. I didn't even know about the money at first! I didn't make much with the Pinkertons, and I had only a little money put away. Then suddenly this beautiful young woman whom I loved with all my heart handed me a fortune. I wanted nothing to do with it. I came awfully close to not marrying her, and that was a terrible time for both of us because she simply could not understand how I felt.

"The truth was that Sky didn't care about the money either. She said we could give it all away if it bothered me that much, that all she wanted was to be my wife. That's when I realized how selfish and immature I was being. Why should my pride prevent my wife from having her inheritance? I came to learn that the money didn't belong to Sky or to me. It belonged to the Lord, and if he was gracious enough to allow us to make use of it, then we needed to use it wisely for his glory.

"I'm not accusing you of acting like I did, Cavan, but I see your struggle, and I want you to know that you're not the only one who has gone through it." He waited, praying he hadn't offended the young man.

Cavan nodded slowly. "I never thought about how it was for you. Does it bother you anymore, Russ?"

"No. Sky and I are united now. Whatever belongs to her is mine, and whatever is mine is hers. You know, Cavan, you should have a talk with Buck Riley sometime. I think he has gone through the same thing you and I have since he married Lucy. I don't think Simon and Emma had any trouble with it, probably because Simon's family had wealth to begin with, but talk to Buck. I think he and you have a lot in common. And never be afraid to talk to me if you'd like."

He patted Cavan on the shoulder. "And one more thing, don't shut Dorcas out of your thoughts. I did that with Sky at first, and it only caused more misunderstandings. Dorcas loves you and wants to work with you."

"Thanks, Russ. I do want you to know that I appreciate the gift you and Sky have given us. I guess I have a lot more pride than I thought. And I do worry about what other people think, and that's another downfall."

They headed back to the house. "It's more important what God thinks of us than what other people think,"

Russ commented. "And like I said, the money belongs to God. I'm not about to let a bunch of thieves take it and use it to satisfy their sinful behaviors, so keep your eyes open."

Chapter 8

Norris

Mattie tucked the short strands of her hair back under her sunbonnet. She grimaced at the feel of the cut ends in her fingers and allowed herself a moment of self-pity as she thought of her long locks now gone. Her mother had trimmed the chopped ends the best she could, but until it grew out some more, Mattie knew she would be hiding her short hair under a bonnet.

Her parents had been stunned by Mr. Granger's report of what happened at the Wynns' home and about the stranger rescuing her from freezing to death. They believed in their daughter's innocence without question, and for that, Mattie was truly thankful. The marriage ceremony left them all wondering about its validity, but Mattie was firm in denouncing that it could be considered legal in any way.

"Mattie!"

She looked up from hoeing in the garden at the call. Her mother came around the corner of the house and motioned for Mattie to come.

"Mr. Granger is here and wants to talk to you, Mattie."

Mattie brushed off her hands and followed her mother back to the house. She stopped to wash in the basin on the porch, where she could hear her mother offering their guest some coffee. Her father joined her at the basin on his way in from the barn.

"He must have some news about that preacher," her father speculated.

"I just wish I had never worked for them. Then none of this would have happened," Mattie told him quietly.

"You can't go on blaming yourself, honey. Maybe it's a good thing you were there so that these people could be exposed for the hypocrites they really are."

They joined their guest in the kitchen, and Mattie hurried to help her mother serve some bread, butter, and jam to go with the coffee.

"I just thought I'd stop by and let you folks know that the church board agreed with me, and we sent the Wynns packing. We put them on the stage last Friday, and where they go from there, we don't know, but at least it's not here." Mr. Granger took a gulp of the scalding liquid. "Meanwhile, I feel bad about your daughter being out of a job, so I took it upon myself to see if I could find her a new one."

Mattie's mouth dropped open in surprise. "Thank you so much for your concern, Mr. Granger, but you don't need to go to any trouble on my account."

"It's the least I can do. The whole church feels responsible for not seeing through that preacher when he first came. We had our doubts about him, but we were all figuring he just needed time to get settled into our ways out here. Turns out he was so self-righteous and self-important that all he was interested in was having everyone else do his bidding."

"And Paul reminds us to have the mind of Christ, who made himself of no reputation and took upon himself the form of a servant," Mr. Morrison added. "What will the church do now?"

"We're going to send out invites to hear some more preachers, and we'll be a lot more careful in our selection this time." Mr. Granger helped himself to the bread. "But as for you, Miss Morrison—"

"Please, Mr. Granger, call me Mattie."

"Well, Mattie, I found out that Sand Creek is looking for a schoolteacher. A friend of mine, Bert Davies, owns the bank there, and he's on the school board. I told him all about you and that you taught in Norris too, so he knows you've got experience, and he wants to meet you and see if you'd like the job."

"That sounds wonderful, but school won't start again until the fall." Mattie looked at her parents. "Maybe I could work in Grandville until then."

"Hold on a second," Mr. Granger continued. "My friend knows that you want to start a job right away, so he thought maybe he could use you at his bank until the school term started."

"At the bank? I've never seen a woman work in a bank before." Mrs. Morrison looked at her husband. "Would that be proper for Mattie?"

"What kind of work does he want her to do?" Mr. Morrison asked. "Would she be cleaning the building?"

Mr. Granger smiled. "No. Since Mattie's had training for school teaching, Bert thought maybe she could work as his secretary for the summer. He has a man coming this fall to fill the position, but he could use Mattie as a temporary employee."

Mattie sat down. She was astounded. The job sounded wonderful and would take her through the summer months until school started, and she loved teaching school. She could hardly believe her good fortune.

"Where would she live?" her mother asked, and Mattie turned to the older gentleman, eager to hear his reply.

"Bert suggested she take a room at the hotel. The owners are good friends of his and won't charge much, plus she'd be nearby both the bank and the school. What do you say, Mattie?"

Mattie smiled. "It seems too good to be true." She turned to her parents. "Ma? Pa?"

Mattie's mother spoke first. "After the last experience you had, I'm a bit reluctant to see you off on your own again." She looked over at her husband for his advice.

"Mattie, what do you want to do?" her father asked.

"I'd like to try it, Pa, if you think it would be okay."

"Then you shall. Thank you, Mr. Granger, for helping our girl. We're indebted to you."

"Nonsense. Mattie has proven herself to be worthy of the position." He stood. "Bert said to come as soon as you're able. You can find him at the bank, and he'll help get you settled."

They followed their guest out to the porch, and as he approached his buggy, he said, "I almost forgot." He reached into the backseat of the buggy and pulled out a garment. "I pulled Mattie's coat out of the mud. I don't know if you want it or not. It will need cleaning and repairing, but here it is."

"Thank you, Mr. Granger." Mattie took the heavy coat from him. "And thanks again for finding me the job. I'll not disappoint you."

"I don't think you could disappoint anyone, Mattie." He tipped his hat and slapped the reins to send the horse moving.

Mattie's mother took the coat from her hands. "My goodness! You never told me that the man cut the sleeves of your coat."

Her father fingered the coat sleeves. "You must have been trapped in the ice pretty hard for him to have to do this." He looked up at his daughter. "He really did save your life."

Mattie studied the garment with her mother. "I still don't remember anything about it. Is it repairable, Ma? I will need it by winter. I don't know what my pay will be, so I don't know if I'll be able to afford a new one."

"I'll see what I can do, but first, we have to get it cleaned up." She set it on the porch and headed back into the house.

"Ma!"

"Goodness, Mattie! What is it?" Mrs. Morrison turned to see her daughter clutching the bonnet on her head.

"What am I going to do about my hair?"

Chapter 9

Near Grandville

Wally Beck watched the house from the trees. *She should be going to the barn soon to do the chores*, he reasoned. But where was she? He pulled on his horse's reins and led him through the trees to the back of the barn.

The door was closed already. She must be in there.

Normally Wally didn't sneak around; he wasn't afraid of anything and certainly was not afraid of the preacher, but he wanted to see Mattie Morrison alone without getting a lecture from the pompous man.

Mattie had a bit of a sharp tongue too, but he didn't mind that in a woman. She was a spitfire; that was for sure. He liked the way she stood up to him and didn't take any of his flirting. He liked the way her brown eyes sparked when she scolded him. And he liked her trim figure and attractive features.

He tied his horse to a fence post behind the barn and quietly slipped between the rails to the back door.

Slowly he opened it and peeked inside. No one was there. He stepped in and took a good look around. The horses and buggy were gone, so maybe that meant that Mattie was alone in the house. He paused. *Didn't they have chickens?* He walked to the back stall and looked around some more. *No chickens.*

Puzzled, he started for the house. This time there was no sneaking in his manner. He boldly stepped to the door and knocked a couple of times then threw the door open.

"Mattie?" he called.

It didn't take long for him to discover that the house was empty, really empty. The Wynns and Mattie had moved out.

What?

Wally scratched his head as he looked around. "They left in a hurry," he said in the vacant house. The furniture was still there, and some of the bedding was tossed about, but all the clothes in the closets were gone.

He hadn't heard anything about the preacher moving, so it must have happened quickly because usually Wally and his friends knew what was going on in the area. They had to know. It was part of their job to know.

He walked back to his horse, deep in thought. *Where did you run off to, Mattie?* He knew he was going to have to locate her again. Mattie Morrison was too sweet of a prize to let get away.

Wally rode back to his mother's house and found his friends lounging on the front porch, waiting for him. His mother stepped to the doorway when she heard him approach. Her glare plainly told him that she was not happy with the company he kept, but he just grinned at her and at the men who called out greetings to him.

"Hey, fellas," he called as he dismounted. He strode up the steps and leaned against the rail. His mother turned on her heel and slammed the door behind her on her way back into the house.

"Anybody hear anything about that preacher skipping town?"

Otis guffawed as he tipped his chair forward with a thud. "Ya mean, anybody hear 'bout thet bit of skirt who disappeared!"

The others joined in his laughter, including Wally. He referred to these men as his friends, but in reality, he would always watch his back around them. He crossed his arms in front of him and grinned at Otis.

Otis was the oldest, a heavy-set man always sporting a couple of days' growth of whiskers. He wasn't quick on his feet but quick enough with a gun and could fell a man with a backhand from his meaty fist.

As heavy as Otis was, the opposite was true of Asa, who was lean. Wally glanced over at the man beside Otis. What Asa lacked in fat, he made up for in muscle. Asa was a handsome, dark-haired man, who had a way with the ladies, a trait that often upset his better judgment. He was the self-proclaimed boss and brains of the group and took no backtalk from any of them.

Without turning to look at him, Wally was aware of the third man on the porch. Standing near the wall was Lonan, a half-breed from the Dakota tribe. All Wally knew about him was that Lonan never knew his white father and was raised with the tribe but never fully accepted as one of them. His native features were in contrast to his curly, black hair, so different from the straight hair of his Indian relatives. For that reason, he wore his hair short and found he could pass as a white man when the need arose. Lonan rarely spoke. His command of the English tongue was fluent enough; he simply preferred not to speak.

Wally was the youngest, the kid of the group. His good looks and jovial ways made him the favorite, but exposure to the temperaments of the others had hardened his character so that underlying his cheerful demeanor was a steely heart void of conscience.

"Forget the girl, Beck. I've told you before that you don't do your best work if you're chasing a skirt," Asa warned.

Under his breath, Otis muttered, "Pot callin' the kettle black."

"What was that?" Asa turned his head to look at the larger man.

"I said, 'Beck better keep on track.'" Otis waited until Asa turned away then grinned at Wally.

"We've got business to discuss. Send your mother to town."

"Ma won't talk, Asa. Why not leave her alone?"

The leader raised an eyebrow at Wally.

"All right, she'll go. Just give me a minute."

Wally stepped into the kitchen to face his mother's back as she stirred something on the stove. "How about going into Grandville, Ma? We could use some supplies. I got some money here you can use."

Without turning around, Mrs. Beck spoke. "I don't want your money, Wally. And I don't need any supplies from town." She tapped the spoon on the pot and set it down and then moved to the table.

"Ma, now don't go giving me any trouble." Wally threw an arm around his mother's shoulders. "You know I think you're the best and only woman in the world for me. Can't you do me this one little favor?"

Mrs. Beck sighed. Her son had always been able to get his way with her. Since his father died when he was a boy, she had raised him on her own and been spoiling the fatherless boy all his life. His recent behavior concerned her, and the men occupying her front porch worried her. She was afraid her boy was going to get into trouble.

"Here, Ma." He placed some money in her hand. "Get yourself some new fabric and make a new dress or, better yet, just buy a dress."

She looked at the money in her hand. "I don't understand how you make so much money as a farmhand." She shook her head. "And I suspect that I don't want to know where it really comes from. All right then, I'll go. But I want these men gone when I get back, you hear?"

He gave her a quick squeeze and said, "I'll hook up the buggy for you, Ma."

After Mrs. Beck left, the men moved their business into the house. Otis went to the stove and tasted the broth cooking in the pot. He stirred the contents and found chicken, potatoes, and carrots, so he rummaged through the shelves until he found a bowl and scooped a healthy portion in it for himself. He brought it to the table where he proceeded to wolf it down.

Asa motioned for Wally to get some stew for the rest of them while he shook his head at Otis. "Were you even thinking of sharing that with us?" He smacked the larger man on the back of the head and pulled up a chair beside him. Otis just kept eating.

"Got any bread?" Asa asked as Wally placed a dish in front of him.

"Sure do," Wally responded. "Ma's a great cook!" He placed a loaf of bread on the table, but before he could turn to grab a knife, Asa pulled one out of his belt and hacked a hunk of the bread off. He dipped it in his chicken stew. Lonan grabbed the loaf and tore off his portion. Before Wally was even seated, Otis took what bread remained and wiped his bowl clean with it. Then he rose and refilled his bowl.

Asa finished his meal and pushed the bowl away from him. He took a paper out of his shirt pocket, unfolded it, and laid it on the table in front of him. He waited impatiently for Otis to stop scraping out the last drops from his bowl, and finally he snapped, "You're like a pig in a feeding trough, Otis! Now pay attention!

"The way I got it figured is that Sand Creek will give us the biggest payoff. We'll wait until there are no customers in the bank. Then we'll send one person in. That's going to be you, Beck. Of the four of us, you look the least like a bank robber."

Wally grinned.

"I'll be covering the front door, and you two will take the back. After Beck gets control of the bank, he'll open the back door for Otis to help him. Lonan, you have to have the horses ready to ride, you understand? As soon as Beck comes out that back door with the money, I expect all of you to be in the saddles and on the move. I'll catch up with you and cover you in case anyone tries to follow."

The men nodded.

"We've still got to decide when the best date will be, but before we even think about taking down that bank, we've got to learn more about the town and the people. That's where you'll come in, Beck. You need to start getting acquainted with some people there, make friends, and learn all you can about the bank without looking suspicious. You need to find out for me the best time when the most money will be there, and I'll work on a little plan I have in mind to make sure the law will be busy somewhere else the day we go in. But before we take on Sand Creek, I've got another little job I want us to do first."

The men were almost done with their planning and had begun sharing a bottle of whiskey Otis pulled from inside his coat when Mrs. Beck returned. The men, including Wally, filed out and got on their horses. Wally turned in the saddle to speak to his mother as she climbed down from the buggy.

"I'll be in late tonight, Ma. Don't wait up."

Mrs. Beck sighed as she watched her son ride away with the men. She unloaded the supplies she had purchased in town and set them on the porch. Then she unhitched the horse and brought her to the barn and took care of the evening chores before going into the house. She stopped in the doorway. Dirty dishes were scattered all over the table, and the room reeked of liquor. She walked to the stove and lifted the lid on the cooking pot. It was empty.

Chapter 10

Sand Creek

Abel stood outside the doctor's office, excited about finally beginning his practice and nervous about it at the same time. He respected the older man who served the medical needs of Sand Creek and the surrounding areas and wanted to live up to the expectations the doctor had for him. Abel had been in this office many times before, often in his childhood as a patient with his cuts and scrapes but also as a curious onlooker into the mystery of doctoring. Old Doc Casper had been delighted in his interest and had encouraged the young boy by teaching him what he knew.

Today was the beginning. Abel took a deep breath and stepped inside.

"Morning, Abel," the doctor called from the open door to the examining room. "Thought you'd be in today.

"Hello, Doc. What are you doing there?"

The older man walked over to shake Abel's hand. "Eager to start, are you?" He chuckled. "Well, I can't blame you. I remember my first few days, so I know how you feel. Come along then. We'll start by inventorying supplies. You'll need to know what we stock in the office and what you'll need to carry in your medical bag when you're on a call."

The men worked together and soon made decisions on how they were going to share expenses and income from patients. Abel was investing in the practice, and his additional money would be a boost to replenishing needed supplies, and they both agreed that because he was the younger man, it would be best if he took most of the house calls, which allowed the older man to remain in the office to handle some of the cases that came to town. Abel would work in the office whenever he was available.

"I guess I should get this order over to Mr. Nolan at the store, and I think I'll stop by the bank to check with Mr. Davies about my funds."

Just then the door opened, and a woman walked in holding her son's bandaged hand. Abel could see blood staining the bandage. His look questioned Doc, who nodded for him to see to it.

Abel bent down to the boy's level. "So what do we have here?"

The woman looked between Abel and the older doctor. "I came to see the doc," she said.

"No need to worry, Ragnhild. This is Dr. Newly. You remember Russ and Sky Newly, don't you? This is their son. He's been away at school and is going to be my partner from now on."

The woman named Ragnhild eyed Abel, and he thought he detected distrust in her perusal.

"It's okay, my dear. Dr. Newly is quite capable."

Abel waited for the mother's approval, and once she nodded, he continued his inspection of the boy's wound. The cut required stitches, and during the process of seeing to it, Abel kept up a steady stream of questions and answers with the small boy while the mother and Doc Casper carried on a conversation. He was done in no time.

"For being so brave today, Tommy, you get to pick a treat from the candy jar." Abel well remembered the doctor's favorite form of incentive to get his young patients to cooperate. "Help yourself, young man, and next time remember not to run with a knife in your hand." He turned to the mother. "Keep the wound clean and bring him back to have the stitches removed in about a week."

"You're done?" She looked at her son, who was proudly showing her his bandaged hand and the peppermint candy. She nodded to him. "You wait outside, Tommy. I'll be out in a minute."

After the door closed behind Tommy, Ragnhild turned to the two men. "I was in a hurry to get Tommy in here and didn't bring any money with me. I'll pay you when I bring him back for the stitches, if that's okay." Even though she was clearly embarrassed to admit her predicament, she kept eye contact with the older man.

"Now, Ragnhild, you know that's not a problem. We always work something out. Why don't you step over to the house and have a cup of tea with Florrie? I know she'd enjoy a visit."

"That would be nice." She looked at Abel. "Thank you, Dr. Newly. I didn't expect Tommy to sit still for you. I can't get him to sit still for two minutes at home it seems."

Abel laughed. "I just told him about my own experience with a knife when I was about his age, and I even showed him the scar, and by the time I got done telling him about how impressed the other kids at school were with my stitches, I was done sewing him up. It's a trick I remember well from Doc Casper fixing me up."

The woman laughed. "It certainly worked for Tommy."

After she left, Doc patted Abel on the shoulder. "Well done. Word will get around now that you are competent, and folks will be more apt to trust you."

Abel was puzzled by the doctor's comment. "What do you mean?"

The doctor motioned Abel to a chair. "I didn't want to worry you, Abel, because I hoped it wouldn't be a problem, and maybe it won't be." He rubbed his chin while he thought on how to form his next words. "You see, when I first started doctoring, I was about your age. I was still back east then, and I worked in a small clinic with two other doctors. We had a policy at the clinic that we would take turns seeing the new patients, but that if a patient was already seeing one of us, he could continue seeing the same doctor."

Abel nodded. "That's how it was in the Boston clinic where I interned."

"Yes, well, I began to notice that I wasn't getting my same patients back. They were asking to see the other two doctors, and at first, I was concerned that I wasn't giving proper care or that my mannerisms weren't pleasing to the patients. It seemed the only patients I had were children or older people. So I asked the other two doctors what to do about it." He smiled. "You see, the other two doctors were older, so people trusted their experience, and"—he paused and pointed at Abel—"they were married men. I was single at that time, and the women didn't want to come to me. Their husbands didn't want them coming to me, and their mothers and fathers didn't want them coming to me."

Abel nodded in understanding. "We talked about this in school," he said. "Did it change after you married?"

Doc sat back in his chair. "It did. It took some time, but it did. And it is good to have a woman as a helper. When I came to Sand Creek, I had to prove myself as a doctor before any woman would come see me, even though by that time I wasn't a young man anymore. Florrie has always helped me when she could, but I hired your aunt Ella at first and then later your mother to work with me, and it seemed to make all the difference to the women patients to have them around. So ever since, I have tried to keep a woman on as a helper, whether she has experience or not. Right now Rhoda Riggs helps out, but it looks like I could be losing her to a suitor in Freesburg."

Abel leaned forward. "Are you saying that until I am married, I won't be accepted as a doctor?" Saying the word *married* immediately brought to mind his recent shotgun wedding, and he felt his face redden. If the people of Sand Creek got wind of that, he would never be accepted as a doctor!

"No, son, I don't mean that no one will want your services, but you may encounter resistance from the mothers and husbands in this town about having their daughters or wives as your patients."

"Have you heard talk?"

The old doctor nodded. "But don't you go worrying about it. I'll be with you and will try to help you win their confidence. It would help if you were married though," he teased.

Abel grinned. "Then let me put your mind to rest, Doc. I'm getting married in the fall." He proceeded to tell his old friend about Delphinia. "So you see, I don't think there will be a problem after all."

The men stood. "We'll pray there won't be, Abel, although it might be smarter for you to move the wedding date up. Now let me show you how I keep the books. See here? I write down today's visit and…"

It was some time later that Abel made his trip to Nolan's store and placed his order. Jonas and Bridget Nolan were friends of his family, and he had always had an easy rapport with them, as he did with most of the people of Sand Creek. Their daughter, Bernadette, was once engaged to his brother Rex, but it hadn't worked out. She instead had married a salesman, and Rex had married Irena.

"Looks like Doc needs more supplies than usual," Jonas commented as he looked over the order.

"We decided, with two of us in the office now, that we should set up two examining rooms instead of just one, so we need to supply both," Abel told him.

"Oh, that's right!" Jonas exclaimed. "You're going to be helping Doc now that you're done with school."

Abel wasn't sure how to take the man's comment. Did he realize that Abel was a doctor now, or did he just think he was Doc's helper? "I'll be seeing patients too," Abel said, "and maybe before too long, Doc and Florrie can take a vacation." He was amused at the store owner's expression.

"You mean Doc might not be here? What if Annie's baby comes when he's gone? Who's going to help her?"

Abel's humor vanished when he saw that Jonas was serious. Annie, their niece, was married to Monty Davies, the bank owner's son. Abel had been in the little Sand Creek school with both of them. "*I* would be here to deliver Annie's baby, Mr. Nolan. I assure you I am fully trained and have delivered babies in Boston. You have nothing to worry about." Now he understood Doc's concern. He hadn't taken the man's words too seriously, but he was seeing firsthand evidence of the people's reaction to him as their doctor.

"Look here, Abel, I believe you went to school and all, and maybe in Boston you're a real doctor, but that doesn't mean you're going to be delivering my niece's baby!"

It was Bridget Nolan who came to Abel's defense. She came from the back of the store where she had been during their conversation. "Now, Jonas, don't give the boy a hard time. Hello, Abel." She smiled a greeting at him.

"Mrs. Nolan."

"Jonas, you know very well that Gretchen and I will be here when Annie has her baby, so whether Doc Casper is here or on vacation won't matter. And I'm sure we can call on Abel if we need him."

Abel felt defeated. "Thanks, Mrs. Nolan. Bye now."

He walked out of the store discouraged by what he had just learned. Folks really were going to be hesitant about accepting him as their doctor here. For a moment, he considered going back to Boston and joining Delphinia's father's practice. Dr. Digby had offered him a position when Abel asked for Dephinia's hand in marriage, but Abel informed the man that Sand Creek's doctor was waiting for him to join his practice, and that was where Abel wanted to be.

But if the people here don't want me… Abel sat down on the bench outside the store to think. *Lord, I've come a long way, and I thought this was where you wanted me. Am I not going to be able to help these people? Help me figure this one out, Lord. You ran me into the side of a building when I asked you. Maybe you're going to have to hit me alongside of the head to see what my next step should be.* He smiled at his thoughts. Then he got to his feet and started for the bank.

The stage had come, and people were descending out of the coach. Abel spoke greetings to the townspeople, who had gathered to see who was getting off the stagecoach, and as he stepped around a group of people, he heard his name called.

"Hey, Abel!"

Abel spun around to see who called his name and bumped into a woman behind him.

"Excuse me, please!" Abel apologized.

The woman's traveling bag dropped from her hand, and Abel bent to reach for it, missing the startled expression on the woman's face as he did so.

"Here you are, miss."

"Thank you." Her head was bent so he couldn't see her face, but he noticed her cheeks were pink, probably with embarrassment. Her hat was large, and he stepped back to avoid being hit by it.

"I hope I didn't hurt you."

"No, I'm fine." She still didn't look up.

"Well, have a nice day then." Abel tipped his hat and stepped around her. He noticed the woman stood still for a few moments before she walked on.

"That you hollering at me, Dugan?" Abel called up to his friend on the stagecoach.

"Yep." Dugan jumped down and shook hands with Abel.

"Sorry about causing you to bump into Mattie there."

"Mattie?" Abel looked over his shoulder to see the woman named Mattie speaking to one of the people on the boardwalk. The person pointed out a building, and the woman nodded and moved on, still carrying her bag.

"Yep. That's Mattie Morrison from Grandville. She used to work for Lucy and Buck at the hotel. Then she quit and taught school in Norris. She told me she's got a job here in Sand Creek for the summer and maybe will be teaching school in the fall." Dugan grinned at Abel. "Too bad you're an engaged man. She's a fine girl."

"You don't have to feel sorry for me. I'm very fortunate to have found Delphinia." Abel grinned. "Did you need me for something?"

"Yep. Emma and Simon asked me to give you a message if I saw you. They went to visit Mr. Halberg, that farmer you helped who got under a tree somehow. They wanted you to know that he's doing well. I hear his wife is quite the woman. Emma said that Mrs. Halberg takes care of all her husband's chores and even went out and finished chopping up that tree he felled. Simon did a bunch of jobs for them while they were there, but he said everything was under control."

"That's wonderful! I'm glad to hear it, but how about the man's wound? Did Dr. Arnett see him?"

"Yep. He told Emma that you had done a fine job taking care of him."

Abel was pleased at the news.

"But."

Abel raised a questioning eyebrow, waiting for Dugan to continue.

"Emma and Simon and everyone else in Grandville want to know how you got home in that snowstorm. The farmer said you didn't stay with them and that you left even when he warned you not to go." Dugan watched his friend's face redden.

"I found some shelter and waited out the storm," Abel said, not wishing to explain. "Look, I've got to get going. I'm on my way to the bank, and then I have to get back to the office. I'm a working man now, you know." He grinned again at Dugan. "Nice to see you, and thanks for the message."

Chapter 11

Sand Creek

Mattie felt her heart pounding as the man reached for her traveling bag. *Oh no, Lord! It can't be him!* She had been behind the man, trying to make her way through the people who were gathered near the stagecoach, when he suddenly turned and bumped into her. She had only a glimpse of his face before he bent to retrieve her bag, but it was *him*!

"Excuse me, please," the man said.

That's his voice! Mattie kept her head bent as he straightened up.

"Here you are, miss."

She took the bag he handed to her. He appeared to be waiting for her to say something, but her wits seemed to have left her. *Oh yes!* She remembered.

"Thank you."

"I hope I didn't hurt you."

"No, I'm fine." She still didn't look up.

"Well, have a nice day then." She saw his hand go to his hat; then he stepped around her.

Mattie didn't know how long she stood there, but she finally forced her feet to move forward again. *Please, Lord! Please tell me that he doesn't live in this town.* Should she leave? Should she go back home? She could turn around right now and get back on the stagecoach.

No, she needed this job, and Mr. Granger had gone to all the trouble of getting it for her. She couldn't let the incident at the Wynns deter her from making a living. The Wynns were long gone, and she had nothing to be ashamed of.

She stopped by a couple who were coming out of a store. "Excuse me, could you please tell me where the bank is?"

They kindly pointed out the way, and Mattie headed to the building a few doors down the street. Her bag was heavy, and she wished she could have left it at the hotel, but Mr. Davies had said to report to him first, so that was what she was going to do. Suddenly she felt her hat tip to one side. She grabbed it quickly with her free hand and looked around her. There was an outhouse behind the store building, and she headed for it.

Mattie would have found her situation funny if she wasn't so nervous about just seeing the man she was supposed to be *married* to and also being anxious about interviewing for her job. She crowded into the little building with her traveling bag. She quickly found her mirror and propped it up on a board in the wall. Then she pulled hat pins out until she could get to her hair. Yes, it had come loose again.

Mattie sighed in frustration at the lopsided bun on her head. Then she chided herself for her ungratefulness. Her mother—her dear, sweet mother—had solved the dilemma of Mattie's short hair. With her husband's permission, she had cut a long tail off of her own hair and formed it into a bun that Mattie could wear on her head. Mrs. Morrison still had enough hair to coil into a bun for herself, and though Mattie felt terrible about her mother cutting off her hair for her, her mother had cheerfully said it made her head feel so much lighter, she should have done it years ago.

Mattie knew her mother was trying to make light of her situation, but it still made Mattie feel bad. However, it was a perfect solution until Mattie's own hair grew out again. If she was careful about pinning the short strands back into place, she could attach the bun to it, and no one would be able to tell that it wasn't her real hair. It had worked fine at home as she practiced with it, but apparently the large hat she wore today, mainly to hide her hair, had pulled too much on the pins and caused the bun to slip. As ridiculous as she felt about the fake hair, it was extremely important to her. No woman, young or old, wore their hair short. It simply wasn't the proper thing to do, and with her needing this job so badly, she couldn't afford to arrive at this interview with her scandalously short hair.

She made the repairs as best she could in the tight quarters and then hastened to the bank. If Mr. Davies knew that the coach had arrived, he would be looking for her. She had sent a wire announcing the day of her arrival.

She pushed open the door and looked around her, unsure of who to speak to first. She stepped over to the teller's caged window and waited for the man to look up.

"May I help you?"

"I'm here to see Mr. Davies, please. My name is Mat—Mathilda Morrison," she informed him with a nervous smile.

"Yes, Miss Morrison. Mr. Davies is expecting you, but he's with a customer right now. I'm Lloyd Humphrey." His smile was welcoming. "Would you mind waiting over there?" He pointed to some chairs in the corner of the bank lobby.

"No, I don't mind waiting. Thank you." She took the seat indicated and set her bag on the floor beside her. She folded her hands demurely in her lap and watched with interest the comings and goings of the people, but her mind kept taking her thoughts back to the man by the stagecoach.

Maybe he is leaving on the stage today. Maybe that is why he is here. Mattie knew she should be concentrating on speaking with Mr. Davies, but she couldn't stop wondering about all the *what ifs* his presence in Sand Creek could mean. *What if he recognizes me? Of course, he couldn't really see my face.* She recalled that he felt the shotgun wedding was as much a sham as she did. Surely there would be no problem even if he did recognize her. *What if other people find out, and I lose this job? What if people hear and believe the worst? What if…*

Mattie realized she was being a worrier instead of a prayer warrior. That was something her mother always told her. She turned her thoughts into prayer and relaxed in knowing that God was going to get her through this no matter what people thought of her.

The door to Mr. Davies's office opened, and the man who was in her thoughts stepped out followed by an older man. The two were shaking hands.

Mattie's heart started thumping so hard it hurt.

"Thanks for taking the time to go over this with me, Mr. Davies," the man was saying. "I'll be seeing you then."

"Anytime, Abel." Mr. Davies was still shaking Abel's hand when he turned and saw Mattie sitting nearby. "Ah, you must be Miss Morrison?"

Mattie stood. "Yes, sir. Mr. Davies?" She held out her hand.

"That's right." He shook her hand. "Here, let me introduce you to Sand Creek's newest doctor, Miss Morrison. This is Abel Newly. Abel, Miss Morrison has come to work for me for a few months and then to teach school, if all goes well."

"I believe I have already introduced myself to Miss Morrison by almost knocking her down a few minutes ago. How do you do, Miss Morrison? Welcome to Sand Creek." Abel waited for the young woman to put out her hand first; then he shook it.

Newly?

"How do you do?" Mattie answered. She glanced up at him and saw the blue eyes that she remembered so well, and now she knew why she had not only remembered them but also thought they were familiar. They were the same color of blue eyes that she had seen in Lucy Riley and in her brother Tyler Newly from Grandville. *He must be their brother.*

Abel smiled. "Nice to meet you, miss." He turned back to Bert Davies. "I need to discuss a few things with my dad first, and then I'll be back in to see you."

"That will be fine. Bye, Abel. Good to have you home."

Mattie and Mr. Davies watched Abel Newly leave; then the banker directed Mattie into his office.

Later that evening in her hotel room, Mattie unpinned her hat and sat down on the edge of her bed. She was worn out from traveling the last two days. She wanted to pull the pins out of her hair that were starting to make her head itch, but she couldn't because she still had to go to the dining room for the evening meal.

She had been concerned about the money for her room and board, but the banker had assured her that her salary would cover it. Still, she knew she could save more money if she found accommodations that would enable her to cook her own meals. She wanted to earn enough to be able to send some money to her parents. She'd have to ask around after she got settled into the job.

She still couldn't believe she would be working in a bank. Mr. Davies admitted it was the first time he had hired a woman, but after speaking with Mr. Granger and now talking with her himself, he felt Mattie was well qualified to work for him.

Mattie was excited about the job, but her thoughts kept bringing her back to Abel Newly. He didn't recognize her! How could that be? She was relieved and happy that her fears of being recognized weren't realized, but at the same time, she felt a little put out. Was she so unattractive then that the man didn't even remember what she looked like? She grinned. Maybe she should be glad he didn't remember her the way she must have looked that day with her short hair sticking up in every direction and a scab forming on the end of her nose, wearing an oversized nightgown. Her face crimsoned. The fact that he was the one to put her into that nightgown still worried her. If he should ever discover who she was, she would be mortified. Doctor or not!

She moved to the chair set before a little desk. A mirror hung over it, and she leaned in to look at her features more closely. Still, was she so nondescript that she had left no impression at all on Abel Newly?

Newly. Mattie stared in the mirror. She knew the Newly family. She had worked for Lucy, who was a Newly, and she was acquainted with Tyler and Jade. She left Grandville before she met Emma and Simon Chappell. Emma was a Newly. She had never met the rest of the family, but the others spoke of them. Lucy told her about her brothers and sisters, and Mattie knew that Rex Newly was the one who married Irena Jenson.

Mattie waited for the stab of pain she usually felt when she thought of Nels Jenson, the man she had once thought she loved. No pain. Was she finally getting over her lost love?

She turned away from the mirror as she thought of Nels. To think of him as her lost love was stretching the truth, for the two of them had never even spoken to each other. They had only shared looks that held a promise of a future together. At least that is what she as a young girl thought. Then one day, she learned that Nels had married Irena, an immigrant Norwegian girl, and that Mattie had meant nothing to him at all.

Mattie left Grandville with what she felt was a broken heart. She got her teacher's certificate and took the school in Norris until that job ended. The day she learned that Nels and his mother had been killed when their wagon overturned, she thought her heart really would break, even though Nels didn't belong to her. But time made her realize that she had only been in love with the notion of having someone care for her. Like most young girls, she dreamed of romance and marriage.

She sighed. And now Nels's widow was married to Rex Newly. Mattie looked in the mirror again. And she, Mattie Morrison, was *married* to Abel Newly. She shook her head and surprised herself by smiling. If Abel Newly didn't remember, she surely wasn't going to be the one to remind him.

Chapter 12

Nolan Farm

Dorcas couldn't keep the smile off her face as she worked around the house. Everything was right again between her and Cavan. She didn't know exactly what happened, but after dinner at her parents' house on Sunday, Cavan had changed back into the man she knew and loved. She wondered if it had something to do with the walk Cavan took with her dad. Maybe it was just having a day to relax with the family. Whatever it was, she was happy to have her husband smiling again.

She hummed as she peeled potatoes for their evening meal. Cavan loved her fried chicken and mashed potatoes, and she was preparing it as a treat for him tonight. A noise outside caught her attention and she went to the window to see what it was.

A man on horseback was talking to Leon. Her first glance told her that the man was no one she knew. She saw Leon point to the field as if telling the stranger that was where his pa was. She hurried to the door and scooped up Fiona on the way.

The man turned to the house when he heard the door open. Dorcas stood on the porch, holding her daughter on one hip. She smiled pleasantly at the stranger but had to shield her eyes from the setting sun to see him more clearly. "Hello! May I help you?"

The man turned and stared. The sun lit up Dorcas's hair so that it glowed like the sunshine itself. He moved the horse closer to the porch and slid his hat off while he took his fill of looking at her.

"Evening, ma'am," he said.

Dorcas took a step back and tightened her hold on her daughter. The expression on the man's face unnerved her.

As if sensing her discomfort, the man smiled.

"I was wondering if your man could use some help with his spring planting."

Dorcas didn't know if Cavan wanted help or not, but one thing she did know was that this man was not going to be hired. She had seen the gleam in his eyes when he looked at her, and she wanted nothing more but to have him leave.

"No, we don't usually hire help," she said.

"Mind if I wait around for your man and speak to him?" He spoke soothingly like a person would to an uneasy horse. "Nice place you have here. Seems like a lot for one man to work by himself."

"We manage, thank you." Dorcas called to her son, "Leon, come in and get washed up now."

"Aw, Ma, do I have to?"

"Leon."

"Always obey your ma, son. That's what the Good Book says. Isn't that right, ma'am?"

Dorcas glanced at the man and then looked away. He seemed neat enough and clean, but something about him made her feel like she had just handled a snake. His reference to the Good Book didn't go unnoticed by her, and she felt he was using the term to make her feel guilty for not being more hospitable. She was sure of it when he continued.

"Something smells mighty tasty. Would that be fried chicken you're making, ma'am? My own sainted mother used to make me fried chicken, God rest her soul. I don't think I've had any since she left for glory a few months back."

The innocent expression on his face didn't fool Dorcas for a minute. She herded her son toward the door without turning her back on the stranger. "My sympathies regarding your loss. If you will excuse me, my children need tending to." She slipped through the door to the house and shut and bolted it behind her. Quickly she set Fiona on the floor and motioned for Leon to be quiet. She took down the Sharps buffalo rifle Cavan kept above the mantle. It was a long-range weapon, but she knew how to use it and knew she would if threatened. Then with her heart thumping, she peered out the window.

The stranger still sat there on his horse. He was smiling at the window.

Dorcas drew back sharply. She should feel foolish, but the uneasy sensation she was feeling wouldn't go away, and she dare not let down her guard. She heard the horse whinny, so she peeked through the curtained window again. He was leaving.

She put the rifle down, out of the reach of the children but close enough to get should the man return. Never before had she felt unsafe in her own house. It disturbed her, and she wished for Cavan to be home.

Asa was still smiling as he walked his horse away from the house. He was scouting the area for a place to stage the second part of his plan, and he had stumbled upon the farm. His request for a job was only a ruse to be able to find out about the people who lived there, and finding the woman was a surprise he hadn't anticipated.

He rubbed at the whiskers on his chin as he thought about the woman. She was sweet, fresh, and young, not the usual type of woman he encountered. If it wasn't for the job he had to do, he'd—

No, he had to stay focused. After the job though, then he'd be back to see about the woman. He wasn't going to let this one go.

Chapter 13

Sand Creek

Abel stabled his horse behind the doctor's house and made his way to the office. He was exhilarated. Three successful house calls behind him gave him the confidence he needed after his discussion with Doc Casper about the people being hesitant about accepting him as their doctor. It was true that all his patients this week were children, but it was a start. He was sure that word would spread of his competence.

"Hi, Doc," Abel called out as he entered. A quick look told him the doctor wasn't alone; Rhoda Riggs was helping him clean up the exam room. "Did you see a patient while I was gone?"

"Yes, Annie Davies came in for her checkup. She's in her last month now before the baby comes, and she's getting nervous. You know how it is for new mothers." Doc smiled.

"Anything special I should know?"

Doc glanced at Abel. He sighed. "I don't think so, Abel. She and Monty are pretty set on having me take care of the delivery. I hope you understand."

Abel stood still for a moment; then he moved on to replenish his medical bag from the stock shelves. "When are they going to accept me, Doc? What do I have to do?"

"Give them more time." Doc thanked Rhoda as she waved good-bye before exiting the office; then he settled into a chair before the desk and started making notes in a book. Without looking up, he chuckled. "Or get married."

Abel looked up sharply and studied the doctor's bent head. *Maybe now is the time.* "Mind if I run some errands, Doc? You need anything?"

The older man waved Abel away and continued with his writing.

Abel strode with purpose through the small town. He was excited about the idea forming in his mind. He stepped around some women on the boardwalk, politely tipping his hat as he did so. He was aware of their averted glances but pretended not to notice.

"Afternoon, ladies."

He made his way on to the telegraph office. "Hey, Bud, I'd like to send a telegram if you don't mind."

"Sure thing, Abel. I mean *Dr. Newly.*" Bud grinned as he emphasized the name. "It's awfully good to have you back in town. I bet ol' Doc Casper is itching to get on the stage and take that trip Florrie is always nagging him about now that you're here."

"And I intend to see that he gets his vacation." Abel scribbled on the paper the telegraph officer gave him. A feeling of rightness, of contentment came over him as he worded his message to Delphinia. Having her come earlier than they had planned was just the thing to get people here to meet her and get to know her and to understand that he would soon be a married man. Maybe if Delphinia was agreeable, they could even move up their wedding date. He couldn't really see any sense in waiting until fall anyway.

Suddenly the image of the brown-haired, brown-eyed bride in his dream came back to him. His hand stopped writing, and he stared at the paper in front of him without seeing the words he had written. He was remembering instead the words the irate preacher said: "What God hath joined together let no man put asunder." Then the frightened face of the girl he rescued crossed his mind. Her big, brown eyes, wide with fright, and the short shafts of her brown hair sticking up in all directions were etched clearly in his thoughts.

"You ailing, Abel?" Bud peered into his customer's face.

"What? Oh! No, I'm fine. Here you go, Bud. What do I owe you?"

Abel left the telegraph office and headed for the bank. He needed to finish his business with Bert Davies, the banker, and then put in another order with Jonas Nolan at the store. Abel and his father had a discussion about his finances, and Abel was more than pleased and forever grateful to a great uncle of his mother's for the bounty with which he had been blessed. *You know, Lord,* he prayed as he shortened the distance to the building with his long strides, *you turned my mom's trials into good and blessed all of us with this money because of her. I know you have good in mind for me as well. I don't understand the setback with the town's attitude toward me, but I trust you to work it out. I just want to keep my attitude right while I wait to see how you do it.*

He entered the bank and was about to knock on the door to Bert's office when a feminine voice spoke to him.

"May I help you, sir?"

He turned to see a woman sitting at the desk next to the office.

A woman?

"Uh, yes, I'd like to see Bert...uh...I mean Mr. Davies."

"Mr. Davies is with a customer right now. Would you care to wait? It shouldn't be long." She indicated the row of chairs.

But Abel didn't move. He kept eye contact with the young lady until she looked down at the papers on the desk before her. He noticed her cheeks were pink and realized his staring was embarrassing her.

"I'm sorry. Do I know you?" He heard her sharp intake of air and was about to apologize again when he remembered. "Oh yes! You're the lady I bumped into the other day, aren't you! And Bert—Mr. Davies—introduced you to me. I'm sorry, what was your name again? I'm Abel Newly."

She looked up at him, and Abel had the feeling that she was uncomfortable. "I'm Miss Morrison. How are you, Mr. Newly?"

"That's right! I'm pleased to see you again, Miss Morrison. I had forgotten that Bert said you would be working for him. I guess you sort of surprised me. I'm not used to seeing a female bank employee."

Mattie smiled. "I've been hearing that a lot, but people seem to be getting used to the idea. Mr. Davies has been a wonderful boss."

"Well, I'm glad to hear it." Abel watched her make a note on a paper and knew he should let her get back to her work, but something made him want to keep her talking.

"Are you enjoying being in Sand Creek?"

Mattie looked up again. Abel watched her reach up to tuck in a pin in her hair and smooth a loose strand back in place. "Yes, everyone has been kind and helpful. The Nolans' hotel is comfortable, and Mr. and Mrs. Nolan have been looking out for me and treating me like a daughter."

"I'm glad to hear it. Say, has anyone invited you to church on Sunday?"

Mattie swallowed and hesitantly spoke, "Um…"

But Abel continued, "I'm sure Harry and Gretchen have mentioned it. Maybe I'll see you there?"

She nodded.

The door to Bert's office opened, and a man walked out. He tipped his head at Mattie and Abel and left. Abel looked questioningly at Mattie.

She rose and went to the door. "Mr. Davies? Mr. Newly is here to see you, sir. Abel Newly, sir."

"Send him in and thank you, Miss Morrison."

Mattie turned back to Abel. "You may go in now."

"Thank you, Miss Morrison." Abel watched her return to her desk. It dawned on him as she was speaking to Bert that she might have thought he was asking her to go to church with him. Was that the reason for her hesitation? He was certainly glad the moment hadn't become awkward. She seemed like a nervous sort of girl.

Mattie waited until the door shut behind Abel; then she clasped her hands together on her lap to try to keep them from trembling. When she first saw him enter the bank, her heart had begun pounding, and when he asked her, "Do I know you?" she thought she wouldn't be able to breathe. And then he wouldn't go sit down! Why did he keep conversing with her? Couldn't he see how nervous she was? And there was that moment when she thought he was asking her to go to the Sunday service with him! She reddened at the thought.

She poked at the pins in hair again and checked that the bun was centered on the back of her head. Up to now she had been comfortable with the fake hairpiece, but as soon as she saw Abel Newly, she had wondered if it was slipping and wondered if he noticed anything awry.

She took a deep breath to calm herself down. He hadn't noticed. He didn't know who she was. She was still safe.

Mattie looked at the closed door. Maybe she should leave Sand Creek. Every day she wondered if their paths would cross, and if they did, she wondered if he would figure out who she was. Could she keep on living like this? Maybe she should just confront him and tell him the truth. Get it out in the open. They could laugh about it, and then she could go on with her life without this gnawing fear of being discovered haunting her every move.

The door opened, and Mattie's heart jumped as Abel stepped out. He turned back to say something to the banker and then closed the door behind him.

He's handsome. Mattie's thought startled her so much she dropped her gaze to her desktop before he could see her face. She felt him stop before her desk, but she kept her head down. She knew he was looking at her, and suddenly she realized that he could see the back of her hair clearly the way she was bent over. She jerked her head up and stared wide-eyed into his blue eyes.

"It was nice to see you again, Miss Morrison," Abel said politely. "I hope to see you on Sunday." He tipped his head, smiled, and moved on.

Mattie let out her breath slowly. *Lord, I'm befuddled,* she prayed as she watched Abel walk away. *I'm confused, bewildered, and discombobulated. What am I going to do?*

Chapter 14

Sand Creek

Mattie pushed through the swinging doors into the hotel kitchen with her arms full of dirty dishes.

"Here are more dishes for you, Mrs. Nolan." She quickly scraped off the plates and stacked the dishes near the washtub.

"Now, Mattie, if you're going to work with me on Saturdays, you're going to have to call me Gretchen. Sure, and if I hear you saying *Mrs. Nolan* all the time, I might be thinking you're talking about my sister, Bridget, instead of me."

Mattie laughed with the hotel owner. She enjoyed the Nolans. Gretchen still spoke with her Irish brogue even after thirty years in America, and Mattie loved the lilting quality of it. Gretchen and her sister, Bridget, had married the Nolan brothers when they came to Sand Creek as mail-order brides years ago. Jonas and

Bridget owned the town's general store, and Harry and Gretchen ran the hotel.

Mattie wiped her hands on her apron and headed back to the dining room to clear more tables. The bank wasn't open on Saturdays and Sundays, so she inquired with the Nolans if they could employ her on her free Saturdays. She really wanted to be able to send more money home to her family, and she also hoped to keep out of Abel Newly's sight as much as possible. She was finding it more difficult as he came to Sand Creek every weekday to see patients in the doctors' office. So far the only time their paths had crossed was when he came into the bank.

"Miss, could we get some coffee here?"

Mattie turned to the couple who had just taken a seat.

"Certainly, just a moment, please."

She hurried into the kitchen with another load of dishes. "Mrs.—no—Gretchen, you have some new customers, and they want coffee," she informed her landlady. "Why don't you let me take over washing those dishes?"

Gretchen shook her head. "No, honey, I'm fine here. If you don't mind doing the running back and forth, I think I'll have you serve today."

Mattie was hoping to hide away in the kitchen in case Abel Newly should show up, but since Gretchen wanted her to serve, she would serve. She grabbed the pot off the stove and headed back into the dining room. Having eaten in the dining room for the last couple of weeks, she knew the menu and how to take the orders, so she returned to the new customers and poured their coffee and then asked what they would like for their lunch. She picked up some more dishes and took a dessert order and headed back to the kitchen. She heard the front door open behind her and knew she had more customers, so she hurried through the swinging doors.

"Two fried chicken dinners and a serving of pumpkin pie," she informed Gretchen. The two worked together quickly to fill the plates. Mattie backed through the swinging doors again with her arms full. She turned and nearly dropped the food when she saw Abel and an older man take seats at a table in the corner. The dishes on her tray rattled a bit as she stopped to set down the dessert in front of a gentleman. She willed herself to calm down and moved on to serve the new couple. Then she took a deep breath and stepped over to Abel's table.

"Good afternoon. Do you gentlemen know what you'd like today?"

Abel had his back to her when she approached, and Mattie was startled when he turned suddenly and grinned at her. He actually looked pleased to see her, or maybe she was just imagining it. He rose from his chair.

"Miss Morrison! How nice to see you again!" He noticed the tray in her arms. "Are you working here as well?"

"Mr. Newly." Mattie nodded to the other gentleman. "Yes, I'm helping here on Saturdays."

"Doc, I want to introduce you to Miss Morrison. She works at the bank for Bert Davies as well as here. Miss Morrison, this is Doc Casper, Sand Creek's physician and my partner." Abel made the introductions all the while unnerving Mattie with his attention. Avoiding him was getting harder to do.

"How do you do, Dr. Casper. Are you gentlemen ready to order? Some coffee maybe?"

The men gave Mattie their orders, and she hurried to fill them and to take care of the other customers. Mattie's heart wouldn't stop thumping hard in her chest. She felt Abel's eyes on her as she moved about the room, and she couldn't help wondering if he was beginning to recognize her as the girl he rescued. She was relieved when he and the other doctor finally left. The lunch business was slowing down, and she was wiping off tables when another customer entered the hotel dining room.

"I'll be with you in a moment," she said over her shoulder.

"Don't take too long, sweet thing. I'm starved."

Mattie's hand stopped moving. *That voice!* She was careful to keep her back to the man as she made her way to the kitchen. Once safely inside, she peeked back into the room. *Wally Beck! What is he doing here?*

"Something wrong, Mattie?" Gretchen came up behind her and peered around her shoulder. "Is he someone you know?" They both watched the young, dark-haired man take a seat at a table by a window. He tossed his Stetson on the chair beside him and leaned back in his chair.

Mattie's hand was pressed over her mouth. She turned to Gretchen with wide eyes. Seeing concern in her employer's expression, Mattie made the decision to seek her help.

"His name is Wally Beck," she whispered. "He's from the Grandville area, and he used to…he…he tried flirting with me several times." She felt her face grow hot. "I never encouraged him. I'm…I'm…not comfortable with him."

Gretchen patted Mattie on the shoulder. "I understand. Sure, and Bridget and I had our share of unwelcome advances in our day. Don't you worry about a thing, honey. I'll take care of him. You just stay in here. Okay?"

"Thank you, Gretchen. I don't mean to not do my job—"

"No worries. There's plenty to do in here too. I'll go see to him now."

Mattie stayed hidden as the doors swung back and forth after Gretchen walked through them. She listened but couldn't hear the exchange between her and Wally. Mattie took a deep breath as she moved to the washtub. She didn't need Wally Beck bothering her in Sand Creek. Hopefully he was just passing through and wouldn't be a problem here. She sighed. Lately her life has been full of problems; Wally showing up was just one more to add to her list. She looked over her shoulder as Gretchen returned.

"I swear that man has more blarney in him than the blokes back in Ireland." Gretchen was shaking her head. "He even tried his flattery on me—the cheeky, young whelp." She talked while she filled a plate. "I don't blame you for wanting to stay out of sight. You just let me take care of him." And she left to serve her customer.

Mattie stayed in the kitchen until Wally left, then she continued helping Gretchen and the cook prepare for the evening meal. By the end of her workday, she was tired but happy. She had earned more money and managed to stay out of the way of Abel Newly and Wally Beck. She pulled the door shut behind her in her room at the hotel and sank into the chair by the small desk. Her hands automatically began unpinning the bun in her hair, and she fluffed her shortened hair with her fingertips. She stretched and yawned. Tomorrow was Sunday, and she looked forward to the Sunday service at church. The pastor didn't just preach at the congregation, but he also taught them to study the Word with him. She had only attended a couple of weeks, but already she was eager to learn and worship with the people of Sand Creek. And she needn't worry about Abel on Sundays; he was always involved with his family members and, other than a nod in her direction, hadn't approached her or spoken to her.

And if Wally was still in the area, she surmised, he wouldn't be anywhere near the church. Despite all the worries she'd had lately, she felt at peace as she slid between the sheets of her bed. Really, what else could go wrong?

North of Sand Creek

Wally dismounted and hitched his horse to the rail in front of the small cabin. Two other horses were already tied to the posts, and he recognized them as belonging to Otis and Lonan. He wondered where Asa was. He grinned. Asa's tardiness was usually due to a woman.

"Thet you, Beck?" Otis's voice boomed out from the cabin.

Wally grabbed the supplies he had tied to the back of his saddle and hurried up the steps. "I brought some grub," he called out.

The cabin was hidden in the woods, away from curious eyes. Wally felt the steps sag under his weight as he cautiously made his way to the door. As his eyes adjusted to the dimness of the interior, he saw Otis seated with his elbows on the table, obviously impatient for a meal. Lonan leaned against the wall near the cook stove where chunks of meat skewered on sticks were propped over the open flames.

Wally sniffed the air. "What's that you've got cooking?" He eyed the mystery meat warily. "Doesn't smell too bad."

Lonan made no reply. He turned the sticks to roast the other side of the meat chunks and leaned against the wall again.

Otis rummaged through the bag Wally brought in, and finding some tins, he tossed them to Wally. "Heat those up," he commanded. He pulled out a knife and jabbed the point into a tin of peaches. Soon he was eating the fruit off the end of the knife and slurping the juice straight from the tin. "This all ya got?" He glared at Wally.

"You're sure a bear when you're hungry, Otis. I'm heating the stew, so just hold your horses, will ya? You know where Asa is?"

"Probably found hisself a sweet treat," Otis chuckled.

"What's that?" Asa's stern voice came from the open door.

"I said, 'Lonan, ain't you done with thet meat?'" Otis turned to glare at Lonan, who remained impassive.

Asa moved into the room and took the chair across from Otis. He straddled the chair backward and stared down the bigger man until Otis's ears turned red. Slowly Asa searched the expressions of the other two men. Finally he spoke.

"What have you learned in town, Beck?"

Wally left the stove to join the men at the table. "It's going to be easy, Asa. There's only a sheriff in town, and he's an older man. The bank has only one teller, and the bank owner has an office, and I think he has a secretary or something because there's another desk outside his door. The safe is in a room behind the tellers, and near as I can tell, it is kept locked, but the teller can open it when he needs to. I couldn't go in the bank on Saturday because they close up both Saturdays and Sundays. Must be a nice life to only work five days a week. I bet that banker lives it up pretty good. So what do you say?

Do we go in soon?" Wally waited eagerly for Asa to lay out his plan.

Asa glared at Wally. "You *think*? *Near as you can tell?* Did you go in the bank at all?"

"Well, no. I didn't want to look suspicious, and then on Saturday, like I said, the bank wasn't open. I just looked in the window is all." Wally sat back in his chair as Asa leaned toward him.

"I expect a better report than that! You get back there and get me everything you can about that town. I want to know what time the bank opens, what time it closes, who goes in and out during the day, and most importantly, how much money is in there."

"C'mon, Asa," Wally complained. "How am I supposed to find out how much money is there?"

Asa sat back and glared at the younger man. "You make friends with someone in the town, you idiot. You be discreet. *That* means you don't let people know what you're up to." He turned to Otis, who was about to ask what *discreet* meant. "I want to know when the most people are in town and when it's the quietest. If you have to, take a room at the hotel and stay there a few days, but next time I see you, you better have answers! Now git!"

Wally mumbled some words under his breath as he slid his chair back.

"What was that?"

"He said he hopes you have a lovely day," Otis quipped with a deadpan expression.

Asa's glare at Otis was icy. As Wally stomped to the door, Asa spoke without turning, "And don't let anyone follow you here."

The door slammed shut behind him. After a moment's silence, Asa spoke again. "Get the food, Otis, before it burns."

Chapter 15

Sand Creek

Mattie finished pinning her hair and looked critically in the mirror. So far no one seemed to notice the fake hair bun, but she still feared that it would slip or get knocked askew, and then she'd have some explaining to do. She did a spin in her new dress. It was a light-blue calico that her mother and she had made together and that she saved for Sundays. Its light fabric was perfect for the warm temperatures as summer started to take hold of the weather. She paused to pin a tiny matching hat at an angle in front of her hair bun. Checking the time, she reached for her Bible and headed out of the hotel to take the short walk to the church building at the end of the street.

People were beginning to gather, she noticed as she stepped along the boardwalk. Buggies and wagons were being unloaded as families gathered their children to go inside. Mattie spied Abel arriving with a couple she assumed were his parents. If she timed her entrance correctly, she could get in the church building ahead of him. She was about to step down from the board-walk when some people near the back of the building caught her attention, and something familiar about them caused her to pause, and then she quickly stepped back so that she couldn't be seen.

The Wynns! Mattie felt her heart start to race. What were Reverend Wynn and his wife doing here in Sand Creek? And who was that they were talking to? She peeked around the corner of the telegraph office to get a better look and ducked back again. They were speaking with Pastor Sweeney, the pastor of the Sand Creek church!

Mattie could only assume the couple was up to no good. Were they looking for her? She recalled the rev-erend's pledge to see to it that she kept the marriage vows spoken on her behalf. Out of the corner of her eye, she saw Abel Newly help his mother down from their wagon. She had to stop him from being seen by the Wynns. But how?

Abel's parents walked away to go into the church, but Abel was still by the wagon, securing the horse. Mattie sought desperately for some way to attract his attention. She backed farther away from the church and started down the steps in front of Nolan's store while she kept track of what Abel was doing. Because she was distracted, on the last step she slipped and found herself in a heap on the ground. She felt a sharp stab of pain in her ankle and grabbed at it with one hand while she spun around to see if anyone had noticed her clumsiness. She drew in a sharp breath as she saw Abel running toward her.

"Are you all right, Miss Morrison? I saw you fall." Abel knelt down beside her and searched her face. Mattie quickly looked past him and realized that the others had all entered the church, and they were alone. She only hoped that the Wynns and Pastor Sweeney were also inside by now. Her attention flew back to Abel. Even though she hadn't planned it, maybe this was her answer to keeping him from being seen by the troublemaking Wynns.

"Here, let me help you try to stand," Abel was saying.

Mattie took his arm and let him help her to her feet.

"Can you stand? Try taking a few steps. Let me see if you're hurt." He kept hold of her arm as she took a step. Her face grimaced when pain shot up her leg.

"Okay, I can see you're hurt. Which leg is it?"

"This one." She tapped her right leg. "I feel so foolish. I wasn't watching where I was going."

"May I feel for any breaks in your ankle, Miss Morrison? Remember, I am a doctor." He waited for her permission. At her nod, he probed the ankle with his fingers. She winced again as he found the tender area.

"I think I better get you over to the office for a better look." As Mattie was about to protest, he added, "I'm afraid you'll have to skip the morning service today."

Mattie clamped her mouth shut. Maybe that would be best. She leaned on Abel's arm and hopped a few steps and then stopped when he did.

"I see this is paining you. Do you mind if I just carry you?"

Mattie couldn't believe she could get more embarrassed, but getting out of sight of the church building was upmost in her mind, so she nodded to Abel. He lifted her easily into his arms and walked to the doctors' office a few buildings away. Mattie realized she was still clutching her Bible in her hand as she clung to Abel's neck to keep from falling. A few more steps, and they were out of sight. She breathed a sigh of relief.

"Am I hurting you? I'm sorry. I'm trying to be careful."

Mattie's face reddened. "You're not hurting me, Dr. Newly, but I have to admit that my ankle is starting to throb," she acknowledged.

Abel set her down in front of the door while he unlocked the office; then he picked her up again and brought her to the examining table.

"Just rest there while I get some supplies for you," he said. "I'll have you feeling better in no time."

Mattie watched as he moved around the room. She breathed a silent prayer of thankfulness that a scene at the church had been avoided. But she still had so many concerns about what the Wynns were telling Pastor Sweeney and where they would be after the service. How was she going to keep hidden and keep Abel hidden from them after he took care of her ankle?

Abel studied Mattie out of the corner of his eye while he readied the bandages he needed. She seemed pretty nervous about being alone with him in the doctors'

office, and he wondered if he should go get Doc Casper or Rhoda Riggs to help ease her fears, but he hated to disturb them for a minor injury like this one. Besides, he was a doctor, a professional, and he could handle this on his own.

"Okay, now let's take a look at that ankle. If you would just raise your skirt a bit; I don't mean to embarrass you, Miss Morrison, but I will need to check the area again." Abel used his most soothing tones to reassure her. She seemed so timid.

"Of course."

Abel carefully removed her boot, unhooking each of the buttons with a button hook he had in the office. He pressed and poked and moved Mattie's foot back and forth. "Does this hurt? How about this?" Finally, he stepped back and smiled at her. "I don't think anything is broken, but I'm afraid you've got a sprained ankle. It's starting to swell a bit already. I'm going to wrap this bandage around it, and I want you to sit with your leg elevated today. It may still be sore for a couple of days, but you should be able to walk on it by tomorrow." He started wrapping a bandage around her foot and ankle all the while talking to her. "It's a good thing today is Sunday, and you're not working. You'll have time to relax and get better."

"Thank you so much," Mattie said when he was finished.

Abel started putting his equipment away, and he watched Mattie bend to see her bandaged ankle. It was then that he noticed that the bun in her hair had slipped and that some of her hair had come loose. Short ends of her hair were sticking up, and Abel noticed that her hair was brown.

Abel's hands stopped what they were doing as he stared at the back of Mattie's head. *Her hair is short! Her brown hair...* His mind whirled. He was puzzled. If this was the girl, how could she have enough hair to roll it into a bun? *And she has brown eyes!* He had put the incident near Grandville in the back of his mind. He hadn't forgotten it; he just tried not to think about it. Could this be the girl?

Wait! Those people called her Mathilda. Abel searched his mind to remember what name Dugan had called Miss Morrison. *Wasn't it Mattie? Mathilda...Mattie.* It could be. Suddenly he saw Mattie reach for her hair and start to right the lopsided bun and hat and frantically poke the pins back in place.

Does she know that I'm the one who rescued her? Why doesn't she say so if she does? Abel didn't know what to think. Should he say something?

He walked around the table to stand in front of her. "Did you get hurt anywhere else, Miss Morrison? You took quite a fall from what I could see." He studied her face, seeing the brown eyes again. *Yes. How could I have forgotten those eyes?* It was then that he saw a tiny scar on the end of her nose. *The frostbite healed well.*

"No, I don't think so, Dr. Newly. I can't tell you how much I appreciate you helping me. It seems that the whole town is either in church or gone on Sunday mornings. I may not have found someone to help me if you hadn't seen me fall."

"I'm glad I was able to help."

"What do I owe you, Doctor?" She reached for the small bag attached to her wrist.

"Nothing."

"No, please. I insist."

"Please, Miss Morrison, I am glad I was there to help you." *Again*, he wanted to add, but he didn't.

"Well…thank you." She seemed to be waiting for something. "Will my boot fit?" she asked.

Abel realized he was staring at her. "No, I don't think so. We have a pair of crutches here that you can use for a day or two and then just return them when you feel your ankle is strong enough." He smiled at her, and when she returned a timid smile, he found it difficult to tear his gaze away. They were both startled when the door of the office opened.

"I need the doc!" A woman rushed in. "My husband chopped into his leg with the axe. He's bleeding something awful! Where's Doc Casper?"

"I'm a doctor. Where's your husband?"

"He's in the back of the wagon. Hurry! He's been bleeding the whole way here."

Abel ran out following the woman. The man in the back of the wagon was still conscious, but Abel could see by the paleness of his face that he was barely holding on. With the help of the man's wife, he hoisted him up, and together they got him into the office. Abel was surprised to see that Mattie was up and hobbling around to gather bandages and his medical equipment close to hand.

He set the man down on the table and helped him to lay back. He turned to get a scissors to cut open the man's pant leg, but Mattie was standing right beside him, and she handed him the scissors without him even asking for it.

"Thanks." He turned back and began examining the cut. "We're going to need to clean this before I can stitch it." He looked up and saw Mattie handing the man's wife a bucket. Then she hobbled over to the woodstove and began lighting a fire. A kettle with water was already on the stove, and Mattie pulled it forward over the flames that were beginning to develop. Then she hurried back to Abel's side by hopping and leaning on whatever surface was near to hand.

"What do you need next, Doctor?"

Abel stared at her for a moment; then he nodded as if accepting that she was going to assist. "Hand me the basin please, and I'll need those cloths over there."

Together they worked on cleaning the man's wound. His wife returned with water from the well, which she replaced in the kettle after she brought the heated water to Abel. Then she stood by her husband's head and talked to him while Abel and Mattie worked together on his injury.

Abel's hands worked automatically, but his mind was distracted by Mattie's presence beside him. He had worked with a nurse before, but Mattie was the most efficient helper he had ever had. She was anticipating his needs and having things ready to hand as he asked for them, and she didn't recoil at the grisly sight the wound presented.

"Jeb wants to know how it looks, Doc," the woman asked.

Abel smiled reassuringly at the couple. "The wound isn't as deep as I thought, ma'am. Thanks to my lovely assistant here, we've got it cleaned, and I'm almost done stitching. You'll need to keep the bandages changed and clean, and I'll be checking on him in a few days. How are you doing, Jeb?"

"Better. Thanks, Doc."

"You're going to have to get some rest and let this heal, you hear? I don't want you ripping open my beautiful handiwork by doing something foolish."

"I got chores."

Abel stepped over to see the man's face as he talked to him. "I'll get you some help while you're laid up, Jeb. My dad and I can take turns, and I have other family and friends who would be glad to lend a hand. Don't you worry about a thing."

Jeb swallowed. "I can't...I can't let you..."

Abel patted his arm. "We help each other out here, Jeb. I'm Abel Newly, by the way." He shook hands with Jeb.

"Jeb Owen. This is Purdy. We bought the farm that belonged to Roy and Nola Hill." Jeb rubbed his face. "The place needs a lot of work because it sat empty for a few years. I got the fields planted, and I was pushing myself to get more done. I guess I got careless." He turned to his wife. "Sorry, Purdy. You told me to slow down."

"This might slow you down a bit, Jeb, but something tells me you'll be up and about before long. Let me welcome you to Sand Creek, and now let me introduce you to Miss Morrison." Abel motioned to Mattie, who was cleaning up the bloody dressings.

"Pleased to meet you."

"Miss Morrison is new to Sand Creek too. She comes from the Grandville area, and she's working at both the bank and the hotel dining room. This fall she'll be our town's schoolteacher. Do you folks have children?"

Purdy blushed, and Jeb answered, "We're expecting a baby."

"Congratulations. You come in and get a checkup, Mrs. Owen. Between Doc Casper and me, we'll take good care of you."

The woman looked at her husband, and he nodded. "Thank you, Doctor."

Mattie was washing in the basin. She dried her hands and then slid over to the woodstove. She spoke over her shoulder, "I have some water ready for tea, Mrs. Owen. Perhaps Mr. Owen should have some water to drink?" She turned to see Abel's answer.

"Yes, thank you, Miss Morrison, but let me get washed up, and I'll take care of that. You shouldn't be on that ankle." He turned to his other patient. "Miss Morrison sprained her ankle on the way to church, and that is why we were in the office today. Otherwise, you would have had to come to church to get a doctor."

Mrs. Owen moved to take the cup from Mattie. "Please call me Purdy," she said. She brought some water to her husband; then she sank down in the chair beside him and sipped at her tea.

Abel studied her a moment. "Are you feeling unwell, Purdy?"

"No, I'm fine. I'm just so relieved Jeb is going to be all right. I was so frightened by all the blood." She smiled at them, and as Mattie turned to sit down in the chair beside her, she exclaimed, "Oh my! Miss Morrison you have blood all over your pretty dress!"

Mattie looked down; then she looked at Abel. She pointed. "Your shirt is bloodied too, Dr. Newly. And there's blood on you, Purdy!"

"And Jeb is covered." Purdy laughed. "My, we're a sight!"

Abel pulled a chair in front of Mattie and, without asking, reached down and lifted her leg onto it. He fixed a cup of tea for himself and sat down too. "I'm thankful we're all doing better than we look."

The four people sat and rested and visited. Abel knew it was important to give the wounded man time before he headed back home in his wagon, and he wanted Mattie to rest as well. She had been on her leg far too long for his liking, and she looked a bit pale now that the crisis had passed.

"Hello? Abel?"

Abel turned in his chair as there was a knock on the door. "Dad! Come on in. I suppose you and Mom wondered what happened to me." He rose to greet his father and almost laughed at the expression on his parent's face when he saw four people covered in blood sipping at teacups.

"Everything all right here?" Russ's eyebrows shot up as he looked from one person to the next. "Looks like there's been a massacre."

Abel grinned at the others. "Everything's fine now, but we've had a bit of excitement. Dad, this is Jeb Owen and his wife, Purdy. Jeb had an accident this morning with an axe. Folks, this is my father, Russ Newly."

Russ walked over to shake hands with Jeb, who was propped up on the table. "You the folks who bought Roy Hill's place?" he asked. After receiving a nod of confirmation, he continued, "Looks like you'll be needing some help for a few days. My boys and I will be over."

"And, Dad, I don't know if you've met Miss Morrison? She works for Bert at the bank. She took a spill on the way to church this morning and sprained her ankle, which turned out to be fortunate for me because she turned out to be an excellent assistant."

Russ nodded to Mattie. "Sorry to hear that you had an accident, Miss Morrison. Bert has been singing your praises ever since you started working for him. I'm glad to meet you."

"Dad, as long as you're here, could you help me get Jeb back to their wagon, and we'll see them on their way?"

"Certainly."

The two men moved to either side of the wounded man and assisted him out the door. Purdy said good-bye to Mattie and followed them out, carrying the crutches Abel had indicated they would need.

The wagon rolled away, and Abel entered his office again. Mattie was up, moving about to clean up the rest of the bandages and was wiping down the table where Jeb had been.

"See here, now, Miss Morrison. You really need to get off that ankle. I'll take care of the cleanup. I can't thank you enough for all the help you've given me— whoa, there!" Abel jumped forward to catch Mattie as she started sinking to the floor.

Russ ran in when he heard Abel call for him. He found his son holding the young woman in his arms.

Abel looked up at his father. "She fainted!"

Chapter 16

Nolan Farm

Asa sat his horse in the woods near the Nolan farm. He had caught a glimpse of the blonde woman a few times as she came to the door to speak to her son, who was playing in the dirt and mud outside, but it wasn't enough. He wanted a closer look, and he wanted to talk to her again, to see the light play on her hair, and to watch the wariness touch her blue eyes. He didn't think she was necessarily afraid of him. More likely she was just being a protective mother hen with her brood of chicks.

He should be out scouting the other farms in the area, but he was drawn back here. This wasn't the first time he had sat and watched her. He needed to get ahold of himself and get back to business. But he couldn't help it.

His horse snorted.

Asa's hand went to his gun. He surveyed the area around him without turning his head, aware that he wasn't alone, but he couldn't see anyone.

"Looking for someone, mister?"

Asa pivoted at hearing the voice. A man stood off to his left. How he got there without Asa hearing him, he couldn't guess. A rifle was held loosely in the stranger's arms, but Asa didn't doubt that the man could whip it up to his shoulder given provocation to do so. Anyone with his woodsman skills would certainly be prepared to shoot his weapon.

Asa backed his hand away from the pistol in his holster. Keeping his tone friendly, he said, "I'm looking for work. Know of anyone who could use a hired hand?"

"I think you better find a different place to look," the man advised.

His meaning was clear to Asa. *He must be the woman's husband.* "That's too bad. I liked the view here." He enjoyed seeing the man's mouth tighten at his taunt. "I guess I'll check on the next farm over. You have a nice day now."

Asa walked his horse away, leaving the man watching his departure. He'd be back. He wasn't about to let some farmer best him, but he knew when to pick his battles, and that was always when the cards were stacked in his favor. He'd be back all right.

Later that evening, he met up with Otis and Lonan at the abandoned cabin.

"Hear anything from Beck?" he asked.

The others shook their heads.

"That whelp better be careful not to arouse suspicion. Everything else is falling into place nicely except for one change I need to make in the plan."

Otis raised an eyebrow.

Asa pulled out his pistol and began cleaning it. "I'm not going to be in town during the robbery, so that means you'll have to cover the front, Otis. As soon as Beck has things under control, you go in and guard the front until you're ready to leave by the back. Lonan will have the horses ready and waiting, and I'll join up with you as you leave town."

Lonan remained expressionless, but Otis had both eyebrows raised as he studied Asa. "What are you gonna be doin'?"

Asa never looked up from cleaning his gun. "I told you. I've got to set up the diversion."

"And I bet it involves a skirt," Otis muttered.

"What was that?"

"I said, 'I think you missed a little dirt.'" Otis pointed to the pistol.

Asa calmly eyed Otis. "You know, one of these times I'm not going to let you get by with that," he said icily.

Otis blinked.

Asa's eyes never left Otis as he said, "Lonan, fix some grub. We've got planning to do."

"I tell you, Russ, there was something evil about that man." Cavan stood by his father-in-law as they leaned on the fence. "I'm sure he was the same one Dorcas told us about, the one who came in the yard that day and made her feel uncomfortable. I swear she nearly shot me when I tried to open the door to get in the house. She'd bolted it shut and had the Sharps ready." He turned to Russ. "I'm afraid for her, but I can't be with her all day long."

Russ nodded. "I know, son. I've been hearing some of the other neighbors talk about seeing a man snooping around their places too. I don't think he's talked to anyone else other than you and Dorcas though. The Owens mentioned it just yesterday when I went to help with Jeb's chores while he's letting his leg heal. Purdy saw someone on a horse just standing in the trees like he was checking if anyone was home at their house. She was pretty upset.

"And I can't help but think this might have something to do with the rumors we're hearing about bank robbers in the area. Have you taken the precautions I mentioned?"

Cavan nodded. "Don't worry. Even though I still struggle with my pride concerning Dorcas's inheritance, I'm not about to let someone else take God's provisions and use them for evil. I've thought a lot about what you said, and I'd like to apologize for my attitude."

Russ clapped his hand on Cavan's shoulder. "We deal with our sinful natures every day, but we have to remember that God forgave our sins through his Son's payment for them on the cross. When we continue in our sin, we grieve him. I'm glad you recognized your pride as sin and made the decision to stop letting it rule you. Have you and Dorcas talked?"

Cavan lifted his booted foot to the fence rail. "I can't thank you enough for raising your daughter the way you did, Russ. She is the best wife a fellow could ever have, and I tell you, I don't deserve her. Once she understood my feelings, she made sure that I knew she didn't care one iota about the money. All she cared about was being happy with me." He shook his head. "She's really special. It pains me to see her afraid of this man. I can't let anything happen to her or the children."

"Don't worry, son. With God's help, we'll protect her, together."

Chapter 17

Sand Creek

Mattie's thoughts kept interrupting her work. She shifted position at her desk to make sure her leg was elevated as Abel had instructed her. If she didn't, she was almost positive that he would appear in front of her and demand that she follow his orders. She looked up at the door to see if her thoughts had materialized him.

She sighed. Something was nagging at her mind, but what?

She felt so foolish for fainting that day. There she was, waking up in Abel's arms just as she had done the night he rescued her from freezing. She blushed as she recalled being held so close that when her eyes opened she was staring directly into those blue eyes.

Mattie, get control of yourself! You're thinking like a schoolgirl!

"Miss Morrison, could you fill out these papers with Mr. Moore and have him sign them when you are through?"

Mattie straightened up in her chair and moved her leg off the footstool Abel had provided for her. "Certainly, Mr. Davies. Please, Mr. Moore, have a seat." She indicated the chair in front of her desk.

"Sorry to hear about your twisted ankle, miss," the blacksmith said politely. "My wife, Belle, wanted me to ask you to come to dinner tonight if you feel up to it."

Mattie smiled with pleasure. "Why, thank you, Mr. Moore. I would be happy to come. I've spoken with Belle several times at the store. How very kind of you, and please call me Mattie. Now, let's see what questions we need to answer on here."

Mattie moved through her day efficiently despite the cumbersome bandage on her ankle. She was able to put her boot on, but she couldn't button it. Not that it mattered; no one could see it under her long skirt anyway. And she didn't think she would need the crutches much longer either.

The crutches. She smiled when she thought of them. Abel had given the pair of crutches in the doctors' office to Jeb Owen, forgetting that she needed a pair too. When they both realized what he had done, she had tried to assure him that she would manage without the crutches and that Jeb needed them more than she did anyway. But he had been so worried about her being able to get around that he gave her a cane to use the first day and even helped her get back to the hotel, where they had to stop and explain her bloody dress to several people.

My dress. Again Mattie smiled, remembering that Abel had insisted on having his mother wash her dress or even that he'd buy her a new one. She had to convince him that she was capable of getting the dress clean herself, even with an injured leg. My! He was persistent, but finally she persuaded him that she would be fine.

And then the next morning, Gretchen had tapped on her door. "Mattie, Abel Newly was here bright and early this morning with this pair of crutches for you to use. I understand he worked on them most of the night to have them ready for you. He said to apologize if they seem a bit crude, but he wanted you to have them right away."

"He made these?" Mattie was astonished. "They're sanded so smooth. How ever did he do it?"

"Oh, you'll find that Abel does everything quite well." Gretchen paused as if thinking about something. "He's probably a very fine doctor, knowing him." The words were said more to herself than to Mattie, and Mattie wondered if the hotel owner was thinking about her daughter, Annie, giving birth soon.

Mattie stacked some papers together while she readied her desk for the end of her workday. There had been no sign of the Wynns after church, but by then, Mattie was safely ensconced in her hotel room. She assumed Abel had avoided meeting up with them too since he hadn't mentioned anything when he came by the bank to check on her, which he had done every day since her injury.

Her forehead wrinkled as the nagging thought that she was forgetting something presented itself again. It was something Abel had said the day she was in his office. *My lovely assistant.* Suddenly his words popped into her head. *Why did he call me lovely?* At the time he said it, she had been too busy to realize what he said, but it must have been stored away in her mind to be examined again later. Was that it?

Mattie bit at her lower lip while she tried to capture the other nagging thought just beyond her mind's reach. *She comes from the Grandville area.* That's what Abel told the Owens about her! How did he know that? Mattie tried to recall if she had ever told him. Has he remembered her then? Does he know that she's his *wife?*

"All done for the day, Miss Morrison?"

Mattie looked up to see Mr. Davies smiling at her. "Yes, sir. Unless there's anything else you need?"

"No, I'm done too. Do you need any help getting to the hotel? Those crutches can be difficult to maneuver on as I can readily attest. I broke a leg once," he told her, and Mattie swore he seemed proud of it.

"I'm sorry to hear that, sir. No, thank you, I can manage quite well now. If you wouldn't mind holding the door is all." Mattie stepped outside. "Thanks again and have a pleasant evening."

"I'll see you tomorrow, Miss Morrison."

Mattie felt a little foolish as she swung her leg along and balanced her stride with the crutches. People moved out of her way and opened doors for her. Everyone was so kind, but she didn't relish all the attention, especially as she feared the Wynns were going from town to town looking for her. She asked Gretchen, quite innocently, if there were any new people staying at the hotel, but no one fit their description. She wondered if they would be back, and recalling the wild look in the stern preacher's eyes, she feared he wouldn't stop his quest to make an example of her and Abel to the community.

As Mattie prepared for the evening, she realized that she was looking forward to visiting with the Moores. It would be nice to have someone to eat with instead of sitting at a table alone in the hotel dining room, which she did every night. Sometimes Gretchen joined her, but usually she was busy seeing to her customers and couldn't stay long. Mattie changed her dress and took the pins out of her hair, brushed it, and repinned it with the bun firmly in place. Suddenly her thoughts took her back to the doctors' office and how she had frantically pushed the pins in her hair as Abel was busy putting things away.

Did he see my short hair? She remembered feeling the bun slip, and when she reached up to right it, she felt her shorter hair slipping out of their pins. If Abel noticed that she had short hair, he was sure to know it was her that night of the storm. No women wore their hair short on purpose. It just wasn't done. *Did he see?*

Thinking of the doctors' office made Mattie recall again the moment she awoke from her faint. How embarrassing! Abel was holding her and talking to her while his dad watched from over Abel's shoulder. When she was finally able to sit up on her own, she asked what happened.

Abel smiled at her, and she noticed that mirth had replaced the concern she had seen at first in his eyes. "My guess is that after the crisis with Jeb was past, it all hit you: the blood, the open wound, his pain. That happens sometimes. I saw it happen in medical school even with doctors who were in training."

Mattie stared at him. "But it's never happened to me before."

"Have you ever dealt with an injury like that one before?" he asked her.

She shook her head. "But why didn't I faint during it? I mean…it was awfully deep…and there was blood—"

"Put your head down," Abel put his arm around her again as she began to sway. "Breathe deeply. That's right. I think, Miss Morrison, that you could handle any crisis that came your way, but your reactions to it will occur afterward." He chuckled. "I'm not sure that nursing is the career for you."

"I don't know," Russ spoke up. "If she could assist with an injury like Jeb's and not faint through it, I would want her taking care of me in an emergency."

They had all laughed together; then Abel brought her to the hotel. Mattie smiled at the memory. She checked her reflection in the mirror. She was ready to go.

It was only a short walk to the blacksmith's house. The door opened before Mattie even reached the end of the walkway, and Belle Moore beamed at her.

"Welcome, Mattie! I should have had my Clyde escort you over here, dear. How thoughtless of me!

How are you getting along on those crutches? Is your leg feeling better?"

Mattie smiled, not having to answer any of the questions as her hostess kept up a steady barrage of them, most of which she answered herself. Mattie was led into the parlor. She stopped short.

"Surprise, Mattie!" Belle exclaimed. "I thought I'd give a little welcome dinner for you to help you get acquainted with some of the other young people in Sand Creek. This is John Trent."

A nice-looking man stood to his feet at her entrance as did the other men in the room. Mattie's initial shock was replaced with embarrassment as Belle went around the room, introducing the other men.

"These two handsome blokes are brothers, Jethro and Parker Riley, and here's Clayton Riggs." The men all seemed as embarrassed as Mattie did as they nodded their heads or said "How do you do?" to her.

"And these are Clayton's sisters Rhoda and Penny. Have you girls met Mattie yet?" Belle chattered on while Mattie tried to make sense of the awkward situation. It looked like the friendly Belle was trying her hand at matchmaking.

"Now you young folks just sit and visit a few moments while Clyde and I finish getting supper ready. It won't be long." Belle scurried from the room leaving them in silence.

An uneasy silence.

"You mustn't mind Belle, Miss Morrison." Rhoda leaned over to speak to her. "She and Clyde don't have children of their own, and they have kind of adopted all the Sand Creek children. She loves to have us all over."

"She seems very nice," Mattie agreed.

"Is Grace your sister?"

Mattie turned to the Riley brothers, but she didn't know which one had spoken. "Yes, how did you know?"

Parker nudged his older brother with an elbow. "Jethro met Grace at Buck's hotel." His tone was full of hidden meaning.

Mattie tried not to notice that Jethro Riley's ears were turning red. "Oh yes, didn't Mrs. Moore say your last name is Riley? You must be brothers to Buck?"

"That's right, Miss Morrison. And John here is a cousin to Lucy, our sister-in-law."

Mattie turned to John Trent. "Lucy is a Newly, right? How are you cousins?"

"My dad and Lucy's mom are twins," John answered.

"So Dr. Newly is your cousin too?"

"Ha! *Dr.* Newly! That sounds so strange."

Mattie swung her head to see Clayton Riggs. "Why is that funny?" she asked him.

"Aw, we all grew up with Abel, so to hear someone call him *Mr.* Newly would be funny, but when you said *Dr.* Newly, it just struck my funny bone. I still see Abel sticking frogs down his sisters' backs." He got a chuckle from the others. "See, we don't call one another mister and miss. We all know one another too well from growing up together."

"Then by all means, please call me Mattie. Did you know that I used to work for Buck and Lucy at the hotel too?"

The conversation flowed easily after that. Mattie found herself enjoying the other young people even though she tried not to notice that John Trent was being most attentive to her. It seemed the others noticed also, as there were some rib nudges between the men. Mattie felt a sinking sensation in her stomach. She liked these people as friends, but she didn't want a romantic involvement.

The evening turned out to be quite pleasant. "Thank you for inviting me, Belle. Everything was delicious, and I appreciate it. You have a lovely home." Mattie was making her exit and saying good-bye to the other guests.

"Let me walk you home, Mattie." Clyde Moore stood.

"I can do it, Clyde." John's rise to his feet was unexpected. "If you don't mind?" he questioned Mattie.

Mattie saw a wink pass between the Riley brothers. *They're as childish as schoolchildren.* "Thank you." She nodded to John. He walked past her with a smile as she waited on her crutches. He opened the door, and there stood Abel.

"Oh, hello. I was just about to knock." Abel smiled at Mattie, then he noticed John holding the door, and the smile left his face. "What are you doing here?" he asked his cousin.

"What are *you* doing here?" John asked back.

"I was about to head for home, and I noticed a shoe was loose on my horse, so I wanted to ask Clyde—oh, hello, Rhoda. Penny." Abel nodded to the ladies. He stepped farther inside and spied Clayton and the Rileys. "You having a party tonight, and you didn't invite me, Belle?" he teased.

"Now, Abel, I thought you had a young lady already. I wanted these young people to get to know one another, you see. If I had known you wanted to be invited, I would have asked you too."

Abel stood still for a moment, and Mattie wondered what he was thinking. He seemed to be trying to decide what to do next. "Well, I don't want to interrupt, but I was wondering if I could leave my horse in the stables tonight and borrow one of yours, Clyde? Maybe tomorrow you could fix that shoe for me?"

"Sure thing, Abel. Take the pinto tonight."

"Thanks, Clyde."

John motioned Mattie to step out ahead of him. He turned back to the others. "Thanks again, Belle, for another one of your delicious meals. Good night."

"Where are you going?" Abel asked him.

John turned back to his cousin. "I'm escorting Mattie home." He grinned and wiggled his eyebrows.

But Abel didn't laugh. "Uh, Miss Morrison, I should really take a look at that ankle." He stepped out the door behind them, missing the looks that were exchanged by the people left in the house.

Mattie looked at Abel in surprise.

"How about I just walk along with you two, and I can check your ankle at the hotel. Do you mind?"

Mattie pretended not to see the look that passed between the two cousins. It appeared that some animosity was building. "That would be fine, Dr. Newly, but my ankle is really starting to feel much better. I have even been putting some weight on it now and then like you said I could."

"Still, I think it would be wise to keep an eye on it."

They moved along together at a slow pace to accommodate Mattie's awkward stride on the crutches. Neither of the men spoke, and Mattie wondered what exactly was wrong and what Belle meant about Abel having a young lady already. She hadn't heard anything about it.

When they reached the hotel, Abel motioned for Mattie to take a seat on the bench on the boardwalk out front. He bent down and removed her boot; then he started unwinding the bandages. John stood to one side and watched in silence.

"Just as I thought. It's a bit swollen, Miss Morrison. Have you been keeping it up like I told you?"

"I haven't been able to this evening as I was out." Mattie watched as he rewound the ankle bandages again. She wanted to tell him to just leave it off as she would be going to bed now anyway, but she kept silent. Abel's behavior was odd, and she wanted to know why.

"Maybe you should avoid evenings like tonight until this is properly healed," he suggested, but instead of looking at Mattie, he was directing his comment to John.

He can't be jealous! The thought startled Mattie.

"It feels fine now. Thanks again, Dr. Newly. Good night. And good night, John. Thank you for walking me to my room. It was a pleasant evening, and I'm so glad to have met all of you." She waited for one of them to open the door to the hotel; then she made her way inside. Before she turned to go down the hallway to her room, she looked back over her shoulder. The two men were still standing on the boardwalk. She wished she knew what they were saying to each other.

"What was that all about?" John crossed his arms over his chest as he examined his cousin's face in the dim light of evening.

"What do you mean?"

"Don't give me that innocent look, Abel. I know when you're up to something. You knew perfectly well I wanted to walk Mattie back here *alone*. Why did you butt in? And what's with all this 'Dr. Newly and Miss Morrison stuff'? Since when did you become so formal? You two act like—wait a minute!" Realization dawned on John's face. "You're sweet on her!"

"Don't be ridiculous! I'm engaged, remember? I'm going to marry Delphinia. I just feel that I should keep an eye on my patient, that's all."

"You can't fool me, Abel Newly." John shook his head. "I know you too well." They started walking to the blacksmith's stables together. "But if you really aren't sweet on Mattie Morrison, then you won't mind keeping out of my way when I come calling on her, and I mean *keep out of my way*. You won't have a problem with that, will you?"

Abel's silence was all the answer John needed. He turned his face away to hide the smirk he couldn't keep off it. He only hoped he was around when Abel's fiancée showed up from Boston.

Chapter 18

Newly Ranch

Russ and Sky Newly sat at their kitchen table, facing Pastor Sweeney. The steaming cups of coffee in front of them were forgotten as they listened with open mouths to what the pastor had to say.

"You say this preacher claims that he performed the wedding ceremony? How can you be sure he was talking about Abel?" Russ asked.

"I'm not. He didn't know the name of the doctor, but he certainly knew the name of the young woman. He called her Mathilda Morrison, and he said she's from the Norris area, and she worked for them. She's got to be the Miss Morrison who works for Bert at the bank, right?"

"I've never heard anyone call her Mathilda," Sky spoke cautiously.

"She says her name's Mattie," Russ admitted. "That could be a nickname for Mathilda." He patted his wife's hand. "Let's not jump to any conclusions, Sky. I think Abel deserves the benefit of the doubt, and I don't like the accusations this man is making about our son. I don't care if he is a preacher."

Pastor Sweeney nodded in agreement. "This is why I've come to you two first with this information. I don't want rumors to get started that could ruin Abel's reputation or Miss Morrison's for that matter."

"What exactly did the man tell you?" Sky's face was pale as she clasped Russ's hand and waited for their pastor to speak.

"He told me his name is Reverend Wynn. He and his wife took the church north of Grandville, you know, the little country church? They hired Miss Morrison to help around their place, do the cooking and farm chores, I guess." Pastor Sweeney stopped a moment as if trying to think how to word his next thoughts. "He made Miss Morrison to sound like a real trouble-maker. He accused her of having a secret rendezvous with some young man in the area, and he said she was obstinate and disrespectful.

"He and his wife were called away before the night of the big snowstorm this spring, and they left Miss Morrison to take care of the house. They said that when they arrived the next morning, they found her and a young man…bedded down together before the fireplace of their home. Forgive me, Sky, for being blunt. I do not wish to embarrass you. He felt it was his duty before God to marry them on the spot, and he did so. They even have a witness."

Sky swallowed. "But why does he think the man is our son?"

"He and his wife have made it their mission to see to it that Miss Morrison and her...lover...as he put it, abide by the vows that were made. All they know is that the man claimed to be a doctor and claimed that he saved Miss Morrison's life that night. Reverend Wynn feels that last claim is a pretense to hide what really happened.

"He's going from town to town looking for them. I didn't tell him about Abel being a doctor, nor did I mention Miss Morrison was in our town. I didn't like the condescending attitude of the man and his wife, and frankly, I was disturbed by the man's mental state. He seemed obsessed with exposing this couple and exacting vengeance upon them. I wanted to talk with you about the situation. I believe they will be back. The people in the surrounding towns may know about Abel being our doctor and send them back here." He paused and took a sip of his coffee. "Could Abel be involved somehow?"

Russ and Sky looked at each other before Russ turned to the pastor. "Abel hasn't said anything about the night of the storm to us other than he found shelter. I don't know where he was or what happened that night, but I can assure you that my son did nothing wrong. We appreciate you coming out here to discuss this with us. Would you mind leading us in prayer, Pastor? I think we need divine help to see us through the storm that's coming."

Sand Creek

Abel waited nervously for the stage to arrive. *I shouldn't be nervous*, he chided himself. He knew he should be delighted that Delphinia and her parents were going to be here soon, but in the back of his mind loomed the problem of his shotgun wedding to Mattie. Having Mattie right here in Sand Creek made for a recipe of impending disaster, yet he couldn't blame Mattie for something that fool preacher thought he ought to do.

Sorry, Lord, I'm borrowing trouble again. Have you got any suggestions on how I can get through this mess without making it worse? Abel smiled to himself. The Lord knew his thoughts before he could even form them into words. He recalled a verse in Romans, "Likewise the Spirit also helpeth our infirmities: for we know not what we should pray for as we ought: but the Spirit itself maketh intercession for us."

Help me as I blunder through, Lord. I don't want to hurt or embarrass anyone. Mattie's face came clearly to his mind, and he looked down the street to the bank where he knew she was working. John's insinuations about him being sweet on Mattie had shocked him. *Absurd!* Maybe he should go talk to her now and get this thing settled. But no, the stage—

"Abel!"

Abel turned as Rhoda Riggs ran up to him. "Doc says to have you come quick." She paused to catch her breath. "The Grays' buggy overturned, and Violet and Taylor are both hurt."

Abel started running back to the office. He found Doc Casper hitching up the buggy. Doc called to him, "You go on horseback, and I'll catch up to you, Abel! They were almost home when it happened."

"Right!" Abel grabbed his medical bag and hurried to the stable where he saddled his horse. He was on the road shortly after Doc and passed him as he galloped on. Thoughts of the stage, Delphinia, and Mattie left his mind as he prayed for the injured couple.

Mattie limped only slightly as she walked to the hotel for her afternoon lunch. Her day at the bank was busy, but she was glad for that. It kept her mind off the problem that continued to linger there.

I should just face it. I should talk to Abel and get it out in the open so I don't have to keep worrying about the Wynns showing up and making a scene.

A crowd was forming in front of the hotel, and that meant that the stage was coming soon. Mattie smiled. It was like this in Grandville and Norris too when Dugan or Gabe would arrive with the stagecoach. People gathered around because they wanted to see who was getting off at their town. People had "nose trouble," as her grandfather used to say. They were just nosey.

Gabe was driving today, Mattie noticed. She stopped and waited with the others because it was too difficult to squeeze through the throng, especially with her limp, but she was just as curious as the rest. There weren't many passengers today: first, a mother with a child; then an older, distinguished-looking couple; and last, a lovely blonde woman, who appeared to be their daughter.

City folks, looks like. Mattie admired the fashionable traveling suits the two ladies wore. She wondered who they were meeting, for they seemed to be looking around for someone. She shrugged and made to move forward again when suddenly she was grabbed by her arm and pulled off the boardwalk to the side of the building.

"Well, looky here! I wondered what happened to you, sweetheart!"

Mattie struggled against the man's hold on her, trying to see his face. She gasped. "Wally!"

Wally Beck tipped his hat back and leaned close to Mattie, pinning her back against the wall. "I looked everywhere for you, Mattie. Why did you run off like that?" He smiled his rakish grin at her.

Mattie wiggled out from under his arm. The only way she knew to handle Wally was to put him in his place. He'd made innuendoes in the past about what he'd do if he got her alone, but she always had the Wynns nearby to deter him. Now she was on her own, but she wasn't going to let Wally know that.

"I need to get back to work, Wally. I haven't time to talk."

But Wally put out his hand to stop her. "Oh no, you don't! You and me are going to finally have some fun. I'm not letting you get away again."

Mattie stomped her good foot, which was stupid because it made her injured foot hurt worse. "Stop it, Wally." She pushed his arm away. "I have to go. My boss is waiting for me."

Wally moved quickly and had his arms around her before Mattie could take a step. "C'mon, sweetheart, let me show you what you've been missing." He stifled her protest with a kiss.

Mattie was outraged. She beat her fist on Wally's head and pushed at him until he pulled away. She drew a ragged breath. "How dare you!" She wiped at her mouth with the back of her hand. "Don't you ever come near me again, Wally. I'm a married woman!"

As soon as the words were out of her mouth, she wished she could take them back, but they seemed to have an effect on Wally. He stepped away from her.

"What do you mean you're married? To who? When?"

Mattie thought fast. She wasn't actually lying, and her declaration had halted Wally's amorous attack. "I'm married to the doctor, Dr. Newly. It's only been a short time." She waited while her heartbeat slowed. "Goodbye, Wally. Please don't bother me any further."

He made no move to stop her as she walked away from him. Her limp seemed more pronounced as she felt herself begin to tremble, the aftereffects of another crisis. She only hoped she'd make it to her room in the hotel before she fainted.

She rounded the corner of the boardwalk and bumped into someone. "Please excuse me," Mattie muttered without looking up. All she wanted was to get away from Wally.

"Quite all right."

After what she had just overheard, Delphinia Digby could barely get the words past her lips as she watched the brown-haired woman limp past her.

Chapter 19

Farm near Sand Creek

"I'm sorry if this hurts you, Mrs. Gray," Abel spoke soothingly to the injured woman.

Violet Gray smiled in return. "Don't you worry about me, Abel. I'm a tough, old lady. Ouch!"

Abel looked up quickly.

"Fooled you, Abel!" Violet laughed; then she grimaced. "Ow! It does hurt."

"Mrs. Gray, you've got to be careful how you move your arm. I've only got a rough splint on it for now until the swelling goes down. Then I'll put a plaster cast on until the bone heals. I'm so sorry about your accident."

Violet nodded. "I'm not really sure what happened. Taylor was just driving us home from town. The horse knows the way so well that we hardly have to guide him at all, but there was a gunshot quite close by, and it startled old Ned into bolting. We must have run a wheel up a rock or something to make us tip over like that."

She turned to her husband, who was being attended to by Doc Casper. "Wouldn't you say that was how it happened, dear?"

"That's about right. I wish I knew who was shooting a gun so near to my house. I don't like that at all." Taylor watched Doc pull out a bottle of liquid and pour some on a cloth. As the doctor moved to dab the cloth on Taylor's cuts, Taylor pulled back. "That's not going to sting, is it, Doc?"

"Taylor, don't be a baby." Violet laughed at her husband. She reached over with her good arm and patted his. "I'm so glad you weren't hurt too badly. We have a lot to thank the Lord for today, don't we?"

They smiled at each other, and Abel couldn't help thinking to himself what a change had taken place in the Gray household since he had been away at school. Violet must have read something in his expression because she smiled at him.

"You look like you were expecting me to react somewhat differently? I think you were in Boston, Abel, when I finally came to know the Lord Jesus. Before that happened, I know I would have reacted differently to this accident. But by God's grace, I'm learning each day to walk closer to him. Remember when Irena's husband and her mother-in-law died?"

"I wasn't here, but I heard about it." Abel continued his work while Violet told her story.

"I was in Grandville with Philippa and Ralph, and I overheard Irena telling Philippa how thankful she was to the Lord even in her heartache, and I had to know how she could feel that way when her husband had just died. She was the one who finally helped me see that my sins were taken care of on the cross by Jesus Christ dying for them. And that sin no longer stood between God and me. But, Abel, even though I knew I wasn't a very nice person, I still thought I had enough good in me to earn my way to heaven. Irena showed me that my goodness could never be better than the Lord's sacrifice for me and that he was all I needed. I put my trust in him, and I haven't looked back."

Violet moved her cumbersome arm to her lap, but Abel shook his head. "You need to elevate that arm to get the swelling down."

She let him reposition it. "Your mother and Randi Riley had been praying for me for years," she continued. "I used to be so cruel to them and to most of the people in town. But when I went to your house to tell your mother how sorry I was for the way I had treated her all those years, she welcomed me and never condemned me." Violet wiped at a tear. "She's been like a sister to me ever since." She reached for her husband's hand. "And Taylor accepted the Lord shortly after I did," she added with pride.

"That's wonderful!" Abel sat down at the table. "My folks told me that both of you had gotten saved, but I never heard the whole story before. It's amazing how the Lord can use a tragedy like Irena's sorrow to help another soul come to him. It helps us have a thankful heart in any situation, good or bad."

"Irena is a wonderful girl, and your brother Rex is fortunate to have her for a wife. How about you, Abel? When are you going to settle down?"

Abel's eyes widened. "Oh no! I forgot the stage!"

Doc Casper turned to his partner. "I've got this covered if you need to go."

"Are you sure, Doc?"

"Go on. I see your folks are coming up the drive now. They must have gotten word about the accident somehow. That's Sky and Russ; they're always ready to lend a hand."

"Thanks, Doc. Mr. and Mrs. Gray, I hope you both are feeling better soon. I'll be back to check on that arm tomorrow."

Abel hurried out the door. He could hear Doc explaining to the Grays why he needed to get back to town. Soon everyone would know about his fiancée being here.

Russ and Sky pulled up by the house as Abel was dashing out.

"Everything okay, Abel?"

Abel stopped briefly to talk to his parents. "Violet's arm is broken, and Taylor has cuts and bruises but no broken bones." He told them about the gunshot spooking the horse. "Someone was too near the house with a gun, Dad. Taylor is concerned about it." He moved to untie his horse. "I need to get back to town. I think Delphinia and her parents might be on today's stage, and I sure hate not being there to welcome them. If they're here, do you still want them to come for supper tonight, or will you stay here with the Grays?"

Sky looked to Russ for an answer. "Maybe we better postpone their visit for a day until we see how things are here. And, Abel, when you get a chance, we'd like to talk with you."

"Okay. I'll see you later tonight." Abel rode off while his parents watched him with concern in their faces.

Sand Creek

Abel tied his horse to the rail in front of the hotel and hurried up the steps. He gave no thought to his appearance as he crossed to the hotel desk and greeted Harry Nolan, but the hotel keeper's raised eyebrows warned him that something wasn't right. Abel looked down and saw that his rumpled shirt was bloodstained, and his pant legs were dusty from running his horse on the dirt road. He smacked his leg with his Stetson only to have Harry shake his head at him.

"Sorry, Harry. I didn't realize I was such a mess. Did the stage come in yet?"

"Uh-huh." Harry was frowning at the dust and dirt dropping from Abel's boots.

"Were the Digbys on it? Did they register here?"

"Uh-huh." Harry walked around the desk and guided Abel back to the door. "They're resting right now in their rooms, so why don't you go on back to the doc's office and get cleaned up a mite. Gretchen just had this floor swept clean until you came in."

Abel allowed himself to be moved along, but when they reached the door, he turned back to Harry. "Did they look upset that I wasn't here to welcome them? You see, the Grays had an accident with their buggy, and Doc and I had to go and—"

"Were they hurt badly?

"Violet's arm is broken, and Taylor has cuts and bruises, but other than that, they are fine. A gunshot spooked their horse."

"A gunshot? Where—"

"Harry! What about the Digbys?"

"Okay, okay, hold your horses. They asked me if they were in the right town since no one was here to greet them, but I just told them that you were out doctoring somewhere and would join up with them later. They wanted to rest anyway, so I don't think they were upset. They really didn't say much to me. Pretty daughter they have. Is she the one you're supposed to marry?"

"Thanks for taking care of them, Harry. I'll get cleaned up and be right back, so if they ask for me, tell them that, will you?"

"Sure thing, Abel. Take your time."

Abel took time to bring his horse to the stable and care for it before he went back to the doctors' office to wash and change into another set of clothing he kept there. He even remembered to soak the bloodied shirt in some cold water as his mother requested he do. She was having a time getting out some of the stains he encountered in his profession. While he swished the shirt around in the cold water, Abel's thoughts turned to Mattie, and he wondered if she had gotten the bloodstains out of that pretty blue dress she wore.

He stopped. Why was he thinking of Mattie when he should be getting ready to see Delphinia? He knew why. He still needed to deal with that whole wedding thing he and Mattie were a part of before it became known. That reverend fellow had been adamant about them abiding by it, and Abel wondered what would happen if the Wynns showed up in Sand Creek one day to broadcast it to the town. He couldn't let them embarrass Mattie. He didn't stop to think why Mattie's reputation came first to his mind rather than his own being a concern.

He quickly combed his hair and even took time to rub a polish on his boots. *Delphinia is going to love Sand Creek! I just wish we had gotten off to a better start by me being here to welcome her.* Abel checked his reflection one more time and then headed back to the hotel.

Harry was still behind the desk when he entered, and Abel saw him motion with his head to the dining room. He followed where Harry pointed and saw the Digbys seated at a table. He rushed over to them.

"Dr. Digby! Mrs. Digby, Delphinia, welcome! Welcome to Sand Creek! I apologize for not being here when you arrived. I was called away for medical reasons."

The older man stood to shake hands with Abel, then Abel took the hand Mrs. Digby offered, and lastly, he turned to his fiancée. She smiled a greeting and then looked down at her plate. Abel was uncertain what to do. She had never been shy around him before. Perhaps the length of time since they had last seen each other had made her bashful.

"How was your trip?" he asked as he took the chair beside Delphinia.

The older couple made general comments about the discomforts of travel. It seemed the last leg of their journey by stagecoach was the most rigorous for them. All the while they talked, Delphinia kept silent. Abel only half listened to what the others were saying. He studied Delphinia covertly and marveled again at how beautiful she was. Her dress and her mother's were of some kind of shiny fabric that shimmered and rustled faintly when they moved, a far cry from the simple cotton dresses that Mattie wore. *Mattie again?*

Abel cleared his throat. "My folks want me to ask you to come to the house for dinner tomorrow night, but I thought we could look around the town during the day, and I'd love to show you my office, and perhaps we could check on some houses that are for rent in town?" His last question was directed to Delphinia.

"Perhaps," she replied.

Abel was puzzled. He had thought their reunion would have been exciting and joyous, but Delphinia seemed distant. Maybe she was just tired from the journey.

"I believe I am ready to retire," Mrs. Digby was saying. "It is good to see you again, Abel. We'll look forward to our tour tomorrow. Good night."

Abel stood and was dismayed when Delphinia rose too.

"I think I will join you, Mother. It is good to see you again, Abel. Good night."

"Good night." He couldn't keep the disappointment from his face, and Dr. Digby who had also risen to see the ladies off turned to him with a questioning expression.

"You and Delphinia have an argument?" he asked.

Abel shook his head as they sat down again. "No, sir. At least I don't think so." His confusion was so genuine that the doctor laughed.

"It is not for us to understand the mysterious way of women, my friend. Delphinia may just be weary from travel, although she was eager to come." He was pensive a moment as he pondered his daughter's behavior. "Ah, well. Tell me about your practice, Doctor. Have you reconsidered my offer to work with me in Boston?"

Abel struggled to keep his thoughts on what Dr. Digby was saying; he was trying to figure out what was wrong with Delphinia. All the anticipation of seeing her again was tarnished by her lack of response. Had she changed her mind about marrying him? Had he changed his mind? *Whoa! Where did that thought come from? Lord, I'm confused.*

Dr. Digby covered a yawn with his hand. "I'm sorry, Abel. I'm going to have to excuse myself too. We'll catch up more tomorrow, and I trust you'll be available? You do have an assistant who can fill in for you, do you not?"

Abel heard the slight reprimand in the doctor's voice. "Doc Casper will be happy to handle the office tomorrow, sir, but I told him to feel free to call on me should there be an emergency as there was today."

"Of course, my boy, of course. Well, good night." He surveyed the dining room as they walked together to the door. "You say this is the only dining establishment in town?"

"Yes, sir."

The older man sighed. "It will have to do then, won't it? See you tomorrow, Abel."

Abel stepped outside the door of the hotel and drew a deep breath. Something was wrong, but he didn't know what. The Digbys didn't get a good first impression of Sand Creek, they weren't happy with the accommodations, and something was bothering Delphinia. He noticed a light on at the doctors' office, so he headed that way.

The Digbys were used to Boston, and Sand Creek was a far cry from the city. Was that it? Were they expecting the town to be bigger? He thought he had told them all he could about his town and his friends and family. He thought they understood.

Doc Casper called out, "Who is it?" when Abel opened the door to the office.

"Just me, Doc. How did it go at the Grays?"

"Abel?" The doc was wiping his hands on a towel as he stepped out of the examining room. "I thought you'd be busy all evening."

"The Digbys are pretty worn out after their trip and decided to retire early." He went to the basin his shirt was soaking in and began wringing the garment out. "Anything new to tell me about the Grays?"

"No. I finished up with Taylor, and he'll be sore from falling, but other than that, he should be okay. I was a little concerned about his right shoulder."

The doc went on to describe the man's symptoms to Abel, and Abel listened and nodded at the appropriate times, but he wasn't really hearing him.

He was disappointed. Instead of the elation he had expected to feel when seeing Delphinia again, he only felt let down. Her attitude toward him, whether it was bashfulness or something else, was part of it, but also he didn't experience the joy of being with her that he should have had. Were his feelings so fickle that they could change so quickly? How could he know if he should marry her?

"So I'll drive out to the Grays tomorrow to check on them. That way you can stay in town with your guests and not be bothered. We have no appointments to speak of."

Abel pulled his thoughts back to what Doc was saying. "Of course. Well, I'll see you sometime tomorrow then. I'd like to bring the Digbys by to meet you."

"That would be fine. Good night, Abel."

Abel walked his horse slowly toward home in the darkening evening. He had much to pray about.

Chapter 20

Sand Creek

Mattie yawned at her desk. She slept poorly the night before; her thoughts were racing with what had happened with Wally Beck. She still couldn't believe that she had told him she was married to Abel Newly. What if Wally should say something to someone in town? What was she thinking? Having Wally back off and leave her alone was a blessing, but did she just make matters worse for her and Abel?

"Excuse me? Miss Morrison?"

Mattie lifted her head from looking down at her paperwork. The woman standing before her desk was the woman she believed to be Abel's mother. *Oh dear!*

"Yes, may I help you?"

Sky smiled warmly. "I'm afraid we haven't met yet. I'm Sky Newly, and my son is Abel Newly, the doctor who took care of your ankle. I believe you met my husband, Russ, when you helped Abel with Jeb Owen's injury."

"Yes, I did." Mattie stood to shake hands with Sky. "It's nice to meet you." She watched in trepidation as Sky bit at her lower lip. Clearly the woman came with a purpose in mind to see Mattie.

"I've heard so many good things about you, Miss Morrison, from my daughter Lucy and her husband, Buck. I believe you worked in their hotel, and your sister is working there now?" She waited for Mattie's nod and then seemed to make up her mind to continue. "Would you have time to speak with me? Perhaps we could take a walk outside?"

Mattie's heart started to thump. *Does she know? Why does she want to talk to me?* "Uh…I don't—" She looked over at the door to Bert Davies's office.

Sky nodded. "I understand. I shouldn't be disturbing you while you're working. Maybe we could visit another time when you're free? I'd love to get acquainted with you." Her smile was so genuine that Mattie relaxed.

"Yes, I'd like that too. Uh…I usually have lunch at the hotel. Maybe you could join me sometime?"

"That would be wonderful, Miss Morrison." Sky frowned. "I'm afraid I can't today though. I have guests coming this evening and need to get home soon. Oh, you must think I'm acting strangely, but I just wanted to meet you, dear, and make sure you felt welcome in Sand Creek. Would it be all right if I stopped by another day?"

"Of course. Thank you, Mrs. Newly."

"We'll plan on it then. Good-bye, Miss Morrison."

"Good-bye."

Mattie sat down slowly as she watched Sky leave the bank. *What is that all about?* Her thoughts were churning with a mixture of delight at the welcoming attitude of the woman and dread that the woman knew her secret and was about to expose her. She was still staring at the door when it opened again, and another woman entered carrying a baby and holding a little girl by the hand.

Irena Jenson! No, she's Irena Newly now. Mattie quickly looked down at her desk and shuffled some of the papers around to appear busy. She heard Irena speak to Lloyd Humphrey, the teller, and assumed she would take care of her business and leave, but after she heard Irena thank the man, she heard her footsteps approach the desk. *What more can go wrong today?*

"Miss Morrison?"

Mattie looked up. This woman had married Nels Jenson, the man Mattie once thought she loved. She had treated Irena coldly the last time they met in Grandville, and she was ashamed of herself for doing so. It was time she told her.

"Mrs. Newly, how nice to see you again." Mattie was relieved when Irena smiled back at her.

"Please, Miss Morrison, call me Irena. I just wanted to welcome you to Sand Creek and to invite you to dinner tonight if you are free."

"How nice of you, Irena! Please call me Mattie, and please, I want to tell you how sorry I am about…about you losing your husband, and I want to…tell you that

I'm sorry for...for not being very kind to you the last time we met."

"Thank you, Mattie, but there's no need to apologize." Irena's expression told Mattie that she understood. "Rex comes to town more often than I do, so this is the first opportunity I've had to welcome you. Please forgive my tardiness, and please say you'll be able to come tonight. We'd love to have you."

Mattie hesitated. "I don't have a way to get there."

Irena shifted the baby to her other arm. "I just spoke to Sky, and she mentioned that she has guests coming to her home tonight. Would you mind very much riding with them? She said they would be happy to pick you up and to bring you home as well."

"I...I suppose that would be fine. Where...?"

"They will pick you up at the hotel lobby about five. Will that work?"

Mattie nodded. "Yes. I'll be in the lobby at five, and thank you, Irena." She leaned over the desk to see the baby. "Who is this little one?"

"This is Niels," Irena said proudly, showing him off. "And this is Anika." She patted her daughter's head with her free hand.

Mattie smiled at the little girl.

"We'll see you this evening, Mattie. I'm so glad you're coming." They waved good-bye, and Mattie sat back, wondering what had just happened. She felt a tremendous burden lifted when she spoke honestly with Irena. Why had she carried that hurt with her for so long?

The day moved by quickly after that, and Mattie was kept busy with bank business and customers wishing to see the bank owner. Later Bert came out of his office with his hat in his hand.

"I'm leaving early for the day, Mattie. My wife and I are going to the Grays to help them since their accident, so after you are finished with that stack of paperwork, please feel free to leave too. Have a nice afternoon, my dear."

Mattie tackled the papers, determined to finish early enough to have some extra time to get ready for her evening. She no longer felt nervous about being with Irena, and so with a thankful heart, she looked forward to visiting her and her new husband. She was almost to the end of the pile of papers when a boy ran into the bank, calling her name.

"Miss Morrison! Miss Morrison! Doc Newly said to come and get you quick! He needs you at the doc's office!"

Nolan Farm

Dorcas smiled at Cavan while they ate breakfast together. Life had been good at the Nolan household since they had talked about the inheritance money and how Cavan had finally come to accept it as a gift. In fact, Dorcas was pleased about how Cavan had compared having this gift to the gift of God's grace.

"Grace means that we get something we don't deserve and didn't earn," Cavan had shared his thoughts. "Because the Lord Jesus Christ made the payment for us with his own life, we don't have to try to earn our way to heaven. We can accept it as a gift. This inheritance money reminds me of that. We were given it freely with no strings attached. I had to swallow my pride and just accept it instead of trying to find some way to earn it. Now I want to use what God has provided for us to glorify his work and his ministry," he added.

"So do I, Cavan," Dorcas agreed.

They ate in silence except for the children's chatter; then Cavan brought up the other subject that was on their minds.

"You're sure you know what to do today should that stranger show up?" Concern creased his forehead as he took his wife's hand.

Dorcas took a deep breath. "I only wish we didn't have to go to such extremes because of my fears."

"Your fears are justified," Cavan assured her. "Don't feel guilty about this. It is not your fault." He squeezed her hand. "I only wish Abel's fiancée and her family hadn't arrived just now. Your parents feel that they have to entertain them, but I know your dad wants freedom to check on the Owens and now the Grays. Seems there are a lot of people needing help these days."

"I know. It makes me wonder what's going to happen next."

Sand Creek

Abel started his day early. He wanted to meet with the Digbys at the hotel for breakfast and then try to restore his relationship with Delphinia so they could proceed with their plan to wed soon. He thought about it a lot during his ride home and far into the night. He had been so sure of his plans for the future when he came home from school, and then things had gotten complicated because of that spring snowstorm and Mattie and the wedding and the women in town not wanting him to doctor them. It seemed that more and more problems were piling up in his mind.

Abel corralled his thoughts as he rode into Sand Creek. *Things* had interfered with his plans, but that didn't mean that he had to change all that he wanted because of them. He had planned to marry Delphinia and set up a practice in Sand Creek, and that was what he was going to do. He wasn't going to allow a few minor incidents to upset his plans. He felt better after making his decision.

The town was quiet when he rode in, and he realized that in his haste to put his plans into action, he had arrived too early. The Digbys wouldn't be up and ready for their breakfast yet. He decided to head to the office to catch up on some work there while he waited. He walked his horse slowly down the street and noticed Lloyd Humphrey was unlocking the door to the bank, and Mattie was starting down the boardwalk to go to work. He almost called out to her but stopped himself. If he was going to concentrate on Delphinia today, he better not complicate his day by conversing with

Mattie, as much as he'd like to. That thought startled him into stopping his horse. He watched Mattie limp along, oblivious to his attention, as oblivious as he was to the attentive eyes following him.

Abel worked until he felt the town begin to stir; then he made his way to the hotel. He was surprised to see Penny Riggs, Rhoda's younger sister, working behind the desk.

"Morning, Penny. Where's Harry and Gretchen this morning?" he asked as he strolled through the lobby.

"Hi, Abel. The Nolans are out at Cavan and Dorcas's for the day. Didn't you know? There's been a stranger hanging around Dorcas, and Cavan didn't want her to be alone."

Abel was startled. "No, I didn't know. What's going on?"

"I guess you've been too busy with doctoring, but Gretchen told me that Cavan asked them to come and help, so I'm filling in here, and my ma is taking care of the kitchen today."

"Is Dorcas in danger? Should I be there too?"

"I don't think so. Your dad and Cavan are keeping an eye on things."

"My dad?" Abel was stunned. How could this be going on without his being aware of it? He realized that he didn't spend much time at home these days, and he hadn't had a good visit with his folks for several days. He remembered that they said they wanted to talk to him. They probably were going to tell him about this stranger, but he got home late last night and left early this morning. He was worried about his sister and her family and not sure what he should do.

"Your friends haven't come to the dining room yet," Penny informed him.

Abel turned his attention back to Penny. Who was she talking about? "Oh, you mean the Digbys."

Penny looked at the distracted man. "Don't worry about Dorcas, Abel. It sounds like they've got things under control."

He smiled his thanks at her for her concern.

"It seems like a lot of things are going wrong in town lately," she commented. "There's Jeb Owen's injury and then the Grays' buggy accident and even Mattie hurting her ankle. My pa always said that things happen in threes. I hope this is the end of it."

Abel grinned at her. "I hope you're right too, Penny."

They both turned as they heard voices coming down the hall. Abel hurried forward to greet Dr. and Mrs. Digby. He looked past them, but there was no sign of Delphinia. He raised questioning eyebrows.

"I'm sorry, Abel, but Delphinia is under the weather today. I fear the travel has been too much for her. Please excuse her." Mrs. Digby made the excuses.

Abel was crestfallen, and Dr. Digby was quick to note it.

"Don't worry about her, Abel. I'll check on her later, and I'm sure she'll be up and about by lunchtime. Shall we have breakfast, and then you can show me around?"

It wasn't the morning Abel had planned, but he shared the morning meal with Delphinia's parents, and then they excused Mrs. Digby to care for her daughter, and Dr. Digby joined him in a tour of the medical facilities. The doctor was less than impressed.

"I don't understand your desire to stay in this small town when you have the opportunity to better yourself by working in Boston. Surely you can see that you won't be able to provide well for my daughter with what you will earn here, whereas in my practice in Boston, not only will you make more money, but also you will have more free time. Just see how these people are running you all around the area now. It will only get worse if you let it."

Abel had always assumed that the Digbys understood that his ambition was to serve the people of Sand Creek. To have the doctor belittle what he did here was insulting as well as eye-opening for him.

"I hope that as you get to know the people of this town, you will understand my love for them and why I wish to settle here. I know Delphinia shares my vision," he informed Dr. Digby.

The older man raised an eyebrow. "Speaking of Delphinia, I will go check on her now. We'll try to get together later today, Abel. Think of what I've said." He stood and looked Abel in the eye. "Is this really what you want for Delphinia?"

Abel was shaken as he watched the doctor walk across the street to the hotel. *I know this isn't like Boston, Lord, but surely Delphinia will adjust, won't she?* Suddenly he was full of doubts. He was about to step back into the office when he saw someone race his horse up the street and stop at Nolan's store. He recognized his cousin John Trent, and he ran over to see what was wrong.

John was running up the steps to the store when Abel called out to him. He turned and called over his shoulder, "Fire at the Spencers!"

Abel hurried after him into the store and heard him call out to Jonas Nolan, "Jonas! Can you come quick? George Spencer's barn is on fire, and we need help keeping it from spreading to the house."

Jonas called to Bridget, and they quickly made the decision to close the store so that Bridget could go along to help Janet Spencer. They gathered more men, and Abel grabbed John.

"I'll get my bag and join you," he yelled.

"No! Doc Casper is on his way there from the Grays, and he said for you to stay in town in case you're needed here."

Abel nodded and watched as the men and women readied horses and buggies and rushed out of town to help their neighbor. He turned back to the office and sat down to fill out the next order they would need. He was sure that Doc would need extra bandages on hand after today. After that, he sat and stared into space as his thoughts ran back and forth between his personal problems and the problems of the people in town. Suddenly he realized that instead of worrying, he should be praying, and he immediately sent his requests to the Lord.

He was startled when the door to his office swung open, and Monty Davies helped his wife, Annie, to enter. She was doubled over in pain, and Abel hurried to help.

"It's the baby, Abel! Where's Doc?" Monty shouted his announcement.

"Doc's out at the Spencers." Abel made sure he appeared calm to the frantic man. "They have a fire."

Annie was distraught. "He can't be there! He has to be here for the baby! *Oh!*" She grabbed her abdomen and moaned with pain.

"I'm here, and I can help you, Annie." Abel bent to look into his friend's face. "You're going to have to trust me now. Remember, I'm a doctor."

"You're not touching her!" Monty fumed. "I'm going for the doc. You just wait about having that baby until I get back, Annie!"

"*Ah!*" Annie screamed. "I think my water broke. Don't leave me, Monty!"

Monty hurried back to her side and cried out to Abel, "Do something, Abel!"

With Monty's help, Abel got Annie to the examining room table. He thought fast: Annie's folks, Harry and Gretchen Nolan, were at Dorcas's house for the day. Annie's aunt and uncle, Bridget and Jonas Nolan, had just left because of the Spencers' fire, Monty's parents were at the Grays, and Doc Casper was gone. It crossed his mind to enlist the help of Dr. Digby, but he quickly dismissed the idea. Dr. Digby only did surgeries and had made it clear that his practice did not extend to obstetrics. Abel made a decision and turned to Monty.

"Run to the bank and get Mattie Morrison to come help. She's assisted me before."

Monty stared at him. "I'm not leaving Annie!"

"Then find someone else to send, but go!" he demanded.

Monty hesitated only a moment and then ran out the door. He was back in seconds. "I found Tommy and sent him." As Annie groaned again, he reached for her hand. "Are you going to help her or not, Abel? Can't you see she's in pain?"

"She's going to be fine, Monty." Abel readied the room for the delivery while he kept an eye on the couple. He could see that his biggest problem was going to be getting rid of Monty so that Annie could have her baby. "What were you folks doing in town today? I thought Annie would be staying close to home with the baby ready to come."

"We came to town to stay to be close to our folks and Doc Casper for the delivery. Why aren't they here?"

Abel explained where everyone was while he monitored Annie's pains. "You're doing great, Annie." He knew he needed to examine her, but not with Monty breathing down his neck. He had to find a way to get him out.

Mattie arrived, a little out of breath from running, and assessed the situation in no time. Abel caught her eye, and she stepped over to the side of the room with him.

"I'm sorry to ask, but can you help me today, Miss Morrison? I'm a little shorthanded, and you were the first person I thought of to help."

"Of course, Doctor. I'll do what I can."

"Well, first off, how do you suggest we get Monty out of here so I can examine Annie?"

Mattie gaped at Abel, and he could see she was contemplating his question. "What if we sent him to Mrs. Casper?"

"Florrie? Of course! She'd be glad to help us out!"

"I'll just step over there and be right back."

Abel watched Mattie leave. He felt a renewed confidence now that she was here.

Soon Mattie returned with Florrie scurrying behind her. "Why, Monty Davies! Isn't this wonderful! You and Annie are having a baby today!" Florrie beamed at Monty in delight. "Now, Monty, I need you to come with me while the doctor and Mattie take care of Annie. She'll be just fine."

As Monty started to protest, Florrie took him by the arm and continued, "I always take all the fathers over to the house during this time, Monty. Having a baby takes awhile, and Doctor Abel and Mattie are going to take good care of Annie. Oh! I can hardly wait to find out if you have a son or a daughter. I remember so well when *you* were born. I waited in your parents' parlor with your father, and he paced up and down…" Florrie's voice trailed off as she led Monty out the door.

Abel breathed a sigh of relief. He turned to Mattie. "I need to examine Annie now."

Mattie nodded, and Abel watched as she moved to Annie's side and took her hand. "Hi, Annie. So it's time! Are you excited? I know your parents talk of nothing else but their new grandchild. Won't they be thrilled! And your father-in-law mentions it every day at the bank. He'll be such a doting grandpa!" Mattie continued chatting with Annie while Abel prepared for the exam.

"Okay, Annie. I'll be checking the baby now as soon as this contraction is over. Try to relax."

There was fear in Annie's voice. "I want my mother!"

Mattie's next words surprised both Annie and Abel.

"I'll have her ready for you in just a minute, Doctor." Mattie led Abel to the door and gently pushed him through it. Quietly she spoke to him. "My mother had seven children, and when the midwife came to help the doctor, she always sent him out until she had everything ready. Trust me, Abel, Annie doesn't want you in here until she's been prepared."

Abel was astonished, but he wasn't allowed to express himself because the door shut in his face. He supposed Mattie was right that Annie would like a woman's help before she was examined. He knew all about delivering a baby and taking care of his patient, but he realized he still had a lot to learn about a woman's feelings. Mattie was really a godsend. He admired the way she calmed Annie down and how she took care of getting Monty to Florrie. She really was wonderful, and he was so glad she was here. He wouldn't have dreamed of asking Delphinia to assist him. She was great about visiting patients at the hospital and helping to distribute flowers to their rooms, but now that he thought about it, he had never actually seen her help medically in any way.

Suddenly Abel's thoughts halted, and he stared at the closed door. *She called me Abel!*

Chapter 21

Nolan Farm

"I can't tell you how much I appreciate you coming to spend the day with the children," Dorcas told her in-laws. "I know Cavan has told you all about our situation, and it relieves my mind no end to know that the children will be taken care of should the need arise today."

Gretchen reached for Dorcas and hugged her. "I must say that I'm worried about you, my dear. You know that we'll watch Leon and Fiona so that nothing happens here, but I feel it is foolish for you to be taking this risk." She turned worried eyes to her husband. "Harry, isn't there some other way than to put Dorcas in danger?"

Harry slipped his arm around his wife, and she rested her head on his shoulder. "I know that Cavan and Russ have thought this through. The only way they are going to stop this man from bothering Dorcas is to confront him head on. She can't go on living in fear that he'll show up at her door when Cavan is away. Sometimes the best way to get rid of a problem is to root it out at its source instead of tiptoeing around it."

Gretchen smiled at Dorcas. "You're braver than I am, dear."

"I don't know that I'm so brave," Dorcas admitted, "but I have every confidence in Cavan."

"So do we, and we're delighted to help out. Let's just hope Annie doesn't pick today to have that baby! We have enough excitement going on right here." Gretchen reached for Dorcas's apron. "Now, I'm going to start some bread and a kettle of soup. No matter what the day brings, we're going to need to eat."

It wasn't until nearly lunchtime that Cavan strolled in from the fields. He washed up in the basin outside and entered the house as he would normally do any day, but once inside, his casual demeanor left.

"He's here."

"He is? Where?" Harry asked.

Cavan tilted his head to indicate the grove of trees behind the barn. "He's been there for a while watching the house."

Dorcas reached for her husband's hand, and Gretchen put a hand to her mouth. The children were playing on the floor in the sitting room, and both women turned as if to check that they were safe.

Cavan looked at his father. "Your buggy is obvious out front, so he knows someone is here. I think it's time we make our move." He turned to his wife. "Are you ready, Dorcas? You don't have to do this if you've changed your mind or if you're afraid."

Dorcas squeezed Cavan's arm. "I'm ready. I won't pretend that I'm not afraid, but I know we have to do this to protect our family."

Cavan smiled at her. "Let's pray before we go. Dad, would you lead us?"

They joined hands, and Harry led them in prayer; then Cavan hugged Dorcas and kissed her. "Remember, I'll be nearby at all times. Have you got the derringer your father gave you?" At her nod, he continued, "Be prepared to use it."

Harry and Gretchen both hugged their daughter-in-law, and when Gretchen started to tear up, Dorcas shook her head at her. "Don't worry the children now. I'm counting on you."

Cavan left the house first and went to the barn for their wagon. He hitched a horse to it and brought it around to the front of the house beside his parents' buggy. Dorcas came out of the house with her handbag attached to her wrist and a sunbonnet on her head. They spoke a few words to each other; then Cavan kissed her and helped her up into the wagon and handed her the reins. He called out, "I'll see you when you get home!"

Dorcas turned to the house and waved to Harry and Gretchen, who stood on the porch with the children and waved good-bye to her. As Dorcas snapped the reins and drove out of the yard, they then returned to the house and shut the door, and Cavan made his way back to the barn to go back to his chores.

"I hope this works the way they have it planned," Gretchen fretted as she started feeding the children and Harry their lunch.

"Shh!" Harry motioned to the children, and Gretchen nodded, but the worried look didn't leave her eyes.

Sand Creek

Delphinia stared out the hotel window. Her mother had finally left her alone while she went to lunch with her father, and Delphinia was relieved. She was tired of her mother's probing questions about her health and her obvious reluctance to see Abel interlaced with comments about the dingy, dirty little town and its substandard cuisine and lack of culture. The view out Delphinia's window spoke volumes about the town's absence of refinements. A sagging clothesline held the hotel's daily wash, a pile of wood littered the yard around the chopping block and axe, and an outhouse with a creaking door announced each time it was in use.

Delphinia sighed. Abel had described Sand Creek as a charming place and told her that she would love it. He made it sound picturesque, and while it was true that the countryside abounded with a variety of sights from lakes and rivers to forests and fields, the living conditions were far below what she had expected. How could Abel even think she would be comfortable in this rustic country environment when he had witnessed her rich lifestyle in Boston? She knew she had told him that she would be willing to go anywhere with him, but she hadn't meant living like this. She had always felt it would be an easy thing to convince Abel to return to Boston and join her father's practice. Surely seeing her in this environment would convince him that she didn't belong here.

But the town wasn't really what was on her mind. She reviewed over and over again what she had heard the woman say before she bumped into her. She said she was married to the doctor, to Dr. Newly! Could there be another Dr. Newly in this town or in another town? Delphinia had to assume that she meant Abel. But how could this be?

Abel didn't give any indication that there was a problem between them when he met them for dinner. Had the woman just invented the story to discourage the man who was talking to her?

Delphinia frowned. It hardly seemed like a spur-of-the-moment declaration. The woman had blurted it out like she was revealing a secret and had no choice but to tell it. But if it was true, wouldn't Abel give her some hint, some clue that there was something wrong that they needed to discuss? She paused. How could he? She hadn't given him an opportunity to talk with her alone since she arrived. Maybe it was time she and Abel had a talk. No secrets. She wanted answers.

She cringed as the outhouse door squealed on its hinges. She reached for her hat and pinned it to her hair and then quietly left her room. Her parents were dining, but she rounded the corner to the hotel front desk without them spotting her.

"Could you tell me where the doctor's office is, please?" she inquired of the young girl who approached when she saw Delphinia waiting there.

"Just across the street, miss. It's the one with the sign that says 'Doctor.'"

Delphinia barely refrained from rolling her eyes. "Of course, it is." She stepped outside and lifted her skirts to descend the wooden steps. She eyed the dusty street with distaste. There was nothing to do but hitch her skirts up again to make the walk across to the building the young girl had pointed out to her. Delphinia's glance around confirmed her dislike of Sand Creek. There wasn't a soul on the street, and the stores all appeared to be vacant or shut up for the day.

She entered the office without knocking and looked around. One of the doors inside was shut, and she could hear voices coming from it, but she hesitated about approaching. If Abel was with a patient, she would have to wait, but how would he know she was there? She took a few moments to look around the office while she debated what to do. It was a far cry from her father's office with its rich interior and gleaming floors. The white walls, wooden floor, and woodstove had little appeal. She moved about the small room with increasing impatience. Finally she went to the door and gave it a sharp knock with her fist.

She stepped back and waited. She could hear the voices still, and it appeared that someone was moaning, but she wasn't sure. Maybe she should have waited longer, but now that she was here, she was determined to speak to Abel. Moments passed, and she raised her fist to knock again when the door was opened, and a woman slipped through, closing it quickly behind her.

"Yes? Do you need to see the doctor?"

Delphinia gasped. "You!"

The woman appeared startled by Delphinia's reaction to her. "Are you ill, ma'am?"

But Delphinia turned and ran from the room.

Mattie hurried back to Annie's side. She didn't recognize the woman who ran from the office, but no matter, she didn't look ill, so she wasn't going to worry about it now. She and Abel had their hands full caring for Annie.

"Who was it?" Abel asked. He pulled the stethoscope away from his ears to hear her reply.

"It was a woman, but she apparently didn't need to see you. She left." Mattie turned her attention back to Annie. She wiped the sweat from her patient's forehead and smiled at her. "You're doing great, Annie. Dr. Abel says it won't be long now. You just have a little ways to go, and you'll be holding your baby in your arms."

"That's right, Annie. Soon now I'm going to ask you to push. Your labor is progressing well. We're almost there."

"Oh! I wish it were done! Ah! *Ah*!"

"Don't fight it, Annie! Just take a deep breath and let it out slowly."

Mattie watched as Abel calmed Annie and talked to her. He kept her informed about what he was doing and what she could expect. She was impressed by his manner and his concern for Annie's modesty. Mattie didn't really know that much about delivering babies. Even though she was the oldest of seven children, she was nine years old when the youngest was born. She hadn't really assisted in her mother's deliveries. Her job was to take care of the other children during the delivery, and the midwife and doctor handled the rest. But Mattie grew up on a farm, and she knew a lot about birthing from the animals in her care. However, she didn't tell Annie that; she let her believe that she knew what she was doing. And all she knew to do was to comfort the young mother and be on hand to help Abel in whatever he asked her to do. And the thought that was in the back of her mind constantly was why Abel had asked *her*.

She listened carefully as Abel showed her the instruments he would ask her to hand to him, and together they laid out the basin and blankets for the baby. He encouraged both the women with a smile.

"Okay, this time when you have a contraction, I want you to push, Annie."

Mattie took Annie's hand and helped her sit up part way. She kept up a stream of cheerful words to encourage Annie as the woman struggled to give birth.

"Stop! Annie, stop pushing!" Abel's command startled both women, and Mattie scanned Abel's face in fear.

"What's wrong, Abel? Is there something wrong with my baby?" Annie cried.

"No, nothing's wrong. I…just need to…there!" Abel exclaimed. "The cord was around the baby's neck, but everything's okay now. Push when you're ready, Annie. Everything's going to be just fine and…praise the Lord! You have a little boy!"

"I do? A boy?" Annie started crying, and Mattie gently helped her lie back on the table. She moved swiftly to Abel's side and handed him the things he asked for as he cleaned up the baby and cut the cord. Soon a small cry announced that the baby was breathing. Abel handed the baby to Mattie, and she stepped up to Annie to show her her new son.

"He's so precious, Annie! Here, let me tuck him in beside you for a few seconds before I get him cleaned up. I think he looks like Monty, don't you?"

Annie was crying and laughing at the same time. "Thank you so much, Abel. I don't know what we would have done if you hadn't been here. I'm sorry I didn't trust you at first, but when the cord was around his neck like that, I was awfully glad you knew what to do." She studied her infant son tenderly and with reluctance handed him back to Mattie.

"Here, now. We need to get you cleaned up to meet your father." Mattie spoke softly to the little boy. "I'm sure he is anxious to know what's going on in here. Do you have a name chosen?" she asked Annie.

Annie smiled. "I'll have to make sure with Monty, but we talked about naming a boy Morty."

"That sounds just perfect." Mattie wrapped the baby up when she was done washing him and brought him back to Annie so she could see him once more. "I know you're tired, so how about if I let him rest in this little bed we made for him here while I get you cleaned up? Then I'll bring him to you so Monty can come meet him."

"I'll leave you two then," Abel said as he took off the apron he had donned for the delivery. "Annie, I'll be in to check on you later, but meanwhile, I have the privilege of telling Monty that he has a son." Abel grinned, and Mattie could tell that he was relishing the upcoming experience.

She quickly helped Annie get washed up, and she found a clean gown to replace the now-soiled dress that Annie had arrived in. Together they managed to move Annie to the small bed in the corner of the room.

"There. I'm sure this will be much more comfortable than that table," Mattie told her. "You're going to need to rest a bit before you try going to your parents' house."

The bedding on the examining table needed to be changed, and Mattie efficiently replaced it. She gathered the items that needed washing and got them out of sight before Monty came, and she took time to fix Annie's hair even without the help of a comb or brush. Just getting the pins out and fanning her hair out over the pillow made her patient feel more comfortable.

As an afterthought, Mattie felt her own hair and quickly made adjustments to the loose ends that had found their way out of the bun. She wished for a mirror so that she could check her appearance. She smoothed out the front of her dress, but it was stained and wrinkled and not very presentable.

"You look wonderful, Mattie. I'm sure Abel will think so too."

"What?" Mattie turned to stare at Annie. "What do you mean by that?"

"You and Abel. I think you two would be so perfect for each other. Look at how well you work together, and"—Annie smiled a knowing smile—"he was watching you."

Mattie was astonished. The baby started to whimper, so Mattie turned to attend to him and to avoid Annie's inquisitive expression. She heard the door open, so she stepped over to the bed and handed the infant into his mother's eager arms. The women shared a long look, then finally Mattie gave a shake of her head, but Annie promptly nodded hers in the affirmative.

"Annie!"

They turned to see Monty standing in the doorway. His face was pale as he stared at his wife and son. His dark hair was standing on end as if he had run his fingers through it time after time. Annie smiled at him and held little Morty up for his view. He rushed to their side.

"Told you they were all right, Monty," Abel said from behind him. He chuckled as he motioned for Mattie to join him in the other room to give the couple some privacy. She smiled back as he closed the door behind her.

"Mattie, I can't thank you enough for coming to my rescue today," Abel said.

Mattie blinked. *He called me Mattie.*

"I know it was a big imposition, and I took you away from your work at the bank, but I don't know what I would have done without your help. You saved the day!"

"I'm glad I was available," Mattie said. Suddenly she felt weak in the knees. *Oh no! I'm not going to faint again!* She sank into the nearest chair and waited for the moment to pass. Fortunately Abel had turned away. Annie's words, "He was watching you," came back to her, and she was nervously aware of his presence and that they were alone.

"Would you like a glass of water? I'm sorry I don't have any coffee made."

"Yes, some water would be wonderful."

Abel spun around at her tone. "Mattie! Are you all right? You're not going to faint again, are you?" He rushed over to her and knelt by her chair.

Mattie felt herself grow hot. She fanned at her face. "I don't understand. I'm just fine when I'm dealing with the emergency."

"Perhaps you should lie down." Abel took her arm.

"No, I'll be fine. Just let me rest here a moment. Then I really should get back to the bank to finish my work for the day. Unless you still need me?"

Abel studied her, and Mattie wondered if he was looking at her like a doctor does a patient or as a man looks at a woman. Not only were Annie's words making her self-conscious, but she was also suddenly remembering the night Abel changed her out of her frozen clothes into Mrs. Wynn's nightdress.

"I better go." She started to rise, and Abel stood with her.

"I suppose I have to let you."

She wished Abel wasn't looking at her so intently. "Would you like me to come back later to give Annie a hand?" she asked.

"Yes. I mean, no, I don't think so. Harry and Gretchen should be back from the fire soon, and Gertie and Bert Davies will come as soon as they return from helping the Grays."

"Fire?"

"Yes, the Spencers had a barn fire today, and most of the town went to help them out, the Nolans included. It's been an eventful day."

Mattie took a few steps to the door. She steadied herself on the door frame while she turned to say good-bye.

"I'm walking you back," Abel declared. "You're not very steady on your feet, and I'd feel terribly responsible if you fainted on the way back to the bank."

Mattie started to protest, but Abel was insistent. "Just give me a minute to let Monty and Annie know where I've gone," he said.

They stepped out of the doctors' office together, and Abel put his hand under Mattie's arm to steady her. Mattie was thankful that he didn't know that his nearness was having the opposite effect on her. She glanced over at him and liked what she saw. He caught her look and smiled.

"Feeling better?"

Mattie cleared her throat. "Yes, Dr. Newly. I'm sorry to take you away from your patient—"

"Dr. Newly?" He grinned as he led her up the steps to the boardwalk leading to the bank. "I think we can forego formalities now and use our first names, don't you? May I call you Mattie, or would you prefer Mathilda? Here we are. Are you sure you're up to working? I know Bert would understand if you retired for the day, especially since you just helped bring his grandson into the world."

Mattie couldn't speak. *Mathilda? No one here has called me that. Does that mean that he remembers?* Her laugh displayed her nervousness. "I feel much better now, and I only have a few papers left to go through. Besides, I left my handbag." She glanced down at her dress. "Oh, I forgot about my dress. I wonder if I should have changed first."

Abel appeared to have noticed her stained garment for the first time. "I apologize for ruining another article of your clothing, Mattie! Please allow me to purchase you a new dress. It's the least I can do to thank you for all the help you've given today."

"No, I couldn't let you to do that." Mattie blushed as she waited for Abel to open the door to the bank for her. "Besides, I have a shawl I can use to cover this for the remainder of the day. I'll be fine. Thank you for walking me over." She turned to say good-bye.

"Let me just walk you in."

Mattie's heart thumped at the expression on Abel's face. He seemed so reluctant to leave her, and she realized that she was enjoying his attentions. Was Annie correct in her assumption that Abel was attracted to her?

They entered the bank together, and Mattie noticed that there were no customers. She turned to Lloyd to explain her absence and found him staring at her with fear in his eyes. She was about to ask what was wrong with the teller when a voice, a familiar voice, spoke behind her.

"Just keep walking and keep your hands where I can see them!"

Mattie gasped. She heard the door being locked, and she turned to see Wally Beck, holding a gun on them.

"The bank is now closed."

Chapter 22

Nolan Farm

Asa studied the house from his viewpoint in the wooded grove behind the barn. He stood near his horse's head, and other than a gentle pat to the animal's neck, he didn't move a muscle. He saw the woman leave with the wagon, and he saw the older couple go in the house with the children. It was the man, the woman's husband, who kept his attention and kept him firmly planted in his hiding place even though he wanted to follow the woman. What the man did next would determine Asa's next move.

Everything else was in place. Lonan, Beck, and Otis were in town and would make their move on the bank in a few hours. That would give Asa plenty of time to complete his part of the plan. His ploys to get people out of town were working just as he had expected. The buggy accident brought out the doctor and neighbors with helping hands, just as he had planned it would do.

He heard talk about people helping another neighbor with an injury, and even though the injury hadn't been his doing, Asa was pleased that it was occupying more of the men from the area. Several more were now busy trying to put out the barn fire Asa had started earlier in the day at the Spencers' farm.

There can't be many left in town. Asa allowed himself a thin smile.

He had to be careful though. He knew the town's sheriff was on the lookout for him. The sheriff was looking for the man who was terrorizing these poor people in the countryside. Asa knew the Grays must have reported the gunshot that upset their buggy, and he knew the woman on this farm was nervous about him and had probably warned her man, and he had no doubt told the sheriff. Asa needed to keep his guard up. That was why he stayed still right where he was and watched out for the man instead of taking off after the woman straight off. Asa well remembered how her husband had come up behind him without a sound the first time. He wasn't going to let that happen again.

Without moving his head, Asa's eyes followed the man's movements as he led a horse out of the barn, a horse hitched to a plow. Asa squinted. A trick? He watched as the man threaded the reins over the plow and took his place behind. He snapped the reins and began walking the animal to the fields.

Asa was impatient to leave. He knew which way the woman was headed, and he knew he could catch up to her, but he didn't know how long she'd be alone. Was she meeting someone? Was she visiting neighbors? Was she headed over to help with the fire?

He almost shook his head but stopped. He didn't think the family knew about the fire; otherwise, the man would have gone to help by now. No, she wasn't going there.

He kept waiting. The man had made his first furrow with the plow and was now turning back. If this was a trick, the man would have assumed that Asa would leave by now, and he'd hurry back to the barn, saddle up, and chase him down. But, no. He slowly plodded behind the plow as if he had all the time in the world. Asa waited through three more rows before he made his move. When the man's back was turned, he mounted his horse and backed him out of the grove away from view. Now he was free to follow the woman.

He needed to hurry. He had wasted too much time waiting, but it had to be done. Patience pays off, and he wanted the reward of this payoff. Asa recalled the expression on Otis's face when Asa changed the plan and said he wouldn't be in town during the robbery. Otis knew Asa's weakness for the ladies and expected he knew the reason for the change. Otis knew too much and was starting to get too vocal about it. One of these days, Asa was going to have to put the bigger man in his place.

Otis and the others would handle the robbery without any difficulty now that Asa had contrived to get the men out of town. If only Beck would keep his head and not do anything foolish. Of the three men, Beck was the most unpredictable.

Asa's concerns about the robbery fled when he spotted the blonde woman's wagon ahead on the road. He held his horse back while he perused the area for any sign of life. No one seemed to be about, and while that was a good thing, he felt uneasy. He kept his horse moving along, but he kept his distance while he studied every tree, every rock, and every bush. Nothing.

He knew where she was going now. This road would take her to the Newly ranch, and Asa had only recently learned that the woman was Dorcas Nolan, and she was a daughter to the Newlys, who had all the money in the bank. And Russ Newly used to work for the Pinkertons. Funny how that should scare him away from her, but instead, it lent to the excitement of kidnapping her.

He knew his plan would work. The men would get the money, and he'd get the woman. They'd meet up at their cabin and split the money. Then they would leave the state without fear of pursuit because of the letter that Asa instructed Otis to leave at the bank, saying that if they were followed, the woman would be killed. But if they were allowed to leave with the money, then the woman would be freed alive. Of course, they'd have to keep her with them for several weeks to guarantee their safety, but Asa had no problem with that.

Dorcas would be nearing the Newly house if he didn't make his move soon. Asa looked all around him one more time and then spurred his horse forward, easily catching the slow wagon.

"Whoa there! Howdy again, ma'am!" Asa watched as Dorcas pulled up on the reins. She seemed startled by his presence, and once again, he saw a glimmer of fear touch her eyes. Her hair was covered by the bonnet she wore, and he wished he could see the sun glimmering off it again. Soon. Patience.

"What do you want?" Her voice was shaky, and the sound of it made him smile.

"It's a beautiful day, isn't it? I thought maybe you and me could take a ride."

"No, thank you!" Dorcas snapped the reins, but Asa anticipated the move and stepped forward to the horse's head and grabbed the harness.

It was just the move Russ Newly had been waiting for him to make. As Dorcas snapped the reins, Russ rose from under a tarp in the back of the wagon with his rifle aimed steadily at Asa.

"Hands up! Now!" Russ ordered.

Asa swung around at the command, reaching for his pistol as he did so.

"I wouldn't!" a voice yelled from the trees up ahead.

Asa debated, his one hand on his horse's reins and the other hovering over his gun. The thunder of a galloping horse coming down the road made up his mind for him. He might get a shot at one, maybe two, but three wouldn't be possible. He put his hands up.

"I'll cover him while you get his gun, Rex," Russ called from the wagon. "You okay, sweetheart?" he asked Dorcas.

"I'm fine now, Dad." She set the brake and looped the reins around it while she hopped down from the wagon and raced to Cavan, who was sliding down from his horse.

"Dorcas! Are you all right?" Cavan grabbed her in his arms and held her tight.

"I'm shaking, but I'm fine. It worked just like we planned." She and Cavan turned to see her brother Rex take the weapons from Asa and order him off his horse. All the while Russ kept his rifle aimed at the man.

Cavan stepped away from Dorcas. "I'll tie his hands. I brought a rope along just for that purpose." In no time, they had Asa captive.

"You won't be accosting women anymore." Cavan's eyes bored into Asa's. "And I'll see to it personally that you never get near my wife again."

"You think your troubles are over?" Asa sneered at the men. "They're just beginning."

"Oh, you mean the bank robbery?" Russ asked nonchalantly. "I think that's under control too."

Asa swung around to look at Russ in disbelief.

"We didn't expect the fire you set as a distraction, but we were on to you after you spooked the Grays' horse. The sheriff and I have both seen evidence of your horse's shoe prints in both places, as well as the ones in the woods by Cavan and Dorcas's house. And once the others are caught at the bank, they'll tell us the rest of the story about how you were planning to use Dorcas as a hostage until you got away."

Asa's mouth was tight, and his face red. "Who was it? Which one of them is a traitor?"

"Did you expect there to be honor among thieves?" Russ turned to Rex. "You have our horses? Let's get him into the jail then. I expect he'll have company soon."

"Thanks, Russ, and you too, Rex. I can't tell you how relieved I am this is over. I don't think I've ever had a more difficult task than to plow a field while I knew a man was after my wife. But you were right, Russ. I had to stay and do my part of the job." Cavan pulled Dorcas close to his side. "The reward was well worth it."

"Thank the Lord," Dorcas put in. She stepped away from Cavan and hugged her father. "Thank you, Dad. We'll go on to the house and let Mom know that she can stop praying for the right outcome and start thanking the Lord for the results." She thanked Rex with a hug next. "Even though I was frightened, I was comforted in knowing that you were always just a little ahead of me and Dad was right behind me."

"And the Lord was always beside you," Rex added. He hugged his sister back. "Would you mind swinging by my place and letting Irena know we're all safe too? I know it would relieve her mind. Tell her I'll be home as soon as I can. We've invited Mattie Morrison over for dinner tonight."

"And we're having Abel's future in-laws to our place, so we better get this business taken care of quickly," Russ said. He got Asa up on his horse and took the reins; then he and Rex led the criminal off to town.

Dorcas returned to her husband's arms and smiled up at him. "I can't believe that after all this happened, they are planning on entertaining guests this evening. I have a strange family."

"Hopefully things in town have gone smoothly too, or they may find their plans have changed. Let's deliver our messages and get you home. I want my wife and my family safely around me at the dinner table tonight"—he paused to kiss her—"and every night for the rest of my life."

Chapter 23

Sand Creek

"What's going on here? Who are you?" Abel stepped between the man with the gun and Mattie, but Mattie moved around him so she could see Wally. She put her hands on her hips.

"What are you doing, Wally?" she demanded.

"You know him?" Abel asked. His hands were still up at his sides because of the man's gun pointed at them.

Wally studied the two of them as he leaned against the front door. He was waiting for Otis to arrive, but his mind was suddenly distracted from the robbery at hand to the two people in front of him.

"Say, Mattie, is this the guy you were telling me about?"

"Wally!" Mattie made a strangling sound in her throat.

Abel's hands started to drop as he looked between Mattie and the stranger in perplexity. "Mattie?"

"Get your hands up, mister! You too!" Wally pointed at Lloyd, who had inched away from his teller's window. "And get back where I can see you," he ordered.

A tap on the door made Wally stop and peek out. He unlocked it and let a large man enter. He locked the door again.

Otis quickly scanned the people in the room, and his eyes rested on Mattie. "Hey, Beck, ain't this the skirt you bin chasin'?"

Now Abel made a strangling noise. "What?"

"No one said you could talk, mister." Otis pointed at Abel. He viewed Wally out of the corner of his eye while he watched the others. "Thought you was gonna wait 'til there weren't no customers."

Wally shrugged. "They came in at the end of the day. Besides, it's Mattie!"

Abel stared at Mattie. Was she part of this? She looked absolutely furious with the man she called Wally. She knows him. Had he somehow been mistaken about her?

Mattie sputtered, "Wally Beck, I swear if you don't put that gun down, I'll—"

"You'll do nothin', sister," Otis butted in. "Now you and your lover boy here jest set down on those chairs. We're gonna have to tie you up. You, come here!" He motioned to Lloyd.

"Don't call him her lover boy, Otis!" Wally complained. He took Mattie's arm and led her to a chair. "He's not the guy you married, is he?"

Abel saw Mattie look sharply at him, but he couldn't hear Wally's words. Mattie avoided answering Wally's question. "What are you doing, Wally? Aren't you smarter than this? You know you aren't going to get away, and then you'll end up in jail."

"Do you care what happens to me? Listen," Wally whispered to her, "you can come with us! I don't have to tie you up if you just do what I tell you."

"Are you crazy? I'm not going anywhere with you!"

Abel tried to hear the exchange between Mattie and Wally Beck as Otis tied him to a chair. He was stunned to hear that Mattie knew these men, or at least one of the men. He struggled with his feelings. *Lord, am I in love with a criminal?* Abel nearly fell off his chair as he swung around to stare at Mattie. *I'm in love with her?* His thoughts raced. *What about Delphinia? What if Mattie really is a criminal? How can I be in love with her already? I hardly know her!*

Otis took Lloyd by the arm and led him behind the counter to the bank's safe. "Open it," he demanded.

Obviously frightened, Lloyd stuttered, "Mr. Davies, the…owner…he…has the…combination."

Otis lifted the end of his pistol and pushed it into Lloyd's neck. "You sure about that?"

"No…no…sir." Lloyd bent down and started fumbling with the knob.

"I didn't think so." Otis grinned and looked over to Wally. "Hey, Beck. Leave the skirt alone and git over here. We got work to do."

"I want to take her with us, Otis."

Otis glared at the younger man. "Asa's already got us a hostage. You know that! Git your mind back on the job and forgit about the girl." Otis shoved Wally. "Start loadin' them bags!"

But Wally stepped back to stand eye to eye with Otis. "Don't go pushing me around. You're not the boss, and I'll do as I please. If I want the girl along, I'll take her, and you have nothing to say about it."

During this exchange Abel slid his chair closer to Mattie. He could see by her face that she was outraged by the conversation, but he still didn't understand her relationship with the man named Wally Beck.

"You okay, Mattie?" he asked quietly.

She pressed her lips tightly together. "I'm fine," she whispered back. "You?"

Abel nodded. They watched the two men arguing while Abel tried to think of what to do. He recalled his father's warnings about a possible robbery, but he hadn't given it much heed. It seems he hadn't been paying attention to anything outside his own problems lately. But thinking quickly now, he realized that the thieves had done a good job of setting up for their robbery. Nearly every able-bodied man in town was out of town helping someone else at the moment, and that meant that he, Mattie, and Lloyd probably weren't going to get much help. He hoped the bigger man named Otis could stop the younger one from taking Mattie with them.

"You know them?" he whispered to Mattie.

She shook her head. "I only know Wally Beck. He hung around the Wynns' place and tried to flirt with me."

Abel saw her eyes widened as she realized that she had mentioned the Wynns' place. She closed her eyes tightly and shook her head.

Abel chuckled softly. "I knew we were going to have to talk about that sometime soon, but I didn't expect to be doing it with my hands tied. It's nice to see you again, *Mrs. Newly*."

Mattie's face turned red as she stared at Abel. "How can you joke about that? Do you realize—"

"Quit the jabberin' over there!" Otis's command halted Mattie's words. "I'll gag you next if I hear another peep, ya hear?"

"Don't you talk to her like that, Otis!" Wally swung his gun around to face his partner.

"Knock it off, Beck. We're s'posed to be workin' together, not pointin' guns at each other." Faster than any of the onlookers thought possible, Otis whipped the gun away from Wally and backhanded him. Wally staggered backward, then in a rage, he lunged for Otis, but the big man cuffed him again and then grabbed him by the shirt.

"Ya wanna keep this up, or are we gonna rob this bank and git outta here?"

Wally felt his head where Otis hit him. He shrugged free of the man's hold and straightened his clothing. "We're robbing the bank and getting out of here," he said angrily.

Otis grinned and slapped him on the back. "Thet's what I thought. Now git busy!" A noise at the back door caused both men to look up, and Otis moved swiftly despite his size to stand behind the door as it slowly opened. He grabbed the arm of the person entering and pulled him in, sticking his pistol in the man's face.

Lonan glared coldly at Otis, and Otis grinned. "Ya shouldn't go sneakin' around when there's a bank robbery goin' on, Lonan." He twisted the handle on the door. "Weren't thet locked?"

Lonan shook his head and made a quick survey of the people in the room. His eyes rested briefly on Abel; then he turned to Wally and looked pointedly at the red mark on the side of his head. Otis explained.

"We had us a little trouble, but it's okay now. Ain't thet right, Beck?" He turned back to Lonan. "Why'd you come in here? You're s'posed to be watchin' out back."

Lonan finally spoke. "You're taking too long."

"You're right. You guard the prisoners. Here, tie this one up." He shoved Lloyd toward Lonan. "Beck and I will have this money ready in no time."

Abel watched with a sinking feeling as Lonan directed Lloyd to a chair. He had hoped to try to stop the men somehow, but with three of them, what could he do? And he was worried about Mattie. That Beck fellow seemed determined to take her along, but Abel knew he couldn't allow that. He had to think of something. Fast.

The man called Lonan pushed Lloyd down into the chair beside Abel. Abel kept an eye on him while he watched the other two men stuffing bags with money. This Lonan fellow looked to be the most dangerous of the three, although that Otis was quick on his feet, and his meaty fists were a weapon all their own. Beck was unpredictable, a hot-headed youngster, and that made him a threat as well. Abel wondered if there was any way to stop them.

He saw Lonan slip a knife out of his belt. Abel's mouth went dry. Was he going to kill the three of them? A slice or stab with the knife would be a silent way to get rid of the witnesses to their crime. He felt the man move behind him, and his muscles tightened as he prepared to fling himself, chair and all, at his attacker. But just as suddenly, he felt the knife slice through the ropes holding him prisoner.

Abel turned swiftly to Lonan, but the man put a hand on his shoulder and held him down. He motioned for Abel to keep his hands behind his back, and Abel was quick to obey. Then Lonan pressed a pistol into Abel's hand.

Mattie's rope was sliced next, and she followed Abel's example and kept her hands behind the chair. Abel gave her a quick smile of encouragement. She seemed unsure and scared, but she nodded back. Lonan placed a knife in Lloyd's hand. They all watched and waited for Lonan's next move.

Otis and Wally were almost done, and Abel wondered if this wouldn't be the right moment to take control, but the men still had their guns in their hands as they shoved the money into bags, and it could be that Lonan didn't want to risk gunplay. Abel glanced at Mattie. He certainly didn't want to put her in danger. He whispered to her.

"When it starts, drop to the floor."

She nodded.

Abel wondered what she was thinking, especially now that she knew he knew who she was. But he couldn't be distracted with that; he had to concentrate on the next crucial moments. The men were finished, and Abel glanced at Lonan. He saw Lonan's slight nod, and his hand tightened on the pistol he held. He was ready.

"You best tie those bags, or money will drop out." The men turned at Lonan's words. He was still holding a gun on the prisoners and spoke over his shoulder at the men. Otis and Wally looked at the bags.

"Good idea," Wally said. He holstered his gun and began wrapping string around the bag's opening. Otis watched him a moment. He grunted his approval of the idea as well, but instead of holstering his gun, he laid it on the counter beside him. As soon as both his hands were busy with the string, Lonan turned his gun on the men, and Abel rose from his chair with his pistol ready. He moved to stand in front of Mattie, who obediently dropped to the floor.

"Get your hands up now!" Lonan spoke with authority.

Otis's hand grabbed for his gun on the counter with a speed that astounded Abel. "Don't try it, Otis!" he warned.

At Abel's voice, Wally spun around and swung the money bag in Abel's face. Shots rang out in the room as Abel was knocked back by the bag and fell to the floor beside Mattie. His arm bumped her head, and she said, "Ow!"

Abel threw the bag off and raised his gun, but Wally dove at him as the gun roared. Abel saw a flash of blood on the man's shoulder as they wrestled together on the floor. They bumped into Mattie again, and again she grunted in pain. Abel pushed Wally off him long enough to swing a fist at his jaw. Wally staggered back, and Abel got to his feet. Abel's gun had fallen, and he stood empty-handed but ready to do combat with Wally. Wally's right shoulder was bleeding, but with his left hand, he reached for the holster on his right hip. He sneered at Abel as he raised the pistol to point it unsteadily at him. Lonan and Otis were on the floor wrestling, but Abel ignored them as he watched for Wally's next move. He was ready to dive at him when a chair flew past him and hit Wally head on. Wally's gun went off, but his shot was wild.

Abel stepped in and landed several punches, finally knocking Wally to the floor. He quickly took Wally's gun and turned to the other two men, who were still fighting. He watched for his moment to strike, and using the handle of the pistol, he smashed Otis alongside the head. The big man slumped to the floor, and Abel pulled him off Lonan, who was pinned underneath.

Breathing heavily, Abel dropped to his knees. The next thing he knew, Mattie had him in a stranglehold.

"Oh, Abel! Are you all right? I was so frightened when Wally was going to shoot you! I threw the chair at him." She hugged Abel with all her might. He held her close, and when she finally backed away in embarrassment, he quickly gasped for air, but he still held her arm. He wasn't about to let her go now.

"I'm sorry!" Mattie's face reddened.

"It's okay, Mattie. Just let me catch my breath." Abel grinned crookedly at her. He could feel his lower lip begin to swell from being hit in the mouth.

Suddenly Mattie reached for her hair, and Abel noticed that the short ends were sticking out in all directions. She pulled away from Abel and began patting at her head, and then she frantically started looking about the room. He watched her in puzzlement a moment and then turned to Lonan when he spoke.

"Thanks for the help. You're... Russ Newly's son... aren't you?" Lonan was trying to catch his breath too after fighting with Otis.

Abel nodded as he rose to his feet. Mattie was moving about the room, looking at the floor, and Lonan and Abel watched her curiously as they shook hands.

"Yes, and who are you?" Abel asked him.

"My name's Carter, and I work with your dad sometimes. I've been undercover with this gang for a while now, just waiting for them to try for this bank. The plan was to make the attempt when there were no customers, so I was concerned when I saw you and the lady here. I knew Otis wouldn't go down without a fight, but I didn't expect that much trouble from Beck. I'm glad you were able to lend a hand."

They were joined by Lloyd, who had picked up the pistol Abel dropped. "I'm sorry that I wasn't of more help to either of you. I had the knife, but I didn't dare get in your way. Miss Morrison was of more help to you than I was." The teller's voice was shaky, and he was about to hand the gun back to Abel when they all noticed that Mattie was reaching for something on the floor.

A voice calling from outside the bank startled them, and Mattie lost her balance and accidently kicked something with her foot. The three men saw a brown, furry critter race across the floor, and as one, they aimed their weapons at it, but it was Lloyd who actually fired the pistol he held. His aim was dead on, and the critter slumped to a halt and sprayed fur across the room.

Abel stepped to the bank door and called out, "We're okay. Everything is under control!" He stuck his head out the door and found his dad and his brother Rex step out from the sides of the building with their guns drawn.

"Abel!" Russ grabbed his son's arm. "What are you doing here? It was our understanding that the robbery was going to take place when there were no customers in the bank." He looked at the man called Carter as if affirming that things were really under control. Abel quickly explained the situation to his father and brother.

Carter and Lloyd eyed the spattered object on the floor. "Good shot," Carter commented dryly. He was aware that Mattie was holding a hand over her mouth as she stared in horror at it. Being a detective wasn't necessary to figure out what happened, but Carter *was* a detective, and he noticed that Mattie no longer had a bun in her hair. He glanced at Abel as he turned back to the room and saw that he too correctly assessed the situation. Abel moved to Mattie's side as Russ and Rex entered. Carter, with the men's help, got Otis and Beck to their feet, tied them, and headed to the jail. Lloyd stooped behind the counter and started returning the money to the safe.

Abel stood beside Mattie and waited for her to speak. Her hand was still over her mouth, and he saw her shoulders start to shake. He put an arm around her, and she put her head on his chest.

"I'm sorry, Mattie. This has been a difficult day... "Abel's voice trailed away. His eyebrows drew together, and he tilted his head to listen. *Is that...?* He took hold of Mattie's shoulders and held her away from him. Her head was down, so he took his finger and lifted her under the chin until he could look in her face.

She was laughing. She was laughing so hard she was having trouble catching her breath.

Mattie looked at Abel's astonished expression and laughed harder. She pointed at the remains of her mother's hair bun, and tears of laughter rolled down her cheeks. Abel couldn't help it. It was contagious. He burst into laughter too.

He pulled Mattie toward him again, and together their mirth blended. Lloyd peeked over the counter at the embracing couple and smiled. He ducked down again before they caught him spying on them.

Their laughter subsiding, Mattie wiped at her eyes and smiled up at Abel. He gazed down at her, and his arms around her tightened as he bent his head to kiss her. Mattie's laughter stopped abruptly, and she stared at Abel as his head came closer. Their lips gently touched.

"Ow!"

Abel touched his swollen lower lip, and Mattie burst out laughing again.

"Abel?"

Abel looked over his shoulder at hearing his father's voice. His arm held Mattie by his side when she would have moved away.

Russ took in the scene before him. "Monty wants me to ask you if he can move Annie and the baby to the Nolans now."

"Oh! I had forgotten all about Annie. Will you be all right?" he questioned Mattie.

She nodded but didn't speak.

Abel held her gaze for a moment. Quietly he said, "We'll talk soon. May I see you later?"

She nodded again.

After Abel left, Russ walked over to Mattie. He noticed her short hair, but refrained from questioning her about it. Instead, he saw the bloodstains on her dress. "Were you hurt, Mattie?" he asked, indicating the stains.

She looked down at her dress. "No. No, this was from holding Annie's baby when I helped Abel with the delivery."

Russ blinked. "You helped? You've had quite a day." He noticed that she was starting to tremble, and remembering the last time she fainted after a crisis, he quickly led her to a chair. "Take deep breaths."

"I'm okay, Mr. Newly. It's just…I've never had a gun pointed at me before."

"Can you tell me what happened?" Russ noticed Lloyd and motioned for him to join them. Together Lloyd and Mattie related the events of the attempted robbery while Russ interjected his questions.

"Thank you both. I'll be reporting all this to the sheriff when he gets back to town. Meanwhile, I'm filling in for him. And we caught the other member of the gang earlier today, so that's all of them. Mattie, can I walk you back to the hotel now?"

Mattie looked at Lloyd. "I really should stay and help you get the bank back in order."

"It won't take me long to finish up here, and besides, it's past closing time. I can manage."

Russ waited while Mattie gathered her handbag and shawl. He still didn't say anything when she positioned the shawl over her hair and arranged it to cover the front of her dress. They started down the boardwalk toward the hotel in silence. Finally, Russ spoke.

"I understand that Irena and Rex have invited you to their home for dinner this evening. Are you sure you're still up to it?"

Mattie stopped walking. "I had forgotten all about it! Do you know what time it is, Mr. Newly?"

Russ consulted his pocket watch. "It appears to be almost five o'clock. We're expecting guests this evening as well, so I better get started for home." He watched as Mattie made a decision.

"Would you mind sending my regrets to Irena? I'm afraid that with all that's happened today, I just wouldn't be good company."

"Are you sure, Mattie? Maybe being around people tonight would be a good thing for you."

Mattie tucked the short ends of her hair back under the shawl. "I'm sure. Thank you, Mr. Newly, for walking me home. I'm feeling better now. Good night."

"Good night, Mattie. You're a brave woman, and I praise God for your safety through this ordeal."

Mattie watched Russ walk away before she entered the hotel. She noticed the couple and their daughter from the stagecoach were waiting in the hotel lobby for someone. She passed by them and happened to glance at the younger woman. Mattie stumbled and righted herself before moving on. The woman had glared at Mattie with hatred in her eyes. But why? Mattie didn't even know who she was.

Chapter 24

Sand Creek

It seemed as though all the townspeople were returning at once. Abel looked out the door of the doctors' office and watched as Monty ran over to his parents' buggy to tell them the news about their new grandson. Next, he waved down Harry and Gretchen Nolan, and before Abel knew it, the office was filled with grandparents and well-wishers. Eager helping hands assisted getting Annie over to the Nolans, and baby Morty was passed from one to another before being brought back to his mother.

Harry held out his hand to Abel. "I'm sorry I didn't trust you before to take care of my Annie, Doc." He slapped him on the back. "She told us what you did to save the baby and how Mattie helped through the whole thing. I can't help but thank God for bringing you back to Sand Creek, Abel."

Abel watched them all go with a smile on his face. It was good to know that his skills had helped someone and that he was needed here. He reached for his doctor bag and started out the door.

"Where are you going, Abel?" Doc Casper was just coming up the walk.

"I need to tend to a gunshot wound on one of the bank robbers over at the jail," Abel explained.

"Bank robbers?"

Abel quickly explained; then he asked, "How did things go at the Spencers? Did anyone get hurt helping to put out the fire?"

"There were only minor burns from the fire, nothing serious," Doc reported. "But don't you have a dinner tonight with the Digbys? Why don't you let me take care of the fellow, and you can get on your way?"

"Oh my goodness! The Digbys! I forgot all about them." Abel looked down at his rumpled clothing. "And I'm out of another change of clothes. Are you sure you don't mind, Doc? The guy's name is Wally Beck, and he has a wound on his right shoulder. Dad bandaged it until I could get to him, but with Annie and Monty and the baby and all—"

"Annie had the baby? When did that happen?"

"That was this afternoon before the bank robbery." Abel related the events of the birth and where Annie and Monty were staying now. All the while he was smoothing out his shirt, and combing his hair and try-ing to make himself presentable for the Digbys, he was also thinking about Mattie. What was he going to do about Mattie?

He said good-night to Dr. Casper and hurried over to the blacksmith to pick up the buggy he had asked Clyde to have ready. He spoke briefly with Clyde and climbed in to drive over to the hotel. He knew he was late. He touched his tender lower lip and remembered the kiss he had shared with Mattie. *Mattie!*

The Digbys were waiting for him in the lobby, and they did not look pleased at being kept waiting, nor did they appear to approve of his unkempt appearance. Abel knew he was in for a frosty reception.

"I'm sorry, Mrs. Digby, Doctor, Delphinia." He looked at each one. "You see, there was a bank—"

"We heard. There was a bank robbery. And we heard the gunshots, Abel! They were right down the street from the hotel! What kind of a town is this anyway? What kind of people live here?"

"Believe me, Dr. Digby, this is not normal for Sand Creek. This is the first robbery we've ever experienced, but it's all taken care of now, and we have the men in jail." Abel tried to calm the agitated man.

"Well, I'm sure it won't be the last experience this town has! Not with the riffraff that I've seen walking about."

Abel became very still. He prayed for patience as the silence lengthened. To his surprise, it was Delphinia who finally spoke.

"Papa! You shouldn't condemn a whole town based on what only a few people do. That wouldn't be Christian."

Abel thanked her with a smile, and Delphinia was reminded of how handsome he was. "I'm sure my mother has prepared an excellent meal for us tonight. Are you ready to go?"

From Delphinia's chair in the lobby, she could see the girl who was in Abel's office leave her room and head for the kitchen. Something was different about the girl. Something about her hair. Delphinia squinted. The girl's hair was short! Why ever did she cut it? Delphinia scowled. The girl was still much too attractive.

Quickly, Delphinia made up her mind. She stood and took Abel's arm. She smiled sweetly at him. *If this girl thinks she's taking away my fiancé, she's in for a fight. I don't care what she said about being married to Abel. Abel hasn't said anything, so she must be lying.* Delphinia saw that the girl was getting closer. She raised her voice slightly as she squeezed Abel's arm.

"Abel, darling, I do hope we can marry soon. Maybe we should have the wedding right here, and we could honeymoon in Boston."

Delphinia was satisfied when she saw the girl stop suddenly and lean against the hallway wall. She walked with Abel to the door. "Of course, we can marry in Boston if you'd rather, but if you want your family to be present, why don't we just get married now?"

Mattie felt as if the breath had been knocked out of her body as she leaned against the wall. That woman from the stage, the one who had come to Abel's office while Annie was having the baby, *she* was the one? The one Belle called Abel's "young lady"? But Mattie hadn't heard anything about Abel getting *married*.

She felt physically ill.

Gretchen passed the hallway just then and noticed Mattie. She hurried to her. "Mattie, is something wrong? Are you ill? Gracious' sake, girl! What have you done to your hair?"

"I'm fine, Gretchen." Mattie straightened up, and her hand went to her hair. She made the decision when she got back to her room after the bank ordeal that she would just have to let people see her short hair. There was really nothing else she could do about it now. "I cut it," she said, trying to sound positive. "What do you think?"

"But why? I mean, it's…you look pretty no matter how you wear your hair." Gretchen fumbled for the right words. She waved her hand as if dismissing the matter. Then she grabbed Mattie and hugged her.

"Wha—"

"Mattie, you dear, sweet girl! Annie told us all about how you helped her when she had the baby. I don't know how Harry and I can ever thank you for being there with our daughter, but we're sure going to try. From now on, you are staying with us for free, and your meals are on us too."

"Oh, Mrs. Nolan, I mean, Gretchen! You don't need to do that. I was so glad I was of some help to Annie, but it was really Dr. Newly whom you should thank. He—"

"I know! Annie told us about the cord being around little Morty's neck and how Abel took care of it. I knew he was going to make a fine doctor. Sand Creek is blessed to have him."

"Yes, they are," Mattie said softly.

"Mattie? Is something wrong? Something between you and Abel?"

"What do you mean?"

"Annie told me that the two of you made a pretty nice couple. Maybe you're sweet on him?" Gretchen smiled coaxingly.

But Mattie shook her head. "I'm afraid Annie has given you the wrong impression." Mattie cleared her throat. "In fact, I hear that Abel is engaged to someone?" She looked questioningly at Gretchen.

"You mean that Miss Digby? Mattie, if I know anything about Abel Newly, I know that he won't partner up with a city girl like that for life."

"But—"

"Trust me. I've had enough of her high and mighty demands to know that she wouldn't last a winter in Sand Creek. No, Abel will send her packing now that he's seen how she doesn't fit in here."

"But maybe she'll take him back to Boston."

Gretchen shook her head. "Don't you worry that pretty head of yours. Now come sit down and tell me about your hair and about this bank robbery everyone is talking about. Were you really there? But first, tell me more about Annie having the baby."

Abel was confused. Delphinia was acting just as she had when they were in Boston. She was sweet and adorable and beautiful and hung on his every word.

He was stunned by her announcement that they should marry right away here in Sand Creek. He hadn't been alone with her to speak with her even once since she arrived, and now she was talking about getting married? He needed to clear up a few things with her to find out what had been bothering her when she arrived, to find out what she really thought about Sand Creek, to know why she was in a hurry to marry.

He glanced at her as she conversed with his mother. Delphinia was charming to his parents, maybe to make up for her own parents' lack of enthusiasm. Russ gave Dr. Digby a short tour of the ranch when they arrived, but clearly the eminent doctor was not impressed with horses and barns and didn't want to discuss crops. And Mrs. Digby seemed fond of the word *quaint* when she was shown through the house. She was also surprised to see Sky cooking and serving the meal without the aid of servants, and Abel recalled that at the Digby home, Mrs. Digby never entered the kitchen.

Whatever had made him think that Delphinia would fit in here? The attraction he once held for her was diminishing, but he knew he wasn't being fair. He knew thoughts of Mattie were clouding his judgment. *I can't be in love with two women; can I, Lord?* He almost laughed out loud at his thoughts, but it was disconcerting to know that he once thought himself in love with Delphinia, but now he wasn't so sure. And he realized that he was falling in love with Mattie, but if his love was so fickle as to change like this, how could he ever be sure if it was real love or not?

As if she knew he was thinking about her, Delphinia turned to him and gave him a coy smile. "I can hardly wait to marry Abel," she announced to the others at the table. "I think we should get married tomorrow."

"Whoa! Wait a minute."

Every eye at the table was on Abel as he made his exclamation. He felt his face grow hot, and he saw Delphinia's gray eyes turn icy although her smile remained on her face.

"I mean, there's no need to rush into things," he explained. He cleared his throat. "That was a wonderful meal, Mom. Thank you. Now if you will excuse us, I'd like to take Delphinia for a walk."

"Of course." Sky nodded. She smiled at the others still at the table. "If you would like to retire to the parlor, I'll be in shortly with coffee. Abel, I'll serve dessert when you and Miss Digby get back."

"Please call me Delphinia, Mrs. Newly. After all, we're practically family being that Abel and I are engaged."

Abel herded Delphinia out the door before his mother could answer. He saw the consternation on her face and knew she was worried about his choice for a bride. Frankly, he was too, he admitted to himself. He prayed silently while he led Delphinia down a wagon trail behind the house. She tucked her arm in his and leaned her head against him, which made walking a bit difficult. He slowed his steps.

"Oh, Abel! I'm so glad you and I are finally alone." Delphinia slid her arm around his waist, and Abel stopped abruptly. She had never been this familiar with him in Boston.

"Delphinia."

"Yes, dearest?"

She raised her face to his. She was much too close. Abel stared into her gray eyes with the fringe of black lashes, her creamy skin, and rosy cheeks. He felt himself bending forward to her pink lips.

He backed away.

"Abel?"

"I think we better talk, Delphinia."

Something flickered in her eyes at his tone, but her voice remained sweet. "Of course, darling. We have much to discuss."

"Okay then. Uh…well…first of all, why wouldn't you see me when you first arrived in Sand Creek?"

They resumed walking, and Delphinia tucked her hand in Abel's arm again and pressed close to him. "You know how tired I get from traveling. I was just so exhausted, and I didn't want you to see me not looking my best."

Abel waited. "That's it? I had the impression that there was something else wrong."

"Of course not, darling. I have been longing to see you and to spend some time alone with you. Now, how do you like my idea of getting married here? You told me in your telegram that you wanted to move the wedding up if we could. Mother wasn't too happy about that at the time, but I'm sure I can convince her to allow us a small ceremony here and a much grander one back in Boston. I have just the right dress with me. You do have a church here, don't you?"

Abel stopped walking. Her question irritated him in that he felt she was belittling his town. "Do you even like Sand Creek, Delphinia? Would you be happy living here?"

She turned to face Abel, and her fingers played with the buttons on his shirt. "I think it's a quaint, little town, Abel. But we wouldn't have to be here all the time. You could do some work with my father too, couldn't you?" She wheedled her question with a pretty pout.

Quaint. Abel felt like his eyes were being opened to the truth. *She doesn't want to live here. She doesn't even want me. She wants someone who will dance to her daddy's tune and be an escort for her in her city. Lord, I think you just answered my prayer.*

"Delphinia." Abel took her hands in his and held them away. "I don't think you would be happy in Sand Creek. You're a city girl, and Boston is your home. I can't ask you to live here."

"Oh, Abel! I knew you would see it my way! We'll live in Boston, and you'll work with Daddy and—"

"No."

Delphinia scowled. "What do you mean *no?*"

"I mean I don't think we should get married. If the Lord wanted us to be together, I think he would put a desire in us to want to live in the same place, but you want Boston, and I want Sand Creek. It won't work."

Delphinia's expression hardened. "Now you listen to me, Abel Newly. You and I are engaged. I am not going to be the laughingstock of Boston just because you would rather be with some little country mouse than to be with me!"

"What?"

"I saw that girl in your office. She had the impudence to send me away so that she could be alone with you!"

"You came to my office?"

"She didn't even tell you, did she? You fool! She's trying to trap you into marrying her! But she won't get you because you're already mine! Being engaged is almost the same as being married."

Abel watched Delphinia rant on as if he were seeing her for the first time. "Delphinia, I'm sorry. I don't mean to hurt you, but you must see that we can't build a relationship together if this is how you feel. We would have to love and trust each other no matter what, but you obviously don't feel that way."

"Don't you turn this around and make me the villain!" She put her hands on her hips and glared at Abel. "Admit it. You like this girl, whatever her name is."

Abel shook his head. "This isn't going to work. I'm taking you back to town, and I think you better go back to Boston. I'm sure the Lord will have someone else—"

"Ha! Don't you even try to tell me what the Lord wants for me. I did all the right things. I attended church, I visited the sick, and I gave to the needy. I'm a good Christian! Isn't that good enough for you?"

"Good enough for *me*? You mean you were doing all those things to please me, not to please the Lord Jesus? Delphinia, that is not Christianity at all. We do things for our Savior because we love him, not because we have to prove something to others."

"I don't need to hear preaching from you!" Delphinia turned away and began to sob. "I can't go back without a husband! I'll be a social outcast."

Abel was shocked. How little he knew this woman he had pledged to marry. "I'm sorry, Delphinia," he said again in a softer tone. "I don't see how a marriage between us would ever work out with you feeling this way about me."

Delphinia swung around to face him, and Abel was shocked to see that there were no tears in her eyes or on her face. Was it all an act?

"You'll never be a great doctor! No one who is important will ever hear of you if you stay in this crummy town! Can't you see that? I'm offering you the opportunity to be someone! If you work at my father's clinic, you will be respected. You'll be rich! Why can't you see that?"

"I don't want those things. All I want is to help people who need it."

They stared at each other, and Abel was sickened by the hatred he now saw in Delphinia's face. Her beauty was gone, replaced by anger in its ugliest form. He prayed for wisdom in what he said next.

"Delphinia, please listen to me. This is not how I want you to feel. I loved you as the girl I thought you were in Boston. You seemed to me to have a love for the Lord and a desire to do what was right in his sight. I thought you loved me too and wanted to be with me wherever the Lord sent me. I believe Sand Creek is where I'm supposed to be. I'm not interested in being rich or famous, and I'm truly sorry if I ever led you to believe that was my goal in life. I'm sorry I hurt you, but under these conditions, we cannot marry. I wish the best for you in your life and pray that you will follow the Lord's leading and live honestly for him and not for the approval of others."

Before Abel even finished his last sentence, Delphinia spun on her heel and walked away from him. He sighed. He should feel a sense of freedom that he had escaped from being bound to her now that he saw her true self, but instead, he felt only sorrow at the shallowness of her life. He followed her slowly back to the house.

The Digbys stepped out on the porch as he was about to climb the stairs. Abel heard his mother speaking from behind them.

"I'm so sorry to hear about your headache, Miss Digby. I do hope it is better soon. It was nice to meet all of you."

Abel met them at the buggy and handed Mrs. Digby in. Delphinia ignored his hand and climbed in beside her mother, which left Dr. Digby to ride in front with Abel—not the arrangement they had on the way to the ranch.

There was silence on the ride back to town. Abel glanced at Delphinia's father occasionally, but the man stared straight forward. They arrived in front of the hotel, and Abel jumped down to help the ladies. Again Delphinia wouldn't allow him to even touch her hand as she climbed from her seat. He turned to Dr.

Digby and held out a hand to stop him from going into the hotel.

"I'm sorry it turned out this way, sir," he said. "I need to stay in Sand Creek, but this is not where Delphinia wishes to be."

"Is that the only reason?"

Abel held the man's gaze for a long moment. "No, sir," he answered honestly.

The doctor nodded. He sighed heavily. "It was nice to know you, Dr. Newly. I have to admit that I admire you. Not many men would turn down what I have offered."

"I do appreciate it."

They shook hands, and Abel led the horse away to return the buggy to the blacksmith. He saddled his own horse and walked to the main street of town in front of the hotel. He had asked Mattie if he could see her later. It was much too late now. He knew they needed to talk about what happened at the bank and what happened months ago at the Wynns. They would have to talk soon, but not tonight. He stepped into the stirrup and swung up to the saddle. He began the trek back home at a walking pace. He had much on his mind that he needed to discuss with his heavenly Father.

Chapter 25

Sand Creek

Mattie couldn't sleep. *He asked if he could see me later. What exactly does that mean?* She waited up. She knew it was foolish, but after overhearing what that Miss Digby said, Mattie wanted to know if Abel was going to marry the girl or not. She knew Abel had taken the family to his parents' home for dinner. And she also figured out that if she had gone to Irena and Rex's home, she would have been riding along with them. How glad she was that she had changed her mind about going!

It was still early when she heard the Digbys coming down the hall to their rooms. Mattie had left her door open just a crack so that she would be able to hear, but she swiftly crossed the room to the door and eased it shut. She didn't need them to discover that she was spying on them. Would Abel ask to see her now?

Mattie waited until she was sure the Digbys were in for the night; then she slipped out of her room and made her way to the lobby of the hotel. There was no one at the desk and no one in the dining room anymore. She crossed to the front windows and peered out. It wasn't dark yet, but dusk was settling in, and it soon would be. The street was empty.

Mattie curled up in one of the softer chairs and stared out the window while her fingers played with the short ends of her hair. She could see the jail from here, and she thought of the men who were incarcerated there. Those men deserved to be in jail, yet it hurt her to think of Wally sitting in a jail cell. Wally wasn't really so bad, he just had poor judgment about the company he kept. Still, he did try to rob the bank.

A movement on the street caught her attention, and she spotted Abel walking his horse. Her heart leapt at the sight of him, but she remained still, waiting to see what he would do. He stared at the hotel for a time before mounting his horse and walking away. Mattie wondered what he was thinking. Did he decide to marry that girl? Did he remember that he wanted to talk to her?

She sighed. Abel knew she was the girl at the Wynns that night in the snowstorm. He called her *Mrs. Newly*, and even though Mattie knew he was joking, she knew that the problem of the Wynns wasn't going to go away.

He kissed me.

Ever since her infatuation with Nels Jenson and the rejection she felt when he married Irena, Mattie had made up her mind to not get involved with romance and thoughts of marriage. But she felt differently about that now.

She had much to pray about, and that was what she was going to do.

Abel sat down at the breakfast table across from his parents. They hadn't asked him any questions yet, but he knew they were waiting to hear what happened with the Digbys and Delphinia the night before. It would be a relief to tell them. Where should he begin? He picked up his coffee cup.

But Russ wiped all thoughts of the Digbys from his thoughts. "Pastor Sweeney stopped here the other day to tell us he had a visit from some people named Wynn."

Abel gulped his coffee too fast and burnt his tongue. The expressions on his parents' faces told Abel that they were worried and needed answers.

"I should have told you about that right away," he admitted.

"Why didn't you?"

Abel's coffee cup clinked when he set it down. "It seemed like such a farce that I never really thought anything would come of it. That reverend fellow was acting crazy and wouldn't listen to anything I had to say. I can't believe he is actually looking for Mattie and me."

"Why don't you tell us the whole story from the beginning?" Russ suggested.

Abel nodded, and the story flowed out. Even he was surprised at how vividly the memory was and how he could relate each detail. It was a relief to finally share it with someone, and he knew his parents would be able to offer him much-needed advice on what to do about the situation.

"Mattie knows that I recognize her now, but since delivering Annie's baby and the robbery and the Digbys and everything, we haven't had a chance to talk."

"When did you know it was her?" asked Sky.

Abel grinned. "I saw the short ends of her hair sticking out of that bun she was wearing, and I knew it had to be her. No other woman I know of goes around with short hair. I wonder where she got the hair to make the fake bun." He started laughing. "When that thing rolled across the floor of the bank and Lloyd shot it, you should have seen Mattie's face!"

But Sky wasn't laughing. "That poor girl! I can't imagine how embarrassed she must have felt when she realized you were the man who rescued her, Abel, and that you live in the town she was planning to live in. Of course, she wouldn't want you to recognize her!" Sky turned to her husband. "What will people think when they hear that Abel spent the night alone with Mattie?"

"But, Mom, I had to save her life, and don't forget, I am a doctor," Abel protested.

Sky frowned at her son. "And she's a young, unmarried woman. I think I can better understand why the Reverend Wynn thought he had to marry the two of you."

"But we didn't do anything wrong!" Abel threw his hands up in the air. "Would it have been better if I had left her there to die?"

"No, son. Calm down." Russ soothed Abel's outburst with his words. He rubbed at his chin and then drank some coffee before he continued. "It seems to me that you have feelings for Mattie."

Abel stared at his father; then he nodded. "I do," he admitted. "But I don't know if I can trust my feelings anymore. After all, I thought I was in love with Delphinia, but look how that turned out. She is nothing like the girl I thought I loved in Boston. How can I change my mind like this? I might have married Delphinia if I hadn't met Mattie."

Sky sighed in relief. "So you and Delphinia are no longer engaged?"

"No. Like I said, she's not the same girl she was in Boston."

"So you think she was just putting on an act for you in Boston?" Russ questioned.

Abel nodded.

"Do you think Mattie has been putting on an act as well?"

Abel shook his head. "Except for pretending she had longer hair than she has now, no. I don't think there is anything dishonest about Mattie."

"Well then."

Abel studied his father's expression. "What?"

"It's not your feelings that are in question here, son. It's what your feelings have been based on. You thought you loved Delphinia based on the person she pretended to be. You found out that she was a liar. But your feelings for Mattie are based on truth. You've seen her true self through some rather trying circumstances, and she shines through them. What conclusion do you draw from that?"

Abel's face lit up with a smile. "I think I've found the girl I want to marry!"

Russ and Sky returned his smile with pleasure; then Sky's face clouded with concern. "But what about the Wynns? They are still trying to find the two of you and spread their poisonous lies about you."

Russ took her hand. "Let's not borrow trouble. We'll give Abel and Mattie time to get to know each other better and see where that leads. If they decide it's God's will that they be together, then we will support that decision and help them through whatever trials may be ahead. We'll keep them in prayer just as we did Dorcas and Cavan, and we'll give God the praise as he works out his will in all our lives."

"What has happened with Dorcas and Cavan?" Abel asked. "Penny Riggs mentioned something about Dorcas, but so much has happened that I haven't had a chance to ask."

He listened as his father relayed the events of the last few days leading up to the robbery. "They were going to take Dorcas as hostage? So that's what Otis meant when he told Wally Beck he couldn't take Mattie. They already had a hostage. Otherwise, Mattie would have been it." Abel sat back in his chair. "You had barely gotten back with the man named Asa when we were in the middle of the bank robbery. And you know Carter? The guy pretending to be Lonan?"

Russ nodded. "He's a US marshal, and we've worked together on a few cases. I knew he was working with the gang, hoping to catch their leader."

"You mean the guy you and Rex brought in?"

"No, we thought there was someone else, but even with Carter undercover with the gang, he never heard them mention anyone else."

"Well, I've got to make some house calls before I go to town today. Before you pray, Dad, I'd just like to say that I'm thankful you both know the whole story now about Mattie and me, and I appreciate the fact that you believe me. And thanks for putting up with the Digbys last night," Abel added sheepishly.

Sky reached over and hugged Abel. "Thank *you* for not marrying that girl!"

Chapter 26

Nolan Farm

Dorcas settled the children in the back of the wagon as she readied it for the trip to town. Leon would watch over Fiona on the short ride so that she could drive. She paused when she saw Cavan come from the barn to tell them good-bye. How she enjoyed having him look over her!

Cavan swept Dorcas into his arms and gave her a fierce hug. "I'll miss you," he said into her hair. He set her down and kissed her. Then he stepped to the wagon and ruffled Leon's hair. "You take good care of your mother for me, okay?"

"I will, Pa. I'm taking care of Fiona too," Leon informed him with pride.

"You're a big helper today. Have fun with Grandma and Grandpa." Cavan tickled Fiona under the chin.

Leon smiled in delight. "Can we go now, Ma? I can't wait to see my new cousin Morty. Hurry before Fiona starts cryin'!"

Dorcas and Cavan laughed at their son. Cavan handed Dorcas up to the wagon seat, but he held onto her hand. "Stay away from the jail." His tone was serious. "Even though he's locked in there, I don't want him seeing you."

Dorcas squeezed his hand. "No more need to worry about that. I'm so glad it's finally over, and we can live normally again. Don't worry. I don't have any plans of meeting up with that man ever again!" She smiled. "Thanks to you."

"Thanks to the Lord and your dad and brother," Cavan added. "You take care now. I'll be watching for you to be back this afternoon. I'll miss you."

Dorcas's admiration glowed in her eyes. "I love you, Cavan Nolan."

"I love you too."

"Can we please go now!" Leon rolled his eyes at his parents.

"We're going." Dorcas laughed. "Say bye to your pa!"

Sand Creek

Mattie woke early. She had a lot on her mind, and something told her that today was going to bring about some changes in her life. She still didn't know what decision Abel had made concerning Miss Digby, but regardless, her life would be affected by it. She had to admit it. She was falling in love with Abel, and if he chose the girl from Boston, she would just have to deal with that. Memories of her heartbreak over Nels Jenson flashed through her mind, but she knew she couldn't let that stop her from loving ever again.

Mattie looked in the mirror and groaned. Sleeping on short hair made it stick up all over her head. *The good thing about it*, she thought as she padded over to the washbasin, *is that I can wash it in the morning and it will be dry in no time.* She shivered as she poured the cool water over her head.

She was nervous as she prepared for her day. She knew that some would ask questions about her hair, and others would politely wonder but not dare to ask. The sooner people got used to her shorter hair, the better. She giggled as she recalled Lloyd shooting her hairpiece. She wondered if he got a closer look at it when he cleaned up the bank and discovered what it really was.

Mattie took out her Bible to read and pray before she left her room. Wally Beck was on her mind again, and as she read Ephesians 3, Paul's words held a deeper meaning to her:

> Unto me, who am less than the least of all saints, is this grace given, that I should preach among the Gentiles the unsearchable riches of Christ; and to make all men see what is the fellowship of the mystery.

Mattie's conscience was stirred. Paul wanted all men to know about the gospel of grace to make everyone see that Christ's death, burial, and resurrection was the means of salvation. That meant Wally Beck too.

Mattie went to the mirror to finish fluffing her hair into place. Would she dare? She checked the time. She could stop by the jail on the way to the bank if she didn't take time for breakfast. She made up her mind.

Lord, I need your wisdom to say the right things. All those men need to know you. Help me to make them see.

Mattie slipped out of her room and made her way to the jail. She hesitated only a second before she opened the door and stepped inside. The sheriff looked up from his desk.

"Good morning." He rose. "You're Miss Morrison, aren't you? Russ Newly told me about your testimony regarding the bank robbery. Is there more you wanted to add to that?"

Mattie twisted her hands together. "No, sir. I was wondering if I might speak to the men for a minute."

The sheriff regarded her with interest. "That seems rather unusual, miss. May I ask why?"

"Yes. You see, I know Wally Beck, Sheriff. And this morning as I was reading my Bible, I decided that I needed to tell him about the Lord. I realized that all the men needed to hear the gospel. I know that won't change their situation, but it could change their lives." Mattie was out of breath after stating her mission to the sheriff, but she knew it was the right thing to do.

"I see. Well, I expect Pastor Sweeney to be by later today, but if you wish to have a word with the men,

I'll grant you that. Don't expect them to appreciate it though," he warned.

Mattie nodded. She waited while the sheriff took the keys and went to the back of the jail. He opened the door that led to the area where the men were behind bars, and she heard him speak to them.

"Look alive here! There's a young lady who wants to talk to you. Wake up!"

Mattie thought she would feel nervous now that the time had come, but she knew this was something she should do and that the Holy Spirit would be the one to give her the confidence in what she had to say. When the sheriff motioned for her to follow him, she didn't hesitate.

"Well, looky here, Beck. It's your girly friend." Otis poked Wally in the ribs. "Looks like she might'n be sweet on you after all."

Wally stood and walked to the bars. "Mattie, what are you doing here?"

Both men had bruises on their faces from their fight with Carter and Abel, and Wally's arm was in a sling. Mattie noticed a third man leaning against the back of the cell. She hadn't seen him before, and she was aware that she was under his scrutiny.

"You men be quiet and listen to what the lady has to say," the sheriff ordered. "Go ahead, miss. If you have any trouble, I'll be right at my desk. You can walk out of here whenever you like."

Mattie nodded her thanks and waited until he stepped out of the room then she turned to the men. She directed her first remarks to Wally.

"How is your shoulder, Wally?"

He shrugged and then grimaced at the pain. "It could have been worse, I guess."

"That's what I wanted to talk to you about. You see, it could have been worse. That bullet could have been a few inches over and would have struck your heart. You came very close to being dead yesterday, Wally, and what I want to ask you is this: do you know what would have happened to you if you died?"

"*Aw!*" Otis stretched. "She's gonna preach to ya, Wally! Ya got yerself a preacher girl."

Mattie turned to him. "And you, Otis. Do you think *you* will live forever? What do you think will happen to you?" She looked at the man in back. "And you?"

Mattie stepped back to Wally. "I know what will happen. If you don't know the Lord Jesus Christ, you will spend an eternity in hell. But that doesn't have to happen. God sent the Lord Jesus to this earth to pay for the sins you and I have committed. He died in our place on the cross, but he didn't stay dead. He arose. He washed the guilt and filth of our sin away forever, and now all he wants from you is your faith in him. Just simple, childlike faith to admit that his sacrifice was enough. He doesn't ask you to work for heaven. He gives it to you as a gift when you believe this message."

She paused, wanting her words to sink in. She expected more ridicule from Otis, but strangely he was quiet.

"Wally, you know you're a sinner, don't you?"

Wally shuffled his feet. Mattie could tell that he was embarrassed that she was singling him out from the others, but she didn't have much time.

"Yah, I guess so. I mean, robbing a bank probably won't get me a mansion in heaven," he joked. Otis chuckled.

"Wally, because you are a sinner, Jesus Christ chose to die." Mattie searched for the right words. "It's like this, Wally. What if I were to say to the sheriff, 'Let Wally Beck out of jail. I'll serve his punishment for him.' All you would have to do is walk out of here and let me step in there in your place. That's what the Lord Jesus did for you, Wally. He doesn't want you to go to hell, so he paid the penalty of your sin for you. He suffered terribly—not only the physical pain but also the spiritual separation from God the Father—*for you*. He wants you to accept the gift of eternal life by believing he paid it for you. Won't you do that, Wally?"

Wally looked down and mumbled, "It might be too late for me, Mattie."

"It's never too late until you're dead. You didn't die yesterday. God has given you another opportunity to believe. Knowing him as your Savior can change your life, Wally."

"Ya mean we'll get outta jail?" Otis scoffed.

Mattie looked imploringly at him. "No. You committed a crime and have to suffer the consequences, but don't you see? You don't have to suffer the consequences of hell because Jesus Christ did that for you. You can enjoy heaven because of him. But he won't make you accept him. He offers it as a gift, and he's polite enough to let you make up your own mind."

Mattie waited, but no one else spoke.

"Thank you for listening to me. I'll be praying that each one of you accepts this gift." She turned and walked out the door.

The sheriff stood and closed the door behind her. He looked down at the young woman before him. "I've never heard it put more sincerely, miss. You've given those men something to think on."

Mattie nodded to the sheriff and left. She prayed as she walked the short distance to the bank that her words would reach the men. She noticed a wagon stop in front of the hotel, and a blonde woman who resembled Lucy Riley stepped down. The woman reached into the back and helped down a little boy and lifted out a baby. Mattie wondered if she could possibly be Abel's other sister, the one named Dorcas. She did look a lot like Lucy, Abel's other sister.

Mattie entered the bank and greeted Lloyd warmly. It was good to know that things were back to normal. Bert Davies was already in his office, and Mattie knocked and called out a greeting.

"Good morning, Mattie!" Bert came quickly from behind his desk and took Mattie's hand in his. He beamed down at her. "I don't know where to begin," he said with a smile.

Mattie was puzzled.

"You helped to bring my grandson into the world. Then you helped to protect my bank from thieves. What can I say? I am indebted to you, Mattie Morrison, and I will not forget all you've done."

"Oh." Mattie blushed at the attention. "I was glad to be able to help Annie, but truthfully she did all the work. Congratulations, sir, on being a grandpa!"

"You are much too modest, Mattie. Lloyd has been telling me about the robbery yesterday. Are you sure you are up to working today? You are welcome to take the day off." He patted her hand.

Mattie smiled again. "No, but thank you for the offer. I am fine. How are you, Lloyd?" She tried to get Bert's attention off her.

Lloyd simply nodded. Mattie saw that he was looking curiously at her hair. Her hand automatically touched it.

"I see you've changed your hairstyle," Bert commented. "Most becoming, my dear."

"Thank you," she said simply. "Any special instructions for the day, sir?"

They got down to business, and Mattie was relieved to have plenty of work to keep her busy. She needed to be busy to keep her mind off the many things that tried to distract her. She wondered when or if she and Abel would get an opportunity to talk, and she wondered if the Digbys left on the stage or if Abel left with them. She thought about the men in the jail, and she wondered what the people that came in and out of the bank were thinking of her short hair.

It was nearing lunchtime, and Lloyd left to go to his home for lunch. Mr. Davies usually closed the bank for half an hour so that they all could have a break, but he was still in his office, so Mattie waited until he was ready to go. A customer entered, and Mattie looked up.

"Mr. Granger!" Mattie stood and walked over to the man who helped her get the job at the bank. "How nice to see you again. What are you doing in Sand Creek?"

"Hello, Mattie!" The older man looked pleased to see her. "I thought I'd stop by since I was in the area and see my old friend Bert. Is he here?"

"Yes, sir. He's in his office right now, but I can take you to him." Mattie led the way. "I can't tell you how much I appreciate you getting this job for me. I was just thinking about you the other day, and I wondered if your church has found a new pastor yet." She knocked on her boss's door before turning back to her visitor.

"Just do what I tell you, Mattie, and you won't get hurt."

Mattie stared at Mr. Granger. He held a gun in his hand and was pointing it right at her. "I locked up the front door when I came in, so it's just us now. Go ahead and open the door."

"Mr. Granger, what are you doing?"

"Open the door, Mattie." His voice brooked no argument.

Mattie opened the door, and Bert spoke to her without looking up. "I'm almost done here, Mattie, but if you want to leave for lunch, you go right ahead."

"Sir."

Something in the way she spoke made Bert look up. He didn't see the gun, but he saw Mattie's white face. Then he saw Mr. Granger, and he stood to walk around the desk.

"Matthias! What a nice surprise!"

"Hold it there, Bert." Mr. Granger motioned with the gun.

"What's this? Matthias, what are you—?"

Mr. Granger took hold of Mattie's arm and shoved her into the room in front of him. "We don't have much time, so you're going to do what I say, and you're going to do it now. Fill these bags with the money."

But Bert was outraged. "I won't do anything of the sort! I thought you were a friend, Matthias. What has happened to you?"

"You won't?" Mr. Granger clubbed him alongside the head with the pistol. Mattie let out a scream, and Mr. Granger swung around to her with the pistol raised. She ducked.

"Keep quiet, Mattie! If you want Bert to stay alive, then you'll fill these bags now. You hear me?"

She nodded, and trembling, she reached for the bags and started shoving bundles of money into them from the safe that was still open. She watched Bert groan as he sat up and put his hand to his head.

"Sorry to do this, old friend, but I can't have you coming after us." Mr. Granger knocked Bert on the head again, and the man slumped to the floor. "Keep filling those bags," he ordered Mattie when she stopped to hold her hand over her mouth. He set the pistol on the desk and quickly tied the bank owner's hands and wrapped a cloth over his mouth. Then he picked up the gun and grabbed the bags that Mattie had filled and set them just inside the back door of the bank. He made sure the door was unlocked; then he turned back to Mattie who hadn't moved.

"I bet you've figured out by now why I wanted you to have this job. It's a lot easier to rob a bank when the people in it trust you. Now you and I are going to take a walk over to the jail together, and I'm going to give you a choice. You can cause me trouble, and if you do, I'll shoot the sheriff before I let the boys out, or you can come along nicely, then I'll only tie him up like Bert here when I let the boys out. The choice is yours. Which will it be?"

Mattie stared in horror at the man she once thought was a respected church board elder. He was part of the gang?

"I don't want you to shoot anyone."

"So?"

"I'll do what you say."

Mr. Granger nodded. "Wise choice. Now take my arm like we're going for a stroll together. If anyone speaks to you, answer politely and keep moving. You got it?"

Mattie nodded. She looked again at Bert. "He's bleeding. Please let me bandage it."

"He's fine. Let's go."

They stepped out of the bank together, and Mattie felt herself tremble as she took Mr. Granger's arm. She saw the woman she thought was Abel's sister go into Nolan's store, but other than that, no one seemed to be about. She wondered where Abel was right now, but then she pulled her thoughts together and petitioned the Lord for help.

Dorcas entered Nolan's store with her shopping list in hand. She had enjoyed visiting with her in-laws and seeing baby Morty and holding him. Annie and Monty were still staying with Harry and Gretchen. They didn't mind at all that she left Leon and Fiona in their grandma's care while she did the rest of her shopping. Since that man had plagued them by hanging around their farm, she hadn't felt safe enough to go to town, and now she was out of everything. She had a lot to do.

She saw the man and woman leave the bank but thought nothing of it at first. She had heard of Mattie Morrison, the new girl in town, but she hadn't met her yet. If what her mother told her was true, it was possible that Abel might be sweet on the girl. She heard about how Mattie helped Abel with Jeb Owen's injury, and Annie just told her all about how Mattie helped with Morty's delivery. Annie insisted that Abel and Mattie were interested in each other. And Dorcas had also been hearing all the stories related to the bank robbery and Mattie and Abel's roles in stopping that.

She looked quizzically at the couple walking down the street. The girl had short hair. That was unusual. Had anyone mentioned Mattie having short hair?

Dorcas handed her shopping list over to Jonas and let him begin gathering her supplies while she stepped over to the fabric. The children were growing out of everything, and it was difficult to keep up with clothes for them. She was fingering some of the material when she happened to look out the window. The man and the young woman were entering the jail together. The jail?

"Jonas!"

"What is it, Dorcas? You need some help?" Jonas walked over to the fabric section.

Dorcas pointed out the window. "Do you know them?"

Jonas looked up and caught only a glimpse before the door shut behind them. "Well, that's Mattie from the bank, but I don't know the feller."

Dorcas looked at Jonas. "Why would she go to the jail?"

Jonas smiled. "I hear that she was there early this morning to talk to the robbers about accepting the Lord. The sheriff's been spreading the story to anyone who will listen. He is mighty impressed with her boldness."

Dorcas was thoughtful. "She didn't look too happy about going in there just now." She watched the door to the jail for a moment. "No one said anything to me about her having such short hair," she commented. "That's unusual enough that someone would have mentioned it."

"Her hair isn't short."

"Yes, it is."

"Then she must have cut it."

"You sure that was her?"

"Yep." Jonas was puzzled. "Why? Something bothering you, Dorcas?"

Mattie watched helplessly as Mr. Granger, one arm holding her in front of him and the other pointing the gun at the sheriff, forced him to unlock the door to the men's cell.

"Asa, tie and gag the sheriff and put him in the cell. Then the three of you get over to the back of the bank. I've got the money ready and horses waiting. Use the side window of the jail office to leave. Don't let anyone see you."

"I was wondering when you'd get here."

Mr. Granger's tone was harsh as he responded to Asa's words. "If you hadn't messed this job up so badly, I wouldn't have to be here now. And keep a respectful tongue in your mouth; you're in enough trouble."

Asa was already doing his boss's bidding when Mr. Granger pushed Mattie to the door again. "Now we're going to take another stroll just like before. If the boys hear that you've raised any sort of alarm, then Asa can slit the sheriff's throat. You don't want that to happen, do you?"

Mattie shook her head and stumbled out the door. Mr. Granger quickly took her arm and balanced her, and they started for the bank.

Dorcas motioned Jonas to her side, and together they watched Mattie and the stranger walk out of the jail again. This time Dorcas could see that the girl was upset.

"Is there a back door to the jail, Jonas?"

"There's no door, but there's a window around the side. You think something's wrong?" He looked out the store window again.

"I don't know why, but I do. Jonas, gather some men together. I think we've got trouble brewing." Dorcas started for the door.

"Where are you going?"

"I'm going to follow them." She opened her handbag and pulled out the derringer that was still in there. She slipped it into the pocket in the folds of her skirt.

"Now, Dorcas, don't go doing something foolish. Your pa wouldn't—"

"Go, Jonas! I think that girl is in trouble!" She paused and turned back. "Have someone check the bank and watch that side window of the jail."

Dorcas stepped out of the store but stayed close to the side of the building. She was aware of Jonas running down the boardwalk behind her to the hotel. Maybe she was being foolish, and there was nothing going on, but she had the strangest feeling that something was wrong.

Mattie and the stranger disappeared behind the bank building. Dorcas felt her heart race as she approached cautiously from the other side. She peeked around the corner and saw the back of the man with Mattie as he entered the building from the back door.

Dorcas pressed back against the outside wall. She reached for the gun in her pocket and drew it out but kept it next to her side. The men from town should be arriving soon, so she would wait. She'd only make a move if the man in the bank started to leave.

Asa shoved the sheriff into the cell, not caring that the man hit his head against the wall from the force of Asa's boot in his backside. He motioned for the other two to follow him.

They didn't move.

"Let's go! You heard Granger. He's got the money and horses."

"I'm not going."

Asa spun around to Wally. "What did you say?"

Wally shook his head and sat down on the bunk. "I said I'm not going. I don't want no part of it anymore."

Asa turned to Otis. "Well?"

Otis looked between Wally and Asa, and the struggle was evident on his face. He heaved a sigh. "I'm stayin' too. It's jest not worth the risk."

Asa was furious. He grabbed the cell door and clicked it shut, throwing the keys across the room. "You had your chance." He stepped over to stand in front of Wally. "I'm going to have fun with your preacher girl," he sneered.

Wally jumped to his feet and grabbed the bars with his good arm. "You leave her alone, Asa! So help me I'll kill you if you even touch her!"

"You had your chance. I'd shoot you both now, but the noise would bring trouble. Have fun rotting in jail."

Asa slammed the door between the cell and the office behind him. Picking up the sheriff's pistols, he was out the window in a flash.

What's taking everyone so long? Dorcas thought as she watched the door of the bank. It was opening now. She inched forward.

Suddenly she was pulled back, and a hand snaked across her mouth. Her head was yanked backward into a man's shoulder and twisted so that she had to look up into his face. Her eyes widened in terror as she stared into the eyes of the man who had tried to kidnap her.

Asa grinned at Dorcas. His voice was only a whisper. "So I win after all."

Dorcas's heart pounded in fear. What had she done? She saw Asa raise a pistol as he searched the area around them. He pushed her ahead of him to stand next to four horses, which were tethered behind the bank, and together they watched as Mattie stepped out of the back door first. She was holding the bags with the money in front of her. The stranger was behind her. He clasped one bag in the hand he kept around Mattie's neck. The other hand held his pistol. He looked around carefully before stepping out behind Mattie.

Dorcas knew she had to do something *now.* Mattie was struggling to walk down the steps with the load she carried and with the man's stranglehold on her. Dorcas saw the man motion for Asa to help.

Asa pulled Dorcas along with him as he approached the other two. For a moment, they would be in the open. Dorcas took her chance.

She gave a quick nod to Mattie; then she pushed away from Asa and raised her derringer. As if in slow motion, she saw Asa's gun raise toward her. She fired, and she heard another shot from behind her fire at the same time.

Mattie saw the woman's nod, and she jabbed her elbow with all her might into Mr. Granger's stomach. He doubled over, loosening his grip on her neck. For just a second, Mattie saw Abel's face and a rifle in his hands. She dropped to the ground and heard the blast of the rifle go off. Mr. Granger landed on top of her, and she felt the wind go out of her lungs in a sudden *whoosh*.

Two more shots went off above her head; then there was a moment of silence.

"Mattie!"

"Dorcas!"

Mattie couldn't lift her head. She felt the man's body being dragged off her; then she was pulled up into Abel's arms, her head cradled against him. She looked up into his blue eyes and gave him a wobbly smile.

"I think we've done something like this before," she said between gasps for air. Abel pulled her closer.

Dorcas stared at the body of the man she had shot. She turned slowly as arms encircled her and found herself face-to-face with her husband.

"Cavan! What are you doing here?" Her voice sounded far away and shaky, not like her.

"Dorcas Nolan! What did you think you were doing?" Cavan held her close to him. "I decided to ride into town to have lunch with you and the children, and just as I arrived, I found Jonas running all over town recruiting men. He told me what you were up to." He stopped and swallowed hard before continuing. "I got here just as Asa grabbed you."

Dorcas felt him tremble.

"Is everyone all right?"

They looked up and found the area filled with the men from town, all carrying weapons of one sort or another. Harry Nolan reached for his daughter-in-law and embraced her. Jonas shook hands with Cavan.

"Good thing you got here in time, Cavan."

Clyde Moore and Doc Casper were there, and Gabe was picking up the weapons off the ground.

Jonas explained. "The coach just got in, and I grabbed Gabe too. We were at the jail and found the sheriff locked in the cell with the other two prisoners." Jonas grinned as if he were going to enjoy telling the next part of his story. "They wouldn't leave the jail. The sheriff said they had the opportunity to escape, but they wouldn't do it. I guess Mattie's talk to them this morning must have done some good. Except for this one." He kicked Asa's boot.

Abel's grip on Mattie tightened. "Mattie?"

"I'll…explain later." She stood to her feet with Abel's arm still around her. "Abel! Mr. Davies is hurt."

"I'll check." Doc Casper went into the bank with Jonas.

Abel led Mattie over to Dorcas and Cavan. He reached for his sister and hugged her; then he stepped back as the two women faced each other.

"Hi, Mattie, I'm Abel's sister Dorcas."

Mattie threw her arms around Dorcas and began sobbing. "Thank you so much for helping me." She felt Abel's hand on her back comforting her. "I saw you go into Nolan's Store, and I prayed so hard that you would find help for us, and you did." She wiped at her eyes.

Dorcas's tears started flowing then, and the men realized they needed to get the women away from the dead men. The sheriff had arrived, and with the help of the other men, they would take care of things. The two couples headed back to the hotel.

The boardwalk was filled with people waiting to hear news about the second robbery attempt on the bank and with people waiting to leave on the stage. Mattie, with Abel's arm around her, came face-to-face with Delphinia and her parents. She took a sharp intake of air.

It seemed as though the crowd parted and left the couple alone with the Digbys. From Dr. Digby's arrogant perusal of Mattie to Mrs. Digby's haughty dismissal of her and finally to Delphinia's look of contempt, Mattie was left feeling disparaged and denigrated. Still not knowing what Abel's feelings were toward the girl, Mattie kept her head down and tried to move away from him. But Abel wouldn't have it.

"Dr. Digby, Mrs. Digby, Delphinia." He spoke to each one while he kept a tight hold on Mattie. "May I present Miss Morrison. Please excuse us. Miss Morrison has just been through a traumatic experience. Have a pleasant journey back to Boston." He then guided Mattie past the astonished Digbys and into the hotel.

Cavan and Dorcas were waiting inside for them and motioned for them to follow them to the private quarters in the back belonging to Harry and Gretchen. They were greeted by Leon, who jumped into his father's arms. Dorcas eagerly picked up her daughter Fiona and held her close.

"Sit down! Here, Mattie. You and Abel sit here." Gretchen stepped out of the room while everyone got settled and was soon back with a tray of cups and a pot of coffee. Her face registered surprise to see Abel and Mattie still standing.

"What's the matter? Abel, can't you see that Mattie needs to sit down? She's swaying on her feet." Gretchen reached for Mattie's hand.

"Please, Gretchen, I can't sit on your nice chairs," Mattie tried to explain to the puzzled listeners. "I...I think there's blood on my back."

Abel turned Mattie and looked her over. "Looks like I owe you another dress, Mattie. Seems I keep ruining yours."

Mattie knew he was trying to make light of the situation, but still, she was starting to tremble. The thought of the dead man pinning her to the ground was only now beginning to sink in. She looked up in relief when Gretchen appeared with a dining room chair. Abel held it for Mattie, and she sank gratefully into it.

Abel knelt beside her and took her hand, ready if she even looked like she might faint. "Can you tell us what happened now? Do you know who that man was?"

"Hold on, Abel."

They all turned as Harry entered.

"The sheriff wants to know if he can talk to Mattie and Dorcas now, and Pastor Sweeney is here. Are you ladies up to it?" he asked.

Dorcas waited for Mattie to nod before she agreed. The sheriff came in and took the chair offered by Gretchen; the pastor declined a chair and stood in the corner. The sheriff held his hat in his hands and was about to speak when a knock on the Nolans' residence caused them all to look up.

Sky and Russ Newly entered. Sky went straight to her daughter Dorcas and embraced her. She hugged Cavan next and patted her grandchildren before turning to Mattie and Abel. "Oh, my dear," she exclaimed as she threw her arms about Mattie. Abel was next; then with a sniff and a dab with her hanky, Sky stepped back and allowed Russ to put his arm around her.

"What happened, Sheriff?" Russ asked. "We were on our way to town when we heard about the jail and the bank and that our daughter and Mattie were in the middle of it."

"I was just about to find out," the sheriff replied before turning again to Mattie.

Gretchen carried in two more chairs for the Newlys. "Sure, and if any more people show up in here, we'll have to move out to the dining room," she joked.

The others laughed with her, easing the tension in the room. They all waited for Mattie to speak, and she felt extremely self-conscious, but she began.

"The man's name is Mr. Granger. Matthias is what Mr. Davies called him. I met him when I worked for Reverend Wynn and his wife. You see, Mr. Granger was an elder at a church between Norris and Grandville, and the Reverend Wynn was their minister." Mattie took a breath and wished she could have a drink of water, but every eye was on her, and she knew they wanted to hear all that she had to say, so she continued. "I…I lost my job with the Wynns, and Mr. Granger offered to find me a new job. He said he knew Mr. Davies in Sand Creek, that they were old friends, and that Mr. Davies was looking for a schoolteacher for the fall. He also said I could work in Mr. Davies's bank until the school term began." Mattie gratefully took the water that Gretchen brought for her and sipped it.

"Thank you, Gretchen." Mattie didn't want to say anything about the situation at the Wynns that would cause questions about the night Abel rescued her, so she chose her words with care. "I also met Wally Beck while I was at the Wynns, and he…he flirted with me, but I never encouraged him. I had no idea that the two men knew each other or were involved in a gang of thieves." She turned to Abel. "Mr. Granger was a respected man in his church. He was kind to me after… well, he brought me to my home after the Wynns no longer wanted me to work for them." She hoped he understood what she was referring to.

Abel nodded, and the others in the room watched, wondering what more to the story wasn't being told.

"What happened today, Miss Morrison?" the sheriff asked.

Mattie turned to him. "Lloyd left for lunch, and only Mr. Davies and I were in the bank when Mr. Granger came in. I was happy to see him…at first." She proceeded to tell the others the events, which led up to the death of the two men. "It seems it was Mr. Granger's plan all along to have me at the bank to make the robbery easier for him. I feel terrible about that! I am ever so grateful for Dorcas seeing that I needed help," she concluded. "But what happened to Wally and that other man, the one who tried robbing the bank yesterday?"

The sheriff explained how both men refused to escape from the jail and how Asa had mocked them and left them there. "Miss Morrison, your visit this morning is the reason those men stayed put. I think they want to change their lives." He looked over his shoulder at the pastor. "It might be a good time for a visit from you, Pastor," he suggested.

Pastor Sweeney agreed. "I'd like a visit with you and Miss Morrison some time as well, Abel," he suggested. "Would this evening be possible?"

Abel looked questioningly at the pastor then at Mattie. "I guess so. What do you think, Mattie?"

She too was puzzled, but before she could reply, Sky spoke up. "Why don't you come out to our place tonight, Mattie? Plan to stay a few days and get away from the town and rest up. Russ will talk to Bert, and

I'm sure it will be okay. Bert will need a few days off to rest as well."

"How is he?"

"Doc Casper says he'll be fine, but he'll have a headache," the sheriff answered.

"So how about it, Mattie? Pastor Sweeney, please join us for supper as well." Sky included the minister.

Before Mattie knew what was happening, she was being brought to her room by Dorcas and Gretchen. They helped her change out of her soiled dress and got her cleaned up and ready for the trip out to the Newlys. Dorcas helped pack a few of her things and declared her ready to go.

"Maybe Cavan and the children and I will come out tomorrow for a visit. I'd like to get to know you better, Mattie," she said.

Mattie reached for her hand. "Thank you, Dorcas. I know you risked your own life today for me. I would like to get to know you and your family better too."

They shared a smile. Dorcas gave her a quick hug and whispered, "I'm glad you and Abel are together too."

"But…" Mattie's voice faded off as Dorcas winked. The next thing she knew, Abel was handing her into the wagon beside his parents.

"I'll be home as soon as I speak with Doc and see what else needs to be done here today. I also want to give him my report on the calls I made this morning. I'll see you soon." He squeezed Mattie's hand and waved as they drove away.

Chapter 27

Newly Ranch

Mattie liked the Newlys. She felt right at home helping Sky prepare the evening meal, and she appreciated that Sky included her instead of refusing her offer to help. They worked side by side and talked about other members of the Newly family who were familiar to Mattie, like Lucy and Buck, and Tyler and Jade.

Sky learned about Mattie's family too and discovered that Mattie was regularly sending money home to her parents to help out with family finances. She admired Mattie's skill in the kitchen and her ability to persevere through the trials she experienced that day. When she learned about Mattie going to the jail to witness to the men who had held her at gunpoint the day before, her respect for the young woman grew even more.

"I feel badly about cancelling on the dinner invitation that Irena gave me the other day," Mattie was saying. "I was looking forward to visiting with her finally. I knew her from when I worked in Grandville."

"We'll make a point of going over for a visit soon," Sky suggested. "Dorcas asked if she and Cavan and the children could come by tomorrow. Would that be all right with you?"

"Yes, of course. I feel such a debt to Dorcas for what she did today. She was very brave."

"So were you, my dear."

Mattie shook her head at Sky. "I was scared. I couldn't do anything to stop Mr. Davies from getting hurt, and I couldn't do anything to prevent the sheriff from being locked in his own jail. I felt so helpless." She reached for a chair and dropped into it. Sky hurried to her.

"This is exactly why I didn't want you to be alone for the next few days. It takes awhile to get over something like this. I know. I've been through a similar experience." Sky talked on while Mattie got control of herself. Soon Mattie was up and helping again, and Sky allowed her to because she knew Mattie needed to be kept busy.

"Why does Pastor Sweeney want to talk to us tonight?" Mattie asked.

Sky hesitated. "I suppose we'll find out soon enough. I'm sure it's nothing you need worry about, dear. Now which table cloth do think we should use? This one?"

Mattie knew Sky was trying to distract her, so she let her. All the while they were working and talking, Mattie had something else on her mind. Abel.

The Digbys got on the stage and left Sand Creek. That meant that Abel wasn't going to marry that girl. At least Mattie hoped that was what it meant. They didn't seem very cordial when they all met on the boardwalk. And Abel had stayed close by her side and held her hand the whole time she had relayed the events at the bank to the people in the Nolans' home.

Mattie only half listened to Sky's chatter. She could hardly wait to see Abel again.

Abel finished his paperwork and went over his calls with Doc Casper. Together, along with the sheriff, they looked in on Bert Davies and heard his retelling of the events at the bank. Bert had nothing but praise for Mattie, and when he learned how the robbery was finally foiled, he declared Mattie and Dorcas to be the heroines of the day. Doc checked Bert's wound and put a clean bandage on it before they left.

On the way back to the doctors' office, the sheriff asked Abel how he happened to be in the right spot to get a shot at Matthias Granger.

"Like Cavan, I had just gotten into town and saw Jonas running around spreading the word that Dorcas had taken off after Mattie and some man. I headed straight to the back of the building and hid in the trees until they came out. I saw that man named Asa grab Dorcas and didn't know what to do until I saw Cavan come alongside the building. Then Mattie and Granger stepped out, and Dorcas made her move. When she and Cavan shot, I popped my head up so Mattie could see me. She dropped to the ground like I hoped she would."

"She's quite a woman. Congratulations, Abel."

"What?" Abel stared after the sheriff as he grinned and walked back to the jail. He smiled to himself. *Yes, congratulations. Lord, I want to marry Mattie…again. Is that all right with you?* He chuckled. *If she'll have me.*

Abel could hardly wait to get home.

The evening meal at the Newlys was full of pleasant conversation, and there was an unspoken agreement that no one mentioned the traumatic events of the day. Abel was dazzled by the beautiful woman at his side and longed for nothing more than the meal to end so that he could take her for a walk and tell her what was in his heart. From the glances she sent his way, he felt that she was eager to talk with him too. But first, they had to hear what Pastor Sweeney had to say, and although Abel admired the man and valued his guidance, right now he wished the preacher had chosen a different night to come calling.

"Shall we retire to the parlor for coffee?" Sky suggested. "It will only be a few moments until I have it ready."

"Let me help." Mattie rose and started clearing away the dishes from the table. Abel had hoped this could be the time for them to slip away, but the pastor engaged him in conversation on the way to the parlor, and he reluctantly followed. It wasn't long until the women again joined the men, and Abel rose to his feet and directed Mattie to sit beside him. She smiled demurely as she sat down. As if on cue, they all turned to the pastor.

Pastor Sweeney cleared his throat. He looked at Abel and Mattie, and almost as an apology, he said, "The Wynns have been to see me."

Mattie gasped, and her hand flew to her mouth. Abel's jaw tightened when he saw her distress, but he spoke calmly to the pastor. "Go ahead and tell us what they said, Pastor. My parents already know all about the situation."

Mattie stared wide-eyed at Abel and then glanced at Russ and Sky. She put her head in her hands. "Oh no," she moaned.

"There's no reason to be embarrassed, Mattie," Sky assured her. "Abel has told us all about the night you spent together and how the Wynns reacted when they found you the next morning. Please believe me that we understand. Abel did what he had to do to save your life."

"I know," Mattie choked out the words, "but will everyone else believe it, or will they jump to the same conclusions that the Wynns did?" She shared a look with Abel. "My parents know all about it too, and they believed me." She wanted him to know. "It's ironic that Mr. Granger was the one who vouched for me."

Abel spoke to the pastor again. "What did they say to you?"

"First of all, I want you to know that I didn't reveal that either of you was in town. I didn't know who these people were, and it was obvious to me that they were looking to cause trouble," Pastor Sweeney explained.

"Second, I didn't know anything of the situation, so when they told me their version, I had a hard time swallowing it, knowing you as I do, Abel."

"Thank you, sir."

The preacher nodded. "Third, I didn't know you very well at all yet, Miss Morrison—"

"Mattie, please"

"Mattie." He smiled at her tight features. "So since I didn't know you, I just let them talk and then sent them on their way. They didn't have a very good opinion of you," he admitted.

"But that's not her fault," Abel began, but the minister interrupted him.

"I know that, and since becoming better acquainted with Mattie, I know that their view of her is slanted." He leaned forward. "They're going to be back."

Mattie felt Abel take her hand in his.

"I know this because of the determination they showed in trying to make me believe their story. Reverend Wynn—if he really is a minister—has made it his mission to see that you two abide by the marriage vows made that day."

Russ spoke for the first time. "I would think that is an odd ministry to have. You'd think he would be more concerned about spreading the good news of the gospel than to hunt down two people and make them abide by his edict."

The pastor agreed. "He's a sensationalist preacher, Russ, the kind that preaches fire and brimstone instead of grace. I believe that he is not used to having his authority thwarted, and it's galling to him. Now his pride is making him seek vengeance on Abel and Mattie. That and the fact that he lost his position at the church because of them. I hesitate to say this, but I think the man is demented. He seems to have lost all perspective on anything save ruining Abel and Mattie's lives.

"I've been thinking about how to handle this when they return, and I think the best thing to do is to tell the town the truth. Rumors are going to spread whether we want them to or not, so let's get it all out in the open and save the Wynns the trouble. What do you say, Abel? Mattie?"

"You mean—?"

"I mean that they can't fuel a fire that has already been put out."

Abel squeezed Mattie's hand. "I hate to put Mattie through the embarrassment, sir. Isn't there another way?"

"I believe that if you tell your story in as honest a way as you can, the people will rally around you and pay no heed to the ranting of this man. You know you're right before God. Remember, the truth shall make you free."

Abel looked at Mattie. "How do you feel about it?" he asked.

"Maybe it would solve things if I just left Sand Creek. Then—"

"No!"

Abel pleaded silently with Mattie until she gave a slight nod. She turned to the others.

"Then I think I would like my parents to be here when we do this," she said.

"What a wonderful thought, Mattie!" Sky exclaimed.

Abel suddenly stood. "Would you all excuse us? I think Mattie and I need to take a walk. Mattie?"

She nodded. "Thank you for a wonderful meal, Mrs. Newly."

Sky smiled at the couple as they made their way out the door. She turned back to the two men left in the parlor with her. "I really like that girl," she said.

Mattie was suddenly shy. She and Abel had been through so much together that she should feel completely comfortable with him, but holding onto his arm now as they strolled down a path was far different from handing a medical instrument to him or facing a robber with him. She knew Abel cared for her. She saw the way he looked at her and how he wanted her beside him and how he held onto her hand when she was frightened. She also knew that he was still or had been engaged to that girl. What she didn't know was what Abel was feeling right now. Did Pastor Sweeney's suggestion that they tell their story to everyone have him wishing she'd never come into his life? It seemed that ever since Abel met her, she's brought nothing but trouble to him.

"I'm so sorry!" Mattie blurted out.

Abel stopped walking, surprised by her outburst. "What's the matter?"

Maybe it was the tension and trauma of the day catching up to her, but Mattie started crying, and she poured out her thoughts. "I've been nothing but trouble to you! You had to rescue me that night, and what did you get for it? You were forced into a shotgun wedding! Then you…you end up in a bank robbery because of me and got tied up and…and in a fight, and you got hurt." She reached up and touched the red mark on Abel's lip. He took her hand and started to speak, but she kept going. "And you had an argument with your fiancée because of me, I think, and…and she left. Then you had to shoot a man because of me. And now…now you have to face the whole town…and…and tell them about that night. They might not want you for their doctor when they hear about it! Oh! I'm so sorry!"

There was a moment of silence; then Abel started laughing.

Mattie wiped at her tears as she stared at him. When Abel pointed at her and laughed harder, her hand flew to her mouth. He stopped suddenly, worry creasing his brow.

"Sorry, Mattie, but I—"

A giggle emerged from behind Mattie's hand. She watched as the worry quickly changed to delight on Abel's face. He pulled her close.

"I don't know when I started falling in love with you, Mathilda Morrison, but I know that I've fallen hard." He held her away and waited for her response.

Mattie gulped. From tears to laughter to this sudden surge of wonderment, her emotions had run rampant. She gazed at Abel, and her mouth went dry. "Really?"

Abel pulled her to him again. "I thought I was in love with Delphinia, but that wasn't love. That was an attraction. She seemed to fit into my plan for my life as a doctor, but you, Mattie, you fulfill my whole life. You make me want to be a better man, to serve the Lord with my whole heart, and to love you for the rest of my days. Will you marry me, Mattie, and be by my side no matter where the Lord leads us?"

Her answer was simple and impish. "Again?"

Abel threw back his head as his laugh rang out, making the joy inside Mattie flow to the smile on her face.

"The answer is yes, Abel."

They embraced, and Mattie felt all the worries and concerns facing them melt away. This was right. She belonged here in this man's arms. They still had difficulties to work out, but they were on the right path now, together. When Abel bent his head to her, she met his kiss with a confidence that this was the man God had for her.

Arm in arm they walked back to the house to share their good news with the others.

Chapter 28

Sand Creek

The next day was filled with fun for Mattie. Abel's parents accepted the news of the engagement with enthusiasm and made her feel as if she were already a part of the family. Sky shooed Abel off to work, saying that she and Mattie had wedding plans to discuss. Since Dorcas was already planning to come for the day, Sky asked Russ to ride over and invite Irena and the children to come too.

Dorcas and Irena were thrilled with Mattie's news even though Dorcas admitted to expecting to hear about her brother asking Mattie to marry him sometime soon. At Sky's suggestion, Mattie explained the whole situation to her future sisters-in-law about the wedding she and Abel were coerced into.

"I wanted to ask about your short hair, but I didn't dare," Irena confessed. "Thank the Lord that Abel came by that night and got you out of the ice."

"I would have frozen to death. But the Wynns didn't see that, or they wouldn't see it. They were convinced that they needed to rectify the wrongs they thought we had done.

"Anyway, Abel is going to tell our story to the whole church on the day of our wedding," she said. "We would like to be married in two weeks on Sunday after the service. That way, my family will have time to find someone to watch the farm for them while they come here for the wedding."

"You're going to have the wedding in Sand Creek? That's wonderful! But I thought you and your family went to the church in Grandville," Dorcas said.

"We attended Pastor Malcolm's church in Grandville on occasion, but my family went to one in Norris most of the time. I guess I'd like to have the wedding here because this has become my home too, and all your family is here. I hope that our other friends and family in Grandville will be able to come too."

"They'll come, Mattie, don't you worry about that! Everyone will be excited to be a part of witnessing your wedding. And it gives us a good reason to get together for a party." Sky laughed. "Remember how we surprised them all with an anniversary party at your wedding, Irena?"

The visit went well, and Mattie learned a lot about the family she was joining. She had a thankful heart when she went to sleep that night in the guest room at the Newlys. Tomorrow she was going to ride to town with Abel and get back to work at the bank. She didn't know if Mr. Davies would want her to continue working after she and Abel were married or if they would still want her, a married woman, as a schoolteacher, but she knew she would be happy with whatever decision they made. She and Abel discussed so many things, and they both felt like they were beginning on an exciting adventure together. Whether she worked or not didn't matter; the important thing was that she was going to be Abel's wife.

Mattie decided that it was fun riding to town early in the morning with her fiancé. Abel kept his arm around her and kept her laughing with stories of his boyhood and questions about her growing up years. There was still so much to learn about each other, but they would have a lifetime in which to learn it.

"Your mom and dad are so sweet. I know my parents are going to love them. And did you know that your mom and Irena and Dorcas and the children are all coming to have lunch with me today?"

Abel scowled. "I wanted to have lunch with you!" he complained good-naturedly.

Mattie smiled. "I thought maybe you could have supper with me at the hotel dining room?"

"Are you courting me, Mathilda?"

Now it was Mattie's turn to scowl. "Oh, please, Abel! Don't call me that! I've never cared for that name. Why do you think everyone calls me Mattie?"

"If the Wynns had called you Mattie that morning, I would have known who you were when you showed up in Sand Creek. As it was, the name Mattie didn't give me any clues, especially since the girl by that name seemed to have long hair. By the way"—he smiled down at her—"have I told you that I think your short hair is adorable?"

Mattie blushed, but she was getting used to Abel's humor. "You should. You cut it! And that reminds me, when did you first realize who I was? I knew who you were right away."

"Well, don't sound so smug, *Mrs. Newly*. You got a pretty good look at me the morning of our unexpected wedding, whereas I only saw a white-faced woman with chopped hair. You barely opened those gorgeous, brown eyes so I could see them."

Mattie laughed at Abel again. "In two weeks, I really will be Mrs. Newly."

Abel grinned. "So when did I first recognize you? Hmm…I guess it was in my office when you sprained your ankle."

"Really? How?"

"Your head was bent over, and the bun in your hair was kind of cockeyed, and I could see some of the short hair poking up. I think once I realized that it could be you, I remembered your face."

"You didn't say anything."

"You didn't either."

They started laughing again.

"I'm glad I found you that night, Mattie. You have made me a very happy man."

Abel stopped in front of the bank and lifted Mattie out. Mattie could tell he wanted to kiss her, but he refrained because of curious eyes on them. She smiled, and they bid each other good-bye for the day.

"I'll leave your bag with Gretchen at the hotel desk, all right?"

Mattie nodded and watched Abel climb back in the wagon and drive the short distance to the hotel. She knew she should go inside, but she enjoyed watching the man she loved.

Mattie was happy to be back at work. Mr. Davies was feeling better, and Lloyd wanted to hear all about the second robbery attempt from Mattie. The three talked for a while before getting down to the business of the day. Time passed quickly with so much to do, and soon it was lunchtime.

"Take some extra time, both of you," Mr. Davies said as he came out of his office. "I'm going to nap after lunch, so there's no need for you to get back before I do. How about we make it an hour-long lunch today?"

Mattie smiled at everyone as she made her way to the hotel dining room. She was looking forward to her lunch with Sky and the girls. She was almost to the hotel when she glanced over at Abel's office. She stopped short when she saw that he was standing outside his door watching her with a huge grin on his face.

She waved, and he raised his hand in return. She saw him cock his head to one side as if listening to someone speak to him. He pointed to the door, indicating that he had to go, and waved once more before entering his office. Mattie smiled to herself. *How thoughtful he is!*

Sky, Irena, and Dorcas were already at a table when she entered the room. The children were either being held or were climbing on the chairs. She hurried to join them.

"We got here early so we wouldn't waste any of your lunchtime since you have to get back to the bank," Dorcas said to Mattie.

"I have a whole hour today," Mattie told them. She greeted everyone and was welcomed. Her heart filled with joy to be a part of this community and to be friends with these people. Gretchen was in and out, taking care of her guests and visiting with the ladies and her grandchildren as she passed by.

"We've sent telegrams to everyone in Grandville about the wedding," Sky told Mattie. "I wouldn't be surprised if they didn't all come early to help with the preparations. I'm sure our houses will be filling up with all the guests."

"Did I hear the word *wedding*?" Gretchen whispered as she stopped by their table with a tray of food.

Mattie blushed, and Gretchen reached over to hug her. "I knew it! I'm so happy for you and Abel, Mattie! Now, I want you to tell your family to come and stay here at the hotel, and there will be no charge. You're our family too."

"Gretchen! That is very generous of you, but did you know that, counting me, there are nine of us?"

"The more the merrier! Oh, excuse me." And she hurried off to take care of her customers.

Sky smiled at Mattie. "Don't look so surprised, my dear. All of Sand Creek is indebted to you one way or another. Those you haven't helped with medical issues, you've managed to help by protecting their money in the bank. You are a hero, and you too, Dorcas, although I still shudder to think of the risk you took."

The lunch went by quickly even with the extended time, and soon Mattie was back at her desk at the bank. She was just finishing for the day when she decided that she better speak to Mr. Davies about needing time off for the wedding. She knocked on his door.

"Come in."

Mattie entered and waited for her boss to finish what he was working on.

At length, he looked up. "Oh, Mattie, what can I do for you?"

"I've finished for the day, sir, but I have a question for you. You see, Abel Newly has asked me to marry him—"

"Well, it's about time! I could see you two belonged together right off! Congratulations, my dear! When is the big day?"

"It's in two weeks. That's why I—"

"Two weeks! What are you doing here? You have plans to make and things to do. I think you better take some time off and get ready, don't you?"

"If you don't mind, sir."

"Not at all! Lloyd and I can manage things here by ourselves for a while. You take all the time you need, and you can expect a bonus for all that you've been through these last days." The bank owner was beaming. "I was going to tell you about that soon, but now is as good a time as any." He took Mattie's hands in his. "You and Abel! I can't tell you how pleased I am. God bless you, Mattie Morrison."

Later, Mattie and Abel enjoyed an evening meal at the hotel dining room, and then Abel took her hand and led her outside for a stroll down the streets of the small town. They came to a modest-looking, white house with a small yard and a white fence surrounding it. They stood back and looked at it together.

"What do you think, Mattie? It isn't very big, but do you think it would do for starting out? My dad stopped by the office today and offered me a piece of land to build on. We probably wouldn't be able to start a house until next year, so this would have to do until then." He waited, watching Mattie's reaction.

"Oh, Abel! I love it! I don't mind at all that it is small. Can we see inside?"

He opened the gate for her and allowed her to go in ahead of him. He pulled a key from his pocket and unlocked the door, and they stepped inside. It was still light enough outside that they could see their surroundings quite well. Mattie walked from room to room, admiring and exclaiming over every little detail. Abel enjoyed watching her.

"The kitchen is just right for the house, Abel! Look here at the icebox. Oh, did you see this?" Mattie was delighted with each new find, and Abel was happy to not hear the word *quaint* even once pass her lips. Mattie was a treasure.

When she was done going through each room, Abel pulled her into his arms. "Mattie, I have something for you." He gave her a gentle hug. "Now, close your eyes."

"Abel, what are you up to now?" She obediently closed her eyes and waited. There was a rustling noise, then Abel took her hand, and she felt something slide on her finger.

"Okay."

She opened her eyes and held her hand up to see a small diamond ring sparkle in the evening light. Her eyes sparkled with tears as she looked at Abel.

"Now everyone will know you belong to me," he said before he sealed his promise with a kiss.

The days leading up to the wedding passed all too quickly. Soon Mattie was surrounded by her family, and guests from Grandville began arriving. There were always people around and things to do, so much so that she and Abel found very little time to be alone.

Mattie soon learned of the generosity of the people in her new town. The Nolans offered the Morrisons rooms in their hotel. Gretchen and Harry also approached Mattie and Abel one evening and told them that they wanted the wedding reception to be held in the hotel dining room and that they would provide the main course for the meal. All the other people in town would bring in the side dishes to accompany the meal. When Mattie began to protest that it was too much to ask of them, they simply replied that they wanted to do it.

Then Bert Davies asked to see the couple, and with a wink, he handed them a fat envelope. "That's Mattie's pay and bonus and a little extra reward for all she did to help during the robberies. I guess you could say it's for all both of you did. Have yourselves a happy honeymoon," he said with a smile.

To top it off, the sheriff approached them with the news that there was a reward on both Matthias Granger and the man named Asa. He said it would be split between them and Cavan and Dorcas. Mattie was overwhelmed.

"Sheriff, what will happen to Otis and Wally?"

"They're in the county jail for now, but because they refused to escape with Asa, their sentences have been lightened considerably."

"I'm so glad. Isn't it wonderful what Pastor Sweeney told us about them?" She smiled at Abel. "After he talked to them that day, Wally accepted the Lord Jesus. And after hearing the gospel explained so simply, Otis placed his faith in Jesus Christ too. They both thought their sin was too bad for them to be able to get saved. I'm so glad Pastor could show them that the Lord Jesus paid for all their sin on the cross and washed it all away."

"And he explained that they will still sin, but that they can walk in newness of life because of Christ," Abel added. "I never thought I'd say this, but I hope we see them again someday."

The night before the wedding, the Newlys invited Mattie and her family to dinner. The house was full of people and noise and excitement. Jade pulled Mattie to the side to show her the wedding cake she had made.

"Lucy helped me with the decorating," Jade told Mattie as she awaited her reaction. "What do you think?"

"It's absolutely beautiful! How on earth will you get this to the hotel dining room in one piece tomorrow?" Mattie asked, awed by the artistic work.

"Oh, that won't be a problem. My biggest worry is keeping little fingers from trying to sample it." Jade and Mattie laughed. "Have you seen Emma? We're praying she doesn't go into labor during the wedding! Simon didn't want her traveling in her condition, but she wouldn't miss Abel's wedding for the world." Jade turned at the sound of a baby crying, and Mattie wondered how she knew it was her baby; there were many cries in the crowded house. "That would be Boone. He's hungry, so I better go find a quiet spot to feed him. I'll talk to you later, Mattie." They hugged. "I'm so glad you'll be my sister-in-law."

Mattie was overjoyed at the love she felt from all the family. She and Abel could barely speak to each other amid all the commotion, but she watched in fascination how well they all got along and managed to help Sky and Russ. The men took the older children outdoors with them to do chores and work off some of the pent-up energy the children had. The women were always busy doing something, yet they managed to visit with one another at the same time. Mattie's mother sank down in a chair beside her.

"Your hair is growing," she commented, which made Mattie laugh. She had shared with her mother the story of Lloyd shooting her hairpiece to bits, and her mother had laughed so hard, she cried. Tears seemed to be a common thing the last few days, but at least they were tears of joy.

"Are you and Abel ready to tell your story to everyone tomorrow?" her mother asked.

Mattie sighed. "It will be good to have it out and over with finally," she admitted, "but I don't look forward to the telling of it."

"Does everyone here know?"

Mattie shook her head. "No, they will find out with the rest."

"Your pa and I will be praying."

Mattie squeezed her mother's hand.

"Who is that over there?" Her mother pointed to Irena, and Mattie waited to answer until her mother looked back at her.

"That's Irena. She's married to Abel's brother Rex now." The two women sat without speaking for a moment.

"It's ironic, isn't it? Irena will be my sister-in-law, and I couldn't be more pleased." Mattie felt her mother's arm go around her and squeeze.

The day of the wedding was sunny and beautiful. The members of the wedding party sat near the back of the church during the service and would walk the aisle after Abel spoke to the people. Most of the people in the crowded building had no idea what Abel was going to say, but Mattie and the few others who knew were praying for him to have the boldness he needed.

Finally the service ended. Pastor Sweeney explained that it was a short service as they had a wedding to perform.

"But first, before we begin the wedding ceremony, Abel Newly has asked if he may say a few words. Abel?"

Abel squeezed Mattie's hand before he rose and walked to the front. He looked so wonderfully handsome in his dark suit, Mattie thought. Her mouth went dry as he turned and looked out at all the people.

"Thank you all for coming today to witness Mattie and I make our wedding vows. We're especially grateful that you are here, because you see, there were no real witnesses the first time we were married."

There were gasps from some of the people, and some snickers from others who knew Abel to be a joker. Most just seemed puzzled by his words. Mattie saw some heads turn to look at her, but she kept her eyes on Abel and waited for him to go on.

"I want to tell you a story about the spring snowstorm we had this year. You all remember that storm, don't you?"

Heads nodded.

"I was warned not to travel that day, but I didn't heed the warning."

Mattie saw Emma put her hand to her mouth.

"I am ever so glad that I didn't," Abel continued. "My horse and I were almost frozen, and I couldn't see to go forward or back, but I had to go on or die. I asked the Lord for help and he answered by having me trip over something on the ground. That something was Mattie."

Now more heads turned to Mattie, and she felt her face redden, but still she kept her eyes on Abel, and she saw him smile at her. She smiled back.

"I learned later that Mattie had seen the storm coming and had gone out to the barn to take care of the animals before the weather got too bad. Well, as you all know, the weather turned ugly rather quickly. On her way back from the barn, the storm hit hard. She pulled a bucket of water from the well to have in the house because she knew she wouldn't be able to go out for it later. She slipped and that bucket completely doused her and knocked her out. When I found Mattie that day, she was solidly frozen to the ground."

Exclamations filled the room. Abel waited for it to quiet so he could continue.

"I was nearly frozen myself, but I knew I had to help her. The Lord provided a clearing in the snowstorm for me to see the barn where I found a lantern and an axe. I had no choice but to cut through Mattie's coat sleeves with my knife to free her. The worse thing was that all her hair lay under a pool of frozen water, and I had to chop it free with the axe."

Mattie heard *ah* as if everyone in the room suddenly understood why her hair was short.

"Now I tell you all this for a reason," Abel continued. "Once I got Mattie in the house in dry clothes by the fire, I took care of her so that she wouldn't die from being exposed to the elements. I stayed with her the whole night. I checked her breathing, I fed her. I saved her life. I am a doctor, but I know that any of you who are not doctors would have done the same thing."

Heads nodded. Everyone who lived in the northern climate understood, but they were still puzzled why Abel was telling the story before his wedding. Mattie could almost sense the tension in the room build as they waited.

"Unfortunately, not everyone looked at it that way. The next morning, we were awakened by the man and wife who Mattie worked for. We were awakened by a shotgun being pointed at us and wedding vows being made on our behalf."

Again the crowd gasped. They leaned forward in their seats for Abel's next words.

"The man was a preacher, and he felt it was his duty to marry us after our night of suspected debauchery. We were unwilling participants in this charade but had no choice in the matter. He performed the wedding ceremony.

"Now I have to admit that I laughed it off. I left there thinking it was a joke and that nothing would ever come of it. However, Reverend Wynn and his wife did not view it the same way. They fired Mattie that day and pledged to make her live by the vows that were made. As a result, they were fired from being the minister at their church, and I believe that is one reason they seek to have revenge on Mattie and me.

"You see, the Wynns have been looking for us, and they want to spread their evil story about us to all who will listen. Mattie and I thought the best way to put an end to the story was to tell it to you ourselves.

"The good news is that even though I didn't recognize Mattie when she came to Sand Creek, I soon discovered in her all the qualities I wanted in the woman I wished to marry. Imagine how we felt when we learned that we were already *married*."

Several people laughed.

Abel studied the crowd before him. "God's ways are not our ways. I want you to know our story so that if rumors go around, you know the truth, and you know that we come today to marry with clear consciences. I thank God for my Mattie, and I am honored to become her husband because this marriage is something we both want. Thank you for listening. Shall we pray?"

Mattie had tears in her eyes when Abel was done. She quickly wiped her eyes and let the others lead her to the back of the church to begin the processional. Abel remained up front, and Rex and Tyler joined him. Pastor Sweeney and Pastor Malcolm Tucker from Grandville were going to share the ceremony, and they stood with the men, ready for the bride and her maids to walk forward. The music began.

Dorcas led the way, followed by Mattie's sister Grace, then Mattie and her father walked together. Sky and Irena worked together on Mattie's white dress, and it floated around her like a cloud. Her short hair was adorned with a flowered headpiece and a flowing veil. She was lovely, and even though Abel had already seen her in her wedding attire, Mattie could see the admiration in his eyes as he watched her approach.

Pastor Malcolm spoke first; then Pastor Sweeney began the vows. Mattie and Abel smiled at each other as they finally spoke the vows that sealed them as husband and wife. Abel kissed his bride, and they started down the aisle amid the cheers of congratulations of their friends and family, but suddenly, a gunshot halted their steps. Abel pushed Mattie behind him as he stared into the crazed eyes of Reverend Wynn.

The deranged preacher stood before them with his shotgun waving in front of him. His unkempt hair was as wild as his eyes. It was beyond belief that he found them on, of all days, their wedding day. Mattie gripped Abel's arm as she watched in horror from behind him.

"How dare you make a mockery of marriage! You are already bound to each other! You don't deserve this celebration, and by my authority, I will see to it that you don't have it! *I* sealed your vows when I found you in your immoral state, and you have no right to make new ones. These people must know who you really are and that you cannot be accepted in their midst. Because there is no end to the lengths you will go to deceive others, I must put an end to you!" He raised his gun to fire at Abel, but as he did so, he stepped forward, leaving himself exposed to the people behind him. Every able-bodied man in the back row of the crowded church dove for the insane man with the gun. No more shots were fired as the gun was wrestled out of his hand, and he was held down on the floor. Mattie felt Abel pull her into his embrace and hold her close. Everyone began talking at once as the men yanked Wynn to his feet to lead him off to the jail.

It was Emma who noticed that the plump woman who had been standing behind the preacher now pulled a gun from her handbag and was raising it to fire at Abel and Mattie. Instinct made Emma move to protect them.

"Abel! She's got a gun too!"

Several shots were fired, and Mattie swore she felt the bullet as it passed by her and Abel, and she heard Abel yell out "No!" as red blood sprayed across Mattie's white dress.

Everything faded into the background—all the noise and screaming, the men who now attacked the armed woman, the sight of her mother and father trying to get through the crowd of people to them. It all stopped in Mattie's mind as she saw Abel look in fear at her. But she didn't move. She stood and looked down at her dress and then back at him.

"It isn't me, Abel," she yelled to him. "It isn't me!"

Next to Mattie, they saw Emma begin to crumble to the floor. Abel reached for her and softened her descent. That's when he saw and felt the blood soaking the side of her dress.

"Get Doc Casper and help me get her to the office! Quickly!"

"Doc got hit too," someone yelled.

Abel looked around to where the older man sat holding his thigh.

"I'll be all right, Abel. Take care of your sister."

Simon handed Trudy and Troy over to their aunts and helped Abel carry Emma out the door. Mattie was right behind them. She rushed ahead and opened the door of the office and quickly ran to the stove and started a fire. She pulled forward the pot of water that was on there and picked up the bucket and handed it to the first person who walked through the door after the men and said, "Go, get more water! And keep the others out."

Russ spun around to obey her.

Mattie moved to the examining table and helped hand Abel bandages to stem the flow of blood from the wound. Emma started to sit up.

"Lay back, Emma. Abel is going to take care of you. You got hit by that crazy woman's bullet, but you're going to be fine."

But Emma looked at her with fear. "The baby!"

"He'll check to make sure the baby is okay too, Emma. Don't you worry. You're in good hands."

"No! The baby! It's—*ah*!" Emma doubled over despite the efforts to keep her back.

"She's going into labor, Abel," Simon said.

"Fortunately the bullet is only a graze, but it was traumatic enough to put her into labor. How quick was your first delivery with the twins, Emma?" Abel asked her.

Simon spoke from the other side of his wife. "It went very quickly, but that was twins."

"Well, this is a second birth, so don't expect it to be any slower," Abel cautioned. "Now that we've got the bullet wound under control, we're going to help Emma have her baby. Time for you to take a walk with Dad, Simon. We've got work to do."

Simon was holding Emma's hand. "No, I'm staying with her."

One look at Simon's face convinced Abel that he was dead serious. He nodded.

Mattie moved about the room, readying things for the baby's arrival as she remembered from helping with Annie's baby.

"Gentlemen, I'm going to ask you to leave for a few moments while I get my patient ready," she said calmly.

"*Your* patient?"

"That's right, my husband. Until I get her ready for you, she's my patient. Now scoot, all of you." Mattie shooed them out of the room. She returned to find Emma laughing at her and then quickly squelching her laughter as another pain hit her. Mattie waited until it was past; then she efficiently helped prepare Emma for the delivery. When she had her ready and modest, she called the men back in.

"Her side is still bleeding somewhat," she told them.

Abel moved to check her wound.

"Where's Doc?" Simon asked.

"He's in the other examination room. My mother and Florrie are in there with him right now. I've cleaned the wound and found that the bullet went all the way through. Mom is dressing the wound now."

"Don't we need him here?"

Abel eyed Simon. "I'm a doctor, remember, Simon? Emma is going to be just fine."

Together they waited, watched, and comforted Emma as her pains progressed. As predicted, it wasn't long before the baby made his appearance.

"You've got a boy, Emma! He's a big boy!"

Mattie was ready with the supplies to clean the baby, and before long, they all heard his cry announcing that he was healthy and breathing. Abel handed him to Mattie who brought him to Emma and Simon.

"Oh, he's a darling, Emma! Do you have a name?"

Emma's hair was damp, and her face was red from exertion, but she reached for her son with eager arms. "Trygve," she answered. "Wait until Troy and Trudy meet you!"

Mattie took the baby again and finished cleaning him up while Abel tended to Emma. "I'll get Emma presentable while you and Simon give the news to the rest of the family. I hope you're up to having a few visitors, Emma. Everyone is here."

"I'm so sorry about ruining your wedding."

"Nonsense. Nothing is ruined, it's just postponed. I'm sure that the guests have eaten their meal and are just waiting to hear how you're doing, so let's get you all prettied up for company. I think it's a lovely wedding present to have a baby born during the wedding." Mattie smiled as she helped Emma get cleaned up and brushed her hair for her.

"Look at your dress! I'm so sorry, Mattie."

Mattie looked down and had to laugh. "Abel and I have ruined more dresses together!" At Emma's startled look, Mattie laughed again and explained about the other incidences.

"I think you better forget about being a schoolteacher, Mattie. You were born to be a nurse. You and Abel work so well together."

Mattie thought about that. "It makes sense, doesn't it! I love working with Abel. Thank you, Emma."

There was a knock on the door, and Simon entered. He went quickly to his wife's bedside and talked quietly with her before moving aside to allow Mattie to hand the baby to him.

"Hey there, Trygve," he cooed.

Abel leaned against the doorframe to watch his sister and her family together. He smiled as Mattie walked toward him and slipped her arms about his waist.

"I love you."

"And I, you, Mrs. Newly." He kissed the top of her head and then looked down at her bloodstained gown. "Looks like I owe you another dress!"

They smiled at each other.

"Your mother is waiting to help you change, and I'll go get a clean shirt on. Then we have guests waiting for us."

"What will happen to the Wynns, Abel?"

"They're in the jail now. I guess I don't know. They will be charged with attempted murder, but the insanity that drove them to it may play a part in their sentencing." He pulled her closer. "It's over now."

They heard the door open behind them, and Sky came out. She went straight to Mattie and Abel and hugged them. She wiped a tear away and smiled at them.

"Doc is a terrible patient," she said unexpectedly.

Mattie tried to hide laughter behind her hand, but Abel laughed outright. "I couldn't imagine him being anything less."

"So how's my new grandson doing?"

"Great. Just tap on the door there, and I think they'll let you in. Mattie and I are going to get cleaned up and join our guests. Will you be coming soon?"

Russ stepped into the office. "We'll be right over after we see our grandson," he said. He held out his hand to Abel. "Good job, Doctor. Did you know your mother and I are proud of you?" He held out his arms to Mattie who gladly accepted his embrace. "And we're proud of our son's wife too. Thank you, Mattie, for being here with Emma. I think Abel has found himself more than a wife. He has a helpmate in you, my dear. He is a very fortunate man."

"She's a blessing from God." Abel took Mattie's arm. "We'll see you both later."

After cleaning up and changing clothes, Mattie met Abel in the hotel dining room. They were greeted warmly by all their guests, and Abel said a few words regarding the two who had been shot and announced the arrival of Trygve Chappell to any who had not already heard.

Then he finished by saying, "Mattie and I are thankful for all of you, our friends and our family here in Sand Creek and those from Grandville. We are truly blessed by the Lord to share our lives with you."

Abel searched the room. When he spotted Mattie's family, he pointed them out to the others. "I'd like to thank the Morrisons for their wonderful daughter and for putting up with all the commotion our wedding has turned out to be."

The group laughed and clapped to make the new family feel welcome.

"And I'd like to thank my family." Abel stopped, and Mattie heard the tremor in his voice. The room stilled. Abel was a joker, a tease, but they could all see the emotion he felt as he looked at the members of his family.

"Tyler and Jade." He motioned to the couple who were seated. Jade held Boone on her lap while Tyler bounced Eddie and Pamela on his knees. Tyler nodded his head to his brother.

"Lucy and Buck." Abel and the crowd looked at the next family. Lucy was seated with Molly, and Buck stood behind her holding Finn. Lucy wiped at a tear as she gave Abel and Mattie a wobbly smile.

"Dorcas and Cavan." Next, they turned their attention to one of Sand Creek's own families. "Thank you, Dorcas, for risking your life to save my Mattie." Cavan grinned at the couple, and Dorcas rushed forward and hugged them both. Leon and Fiona watched their parents as they sat with their Grandpa Harry and Grandma Gretchen.

"Rex and Irena." Rex, holding Anika, stepped forward to shake hands with Abel, while Irena, with Niels in her arms, kissed Mattie's cheek.

"And Simon and Emma," Abel stated soberly. "Emma tried to step in front of Mattie when the shots were fired." He pulled his wife closer to his side. "I have been blessed to be a part of this family, to grow up with brothers and sisters who care for one another, and to have parents who have faithfully guided us and trained us in the way which we should go, as Proverbs says." He rubbed the back of his hand over his eyes and noticed that his mom and dad were standing by the hotel door.

"Well, that's enough blubbering by me. Did you leave any food for us?"

Mattie playfully shoved her husband with her hand as the others broke out into laughter.

Sky stood to the side, watching her children laugh together. Across the room, she saw her brother, Evan, look her way, and they shared a special smile as if reading each other's thoughts. They both had come a long way since that bride train rolled into Sand Creek so long ago.

She felt Russ slip his arms around her, and she leaned back against him, contented. Together they watched their neighbors and friends, children and grandchildren, and they knew that this moment would become a memory they would carry in their hearts forever. God had truly blessed them.

For more information about
A Newly Weds Series or
author Margo Hansen, visit her at
www.margohansen.com

Margo would enjoy hearing
from her readers. Send your
comments or questions to
margo@margohansen.com

Other books by Margo Hansen:
*Sky's Bridal Train, Jade's Courting Danger,
Emma's Marriage Secret, and Irena's Bond of Matrimony*